I0612935

LARGE PRINT
EDITION

REVENGE

AT THE

GALLIANO CLUB

CARMEN AMATO

Also by Carmen Amato

Available in Large print

GALLIANO CLUB SERIES
ROAD TO THE GALLIANO CLUB:
Prequel
MURDER AT THE GALLIANO CLUB:
Book 1
BLACKMAIL AT THE GALLIANO CLUB:
Book 2
REVENGE AT THE GALLIANO CLUB:
Book 3

DEDICATION

The Galliano Club series is dedicated to the memory of

Celine McIndoe

First cousin. First playmate. First and best friend. My maid of honor.

In our hearts forever.

COPYRIGHT

Published 2024 by Laurel & Croton
ISBN Large Print: 979-8-9891403-4-3

Key characters in the Galliano Club series

Luca Lombardo: Orphaned in Italy, Luca doesn't own the Galliano Club, but it's all he has after losing his wife and baby to the Spanish influenza shortly after arriving in America. *His secret:* He killed the man who murdered his parents. *He wants:* To truly be an American.

Karol Dombrowski: From Poland, Karol has one of the most dangerous jobs at the Lido Premium mill and lives in the same boarding house as Luca. *His secret:* Karol is ambitious but sees no opportunity to move ahead. *He wants:* A position of influence to improve the lives of fellow newcomers to America.

Owen Forbes Fisher: A graduate of Syracuse University, Owen is the accountant for the Lido Premium mill. *His secret:* He fears his wife will leave him for a richer and more socially connected man. *He wants:* To be an admired figure in Lido's high society.

Ruth Cross: A former Broadway chorus girl, Ruth rents the apartment over the Galliano Club and runs the Tapping Toes School of Dance. *Her secret:* She was once convicted of public indecency and lewd behavior and spent time in jail. *She wants:* To be more than Luca Lombardo's friend.

Tess Kennedy: A graduate of Vassar College, Class of 1924, Tess works in the prestigious First National Bank of Lido. *Her secret:* She is a brilliant mathematician. *She wants:* To break the bonds of family and societal expectations for women and decide her own future.

Benny Rotolo: Previously a hitman for Chicago's North Side gang, Benny was chased out by Al Capone and came to Lido where his cousin lives. *His secret:* He's wanted for murder in Chicago. *He wants:* To build a bootlegging empire with the Galliano Club as his signature speakeasy.

Hanna Gorski: An artist's model and young widow, Hanna is on the hunt for the person who killed her sister and dumped the body in the Mohawk River near Lido. *Her secret:* She has ties to Al Capone's Chicago Outfit. *She wants:* Revenge for her sister's murder.

Eighteenth Amendment - Prohibition of Intoxicating Liquors, effective 16 January 1920

Section 1. After one year from the ratification of this article the manufacture, sale, or transportation of intoxicating liquors within, the importation thereof into, or the exportation thereof from the United States and all territory subject to the jurisdiction thereof for beverage purposes is hereby prohibited.

Section 2. The Congress and the several States shall have concurrent power to enforce this article by appropriate legislation.

Volstead Prohibition Enforcement Act, 28 October 1919

Sixty-sixth Congress of The United States of America;

To prohibit intoxicating beverages, and to regulate the manufacture, production, use, and sale of high-proof spirits for other than beverage purposes, and to insure an ample supply of alcohol and promote its use in scientific research and in the development of fuel, dye, and other lawful industries.

Be it enacted by the Senate and House of Representatives of the United States of America in Congress assembled, that the short title of this Act shall be the "National Prohibition Act."

. . . The words "beer, wine, or other intoxicating malt or vinous liquors" . . . shall be hereafter construed to mean any such beverages which contain one-half of 1 per centum or more of alcohol by volume . . .

"The trouble with women today is their excitement over too many things outside the home." –Al Capone

CHAPTER 1

From Mr. Capone

Hanna Gorski stared at her husband's body in the satin-lined casket and waited to feel sorrow or regret. The only thing that came to mind was that she could really use a cigarette.

The undertaker had done a good job, making Sam look asleep rather than dead. His wavy hair was brushed back from a high forehead and his eyelashes made a dark fringe against prominent cheekbones. Even dead, the man's lips curved in that signature, heart-melting way.

Always the clotheshorse, he wore a houndstooth suit and a diamond stickpin in his tie. Hands were crossed over the lapels, the nails buffed and shiny. A red carnation bloomed in his buttonhole. His shoes were so shiny they reflected the guttering candles placed around the viewing room.

Sam looked so pretty Hanna could almost imagine his eyes popping open. He'd shout for her to get dressed because they were going dancing at the Boiler Club. Right before his fist connected with her jaw.

"Sammy Vitello was a good soldier." Frank Nitti held an unlit cigarette between restless fingers. Dapper in a black suit with a chalk stripe and a silk square in the breast pocket, the mob boss was a head shorter than Hanna.

"I hadn't seen Sam in months. Maybe a year."

"These things happen." Nitti's voice was flat.

As if the bouquets of white lilies on pedestals at either end of the casket weren't enough, a funeral home attendant crept into the parlor with a horseshoe wreath the size of a kitchen icebox. Samuel Vitello RIP.

"From Mr. Capone," the attendant whispered. He propped the wreath on a stand and left the viewing room.

The new infusion of carnations thickened the already cloying air. Hanna wondered how much longer she was expected to stay.

Nitti surveyed the garish floral display and nodded in satisfaction. "Mr. Capone wants to do right by you, Hanna. Being Sammy's legal wife and all."

"I appreciate his concern," Hanna said. It was the correct response; the one Nitti expected her to say but it was also a joke.

Legal wife. A dozen other women were probably crying over Sam right now, wearing mourning black instead of Hanna's own pale blue boucle winter coat and matching cloche hat.

She'd read about Sam's death in the newspaper. Wouldn't have come to this tacky funeral home in Cicero if Capone hadn't sent a car for her. Two thugs showed up at her Chicago boardinghouse just as Hanna was packing and made it clear she didn't have a choice.

Capone probably owned the place. The wallpaper was purple, the same as the satin lining the casket. The windows were covered in heavy velvet draperies the color of blood.

It was a fitting backdrop for Frank Nitti. There was a quiet forcefulness about the gangster that frightened her, and Hanna wasn't frightened of much anymore. Al Capone was loud and large, but Nitti stayed in the shadows where he managed the Chicago Outfit's bootlegging finances and got rid of Capone's enemies. The Chicago rumor mill said that Nitti was the brains behind the cleverly planned October assassination of Hymie Weiss, head of the North Side gang. Rattling crossfire from adjacent rooming houses took Weiss down, peppering nearby Holy Name Cathedral with bullet holes in the process.

"Sammy was a good button man." Nitti punctuated the slang term with a wave of the unlit cigarette. "The only time he ever let me down was when I sent him after Benny Rotolo. A North Side torpedo who was causing us trouble. Sammy should have filled him with daylight but Rotolo slipped through his fingers."

Hanna bit her lip to keep a burst of hysterical laughter from escaping. Under the suit, Sam was full of daylight himself, thanks to the revenge-seeking North Side gang. No doubt Nitti was planning to return the favor.

That was Chicago. Hit for hit. Again and again. World without end, amen.

She was sick of it.

"The funeral arrangements are made," Nitti went on. "Sam will be laid to rest at St. Mary's Cemetery."

"Thank you," Hanna said.

She had loved Sam Vitello for about five minutes, which was as long as their courtship lasted. He'd waltzed into Marshall Field's one day and Hanna sold him a silk tie. Twenty-four hours later, a justice of the peace pronounced them man and wife.

That's what happened when a girl was young and impetuous and determined to learn about life the hard way.

The first lesson Sam taught Hanna was that she was married to a torpedo for Capone's Chicago Outfit. Sam was a gang killer with special pockets in all his coats and jackets to hide an arsenal of weapons. It was the same reason he couldn't commit to living in one place.

For a time, the glamorous lifestyle was worth it. Sam showered her with clothes and jewelry. They lived in deluxe hotel suites, changing every few weeks, and ate in restaurants like the Walnut Room in Marshall Field's or had meals catered in. He was achingly handsome in his custom suits, pearl gray fedora, and bespoke shoes. When they walked arm-in-arm down the street in Chicago, people thought they were seeing royalty.

The second lesson was that Sam was royal with lots of other women, too.

The third lesson was his temper.

Sam hit her. Hanna hit him back. Husband or not, any dumbbell who grew up on the streets in Chicago's Polish neighborhood knew how to use her fists. But when Sam broke her arm, Hanna left.

That was three years ago. They were both Catholic, so a divorce was out of the question. She smartened up, forgot romance, and parlayed her height and slim blonde looks into a job modeling clothes at Gossard's, the most elegant women's store in Chicago. Earned a little extra posing for artists. Sam showed up now and then, slinging money at Hanna to salve his conscience.

"I'm sorry about your sister," Nitti said. "Sam should be helping you cope, not dead in a casket, eh? Bad timing, eh?"

Hanna hadn't expected Nitti to say anything about her sister Marta, but wasn't surprised. Nitti had eyes everywhere and knew everything about anyone in his orbit.

"I have a train to catch," Hanna said. "They're expecting me in Lido to identify Marta and make arrangements to bury her."

"They know who done her in?" Nitti asked.

"No, not yet."

Four months ago, back in August, Hanna's younger sister Marta had disappeared from her job as a waitress at the Harvey House restaurant in Chicago's Union Station. Marta lived in the Harvey House dormitory, which was supposed to keep a close watch on the girls. Yet three days went by before Hanna was notified that her sister was missing.

The news galvanized her into action. Together with the Chicago police and the Harvey House people, Hanna knocked on doors, posted advertisements in the newspaper, and offered a reward. She sold every piece of jewelry Sam ever gave her to hire a private investigator. Her always slender bank account evaporated as every lead turned into a dead end.

Hanna was still grimly hanging on to hope when she received a letter from Arthur Everly, a well-known portrait artist. She had sat for him the previous summer, earning forty dollars. He sold the portrait to The Red Book magazine for last month's cover.

Arthur's letter recounted a twist in the search for Marta. The magazine's editor, Mr. Harriman, got a letter from a concerned citizen in Lido, New York, stating that the portrait on the cover of the October 1926 edition matched an unidentified female murder victim. The editor wrote to the mayor of Lido and forwarded the letter from the concerned citizen to Arthur, who in turn sent it to Hanna. It was in her purse along with a fresh box of cigarettes.

Apparently, the unidentified female murder victim had been pulled out of the Mohawk River. The Chicago newspapers got wind of the story, which was headline news in upstate New York for some time.

Telegrams were exchanged. Hanna agreed to go to Lido to identify the body. It wouldn't be Marta, her silly, funny, impulsive baby sister. It was impossible to think how or why her sister would have ended up there. Marta had no connection to Lido, New York.

Hanna refused to believe that as she had combed Chicago for months, Marta was already dead in a strange city in a strange state. Marta had talked of going places, but it was always to Europe. Warsaw to see the birthplaces of their late parents. Paris to find romance with a Frenchman. Vienna where the famous

Lipizzaner stallions performed their airs above the ground. Certainly not Lido, New York. From what Hanna had learned about Lido, the place had nothing to offer except copper and brass mills and the Lido Industrial League baseball teams.

But if Marta wasn't the woman lying dead in Lido, then where the hell was she?

"You need money?" Nitti held out a slim fold of bills.

Hanna shook her head and moved away from the casket. Chicago Outfit money came with an obligation that was impossible to repay. "I don't need it," she lied.

Nitti replaced the money in his pocket. "You're a good girl, Hanna," he said approvingly. "You ever need help, you know where to find me. Sam did right by Mr. Capone. We won't forget."

He offered a business card.

She could hardly refuse. Hanna slipped it into her purse without looking at it. "Thank you."

The same two thugs drove her back to Chicago. Two hours later, she was on a train heading east. First stop, Buffalo, New York.

We won't forget. Nitti's words echoed tiredly through Hanna's thoughts. Was he implying that the Chicago Outfit would seek revenge for Sam's death? Or that the Chicago Outfit would do Hanna a favor in honor of Sam if she ever needed help?

Maybe she should have taken Nitti's money. Hanna's worldly possessions had dwindled to a suitcase full of nice clothes and 25 dollars in her pocket, all that remained from her last paycheck and the pitiful remnants of her bank account.

Mrs. Brumley, who managed the models at Gossard's, was quite flustered by the reporters who came to the store. Hanna refused to comment beyond admitting that she was going to Lido, but that didn't stop every newspaper in Chicago from printing what they wanted.

LOCAL HARVEY GIRL FOUND STRANGLED IN NY

MISSING GIRL DEAD IN NY RIVER

STRANGLER SOUGHT IN MURDER OF CHICAGO GIRL

On behalf of Gossard's, Mrs. Brumley was terribly sorry, of course. What a tragedy. Deeply concerned. Best to terminate Hanna's employment so she could devote full attention to resolving her sister's affairs. From the way the woman spoke, Hanna would have thought that Marta was empire-builder Andrew Carnegie instead of a 21-year-old Harvey House waitress serving hot roast beef sandwiches to travelers waiting to catch a train.

Outside the train window, fields and hills dissolved into twilight. The carriage darkened. The clack-clack-clack of the train dulled her thoughts.

Hanna took out the letter from Lido. It was creased and had acquired a greasy thumbprint along its journey from Lido to the magazine editor, then on to the artist and finally to her.

Karl Edwin Harriman, editor
The Red Book
Dear Sir,
I am a resident of Lido, New York, where the murder of a woman remains unsolved. No one knows who she is. The police are investigating but are stumped.

I enclose a newspaper article with additional details.

Here at the Galliano Club, we have reason to believe that the drawing on the cover of your October magazine strongly resembles this unknown dead woman. Could you please advise if the girl who is depicted on the cover is missing or has ever been

to Lido? If not, is she related to anyone who was visiting here within the last few months?

The citizens of Lido would be grateful for your help in this matter.

Sincerely,

Gianluca Lombardo

Galliano Club, Lido, New York

The first thing she wanted to do was talk to the writer and see what he knew.

If the body in Lido was Marta, someone had thrown her into a river like unwanted rubbish. If that was the case, Hanna intended to hunt down Marta's killer and make them pay.

Sam hadn't been much of a husband, but he'd taught Hanna the things that mattered.

CHAPTER 2

Fox in the henhouse

Benny Rotolo had lost track of time. All he knew was that he was freezing cold, dead tired, and his shoes were soaking wet. His wool pants were ruined and the hem of his overcoat weighed a ton as it dripped onto the floorboards of the Cadillac.

He drove past the freight yards, parked rail cars looming like blocky black monsters against the night sky, and turned into Trixie's drive. Passed the sprawling farmhouse and parked the V8 Cadillac by the back door. The only other vehicle there belonged to Trixie, which meant that all her customers were gone. The upstairs windows were dark, too. All the working girls were probably asleep.

It wasn't the kind of fancy brothel he'd encountered in Chicago when he was a torpedo and driver for the North Side gang, but it wasn't no clap house where a fella took his chances for two dollars and a shot of grain alcohol. Trixie ran a decent place.

Benny was her fella, which also made him the proverbial fox in the henhouse.

Trixie was waiting for him in the kitchen. She was a good-looking tomato, but not when she had that cranky look on her kisser. It was the same one she was wearing when he left on his little errand.

"Did you take care of it?" she demanded.

"I said I would and I did." Benny didn't take his coat off. He thumped down a Mason jar of bathtub gin before squelching across the linoleum to the icebox. Found a bottle of apple juice and poured a tot into the gin. The stuff turned the color of piss.

Benny collapsed into a chair at the kitchen table and took a gulp. The cocktail tasted like a bolt of cheap lightning and lit up his gizzard. He coughed a couple of times. It stayed down and he rewarded himself with another slug.

Trixie paced between the table and the icebox. She wore a skimpy lace camisole and tap pants that put her hourglass figure on full display. A loose silk kimono robe flapped in her wake like a cape. Her platinum hair was rolled into pincurls and held in place by a colorful silk scarf. "What am I supposed to tell people if they ask where she is?" she asked.

The next slug of gin and juice fizzed on Benny's tongue. "Who's gonna ask?"

"Her regulars."

"She wasn't here long enough to have no regulars."

"The Polish boys liked her." A red lacquered fingernail tapped on the table for emphasis.

Benny snorted. "They like all your girls."

Trixie stopped flouncing around. "The other girls are going to wonder."

"You're the boss. Tell them to shut up."

But Trixie was determined to be a real sourpuss about this. "What about her brother? What if he comes back, looking for her?"

"Al Genovese isn't coming back, dollface." Benny laughed at the thought.

"Why not? Annunziata was just a kid."

"Al Genovese isn't looking for nobody. Not now, not ever. And you can take that all the way to the bank."

"You sure?"

"Sure, I'm sure." Benny pulled Trixie into his lap and held the Mason jar to her lips. "You know, when I get the Galliano Club and turn it into the best speakeasy north of Manhattan, you and the girls will turn tricks upstairs. Every room with velvet curtains and brass beds. Only high rollers, too. No more Polacks and fellas from the freight yards."

Trixie obediently sipped at the firewater, then let Benny finish what was left. "That sounds real good, Benny," she said, relaxing against him. "But I don't like you doing it with the other girls. I especially don't like you getting rough. When you get rough things get out of hand. Like tonight."

"Hey." Benny shoved Trixie off his lap, making her stumble a bit. "How was I supposed to know she was so flimsy? Girl was built like one of those tank machines the Brits drove over trenches in the news reels."

"I liked her, Benny."

There were two Trixies now. Two turbaned heads, two sets of accusing eyes. Lots and lots of red fingernails.

"You didn't know her," Benny jeered. "She didn't even speak English."

But Trixie and her twin had already left the kitchen.

CHAPTER 3

Accounting issues

Owen Forbes Fisher turned onto Hamilton Street and proceeded through the Italian neighborhood of East Lido to the giant Lido Premium mill at the very end. Smoke curled out of the mill's towering double smokestacks. White vapor curled against a brilliant blue sky.

He set the brake and got out of the Ford, murmuring his daily mantra to keep his nerves steady.

You are a successful man. You are in the inner circle.

And why shouldn't he be all that? He was the accountant for a major New York company, a Syracuse University graduate, a Deke from Delta Kappa Epsilon and a member of the Bison Club to boot. The Membership Committee, no less.

His suit was from Van Dyke's. His beautiful wife Cynthia belonged to all the best charitable organizations. On occasion, she called him *darling*.

He was also the money man for what his partner Benny Rotolo called the beer racket.

The latest problem was that too many of the wrong sort of people knew it.

No sooner had he walked into the office building, stamping his feet to clear the snow off his galoshes, than Miss Camden bolted up from her desk. The secretary, normally a forbidding harridan, looked positively flustered. "Oh, Mr. Fisher! I'm so glad you're here."

"I know I'm late," Owen started, quite surprised at her attention. Miss Camden was generally cool toward him, her loyalty reserved for Henry Blick, the operations manager and nephew of the owner, Nathan Packham.

He wondered if he should explain about the uncomfortable discussion this morning with Cynthia on the need, or lack thereof, for grapefruit spoons in her new Etruscan sterling silver pattern, but the secretary didn't give him time to decide.

"I simply didn't know what to do." The normally unflappable secretary twisted her hands together in distress. 'It's been a positively unusual morning. Mr. Blick isn't here. He's gone to get married!"

"Married? Blick?" Owen actually staggered back.

"He telephoned to say he wouldn't be in because he was getting married." Miss Camden almost plucked at Owen's sleeve. "I could hardly believe it."

"Dear Lord," Owen sputtered.

He was hard-pressed to imagine any woman with the courage to link up with Henry Blick. The man was a West Point graduate who'd lost an eye and gained a chest full of medals in the Great War. Always easy to spot with his black eye patch, silver hair, and tall straight frame, Blick liked nothing better than to roll up his sleeves and sweat all day in the mill alongside the Italian and Polish workers. He was the heir apparent to the Lido Premium fortune, too. The Blick and Packham families had been in Lido for generations.

Owen was both terrified and deeply envious of him. Not only did Henry Blick have money, but people looked up to him. His position in Lido's high society was everything a man could want. The mayor was his best friend and his brother-in-law was the current president of the Bison Club.

Blick wasn't so much in the inner circle. He *was* the inner circle.

"I mean, a wedding!" Miss Camden went on. "A spur-of-the-moment wedding and him such a confirmed bachelor. I hardly know whether to believe it or not."

Owen took off his coat. "Will he be in tomorrow? Did he leave a message for me?"

"Oh my goodness, I nearly forgot. There's a

gentleman waiting for you in your office." Miss Camden rushed back to her desk chair, the eyeglasses on a chain swinging across her bosom, and scooped up a business card. She held it out to Owen. "Inspector Ernest Finch. He's from the Post Office."

Owen forced himself to take the card. "What does he want?"

"Fisher?" Inspector Finch stood in the entrance to the hallway leading to the executive offices. "Good morning--"

"Yes. Well."

Owen stared blankly at Finch, taking in the sturdy corn-fed Midwesterner, with his sandy hair, cleft chin, dark suit and shiny badge. In a two-man race, it was obvious who would win.

"Shall I bring coffee to your office, Mr. Fisher?" Miss Camden asked, cutting through Owen's immobility.

"Yes, yes, of course," Owen gabbled. He extended his hand to Finch. "Nice to see you again, Inspector."

"Likewise." Finch turned and led Owen down the hall to his own office.

The door was open. Owen edged past Finch, hung his coat on the peg and settled into his desk chair, indicating the chairs for visitors by the wall. A tweed coat was already draped over one of the chairs, a dark fedora resting on the seat as well. The postal inspector had apparently been waiting some time.

"I won't take up too much of your time," Finch said without preamble. "As you might recall from our conversation at the banquet, I'm here to investigate a case of mail fraud."

"Yes." Owen vividly remembered their conversation at the Bison Club banquet celebrating Officer Sean O'Malley. A few weeks ago the policeman had stopped a murder and extracted a confession from a killer, leading to the discovery of the body of Lido Premium's missing foreman. Visiting Lido from Gary, Indiana, Finch had been seated next to Owen. "Winding it up, are you?" he asked, trying to sound honest and impressed.

"A few loose ends," Finch said. "As well as a new case."

"Ah?"

"Yes." Finch put a slip of paper on Owen's desk. "Related to my original investigation here in Lido, it appears as if you recently sent money orders to a wholesale grocery business connected to my prime suspect."

Owen managed a weak laugh even as he ignored the paper. "I'm sure there's some mistake."

"Two weeks ago, you sent one thousand dollars to

Longo Wholesale Produce and Imports, 722 Perry Street, Gary, Indiana."

Some explanation was required, but Owen couldn't think of any.

"Longo Wholesale Produce and Imports is a large business," Finch went on. "One of the largest fruit importers in Indiana. It also acts as a front for the Society of the Black Hand, a blackmail and extortion group targeting successful Italians. They call it *La Mano Nera*."

"I wouldn't know anything about that," Owen said.

"You sent a money order there," Finch said. "Can you explain why?"

Before Owen could say anything, agitated female voices filtered down the hall. Miss Camden was using her most authoritative tone, yet another woman was standing up to her.

"I should see if Miss Camden needs my assistance," Owen said and started to rise from his chair.

Finch crossed the small office in two steps and slammed the door. "Mr. Fisher, you may not realize the severity of your situation. The Longo brothers and their partner Vincent Salerno are using the Postal Service to engage in blackmail. If you have assisted them in any way using postal money orders, you could be charged with the federal crime of misusing the mail."

The vehement female discussion was still going on, albeit muffled by the stout wooden door.

"Really, this must all be a mistake," Owen said. "I don't know any of those people."

The postal inspector tapped the paper on Owen's desk. "This is your signature, isn't it?"

Owen took a deep breath and forced himself to focus on the receipt. *O. Fisher.* The signature slanted to the left, with oversized capitals. "No, that's not my signature."

Finch blinked. "Really?"

"Here, I'll show you." Owen opened the binder of quarterly reports that he submitted to the Lido Premium board of directors every quarter. A cover letter accompanied each report, typed by Miss Camden and signed by Owen. After each member of the board initialed the circulation sheet testifying to having read the report, the document was placed in the appropriate annual binder and secured with brass brads.

"There's my signature." Owen showed Finch the cover letter from the last quarter. His signature was at the bottom of the letter in perfect copperplate cursive. *Owen Forbes Fisher.*

On the other side of the office door, Miss Camden's discussion continued, albeit quieter and at a slower pace.

Finch nodded. "I see."

"Obviously there's more than one person named Fisher in the world," Owen said.

"But only three named Fisher in Lido." Finch dropped back into his chair. "Relatives of yours?"

"No, not at all. Simply random." Owen made a production out of replacing the binder in the proper spot on the bookcase next to his desk.

Finch crossed his legs at the knee, evidently in no hurry to get on with his job of terrorizing prominent citizens. "Are you prepared to swear under oath that this is not your signature and that you did not send a money order to Longo Wholesale Produce and Imports in Gary, Indiana?"

"Of course," Owen said. "Why wouldn't I?"

"That's good to hear," Finch said. "We've arrested Vincent Salerno, who has been using the Post Office to send threatening letters, using a network of local accomplices. He received hundreds of money orders through the grocery business without ever having a single bank account. We've seized all manner of evidence and of course will be interviewing him as well."

"Well done," Owen said weakly. "Excellent use of American tax dollars at work."

Finch stood and collected his coat and hat. "Don't

leave Lido, Mr. Fisher. We'll have more questions for you."

"Of course." Owen yanked open the door. "Best of luck, Inspector."

Finch shook hands before striding down the hall. Owen swiped sweaty palms on his trousers and crept a few paces in the man's wake, enough to see him pass Miss Camden's desk and leave the building.

Before he could collect himself, Miss Camden flew at him, agitated once again. "This has been such a trying day and it's not even noon!"

"What's happened now?"

"A young lady was here," Miss Camden confided breathlessly. "A most disturbed young woman. She shouted at me."

"Shouted?"

"She was looking for Mr. Dombrowski. She was quite insistent but of course, I could hardly send her over to the mill."

"A young lady looking for Dombrowski?" Owen left the security of the sturdy wall. "Could our new foreman be in trouble with a lady?"

Miss Camden pressed a hand to her heart. "That's exactly what I thought. Mr. Blick wanted him and the board approved him and this business apprentice program has him in the office every week, so far be it from me to say anything about an unmarried foreman. And one who looks like Paul Bunyan, too. We've never had anyone like that, have we?"

"No, we haven't," Owen said.

Blick had championed Dombrowski and the young foreman had already instituted the safety procedures that everyone was talking about, but that wasn't why Owen was interested in the man.

"The girl was very upset when I told her she couldn't speak to him directly." Miss Camden's hand went from her heart to her head. "She insisted upon leaving him a message. I was just about to walk over to the mill and leave it for him."

"I'll do it," Owen said.

"Oh, Mr. Fisher, I can't ask you to be a messenger boy. I know you have work to do."

"I can see you've had a trying morning, what with Mr. Blick's surprising news." Owen retrieved his hat and coat.

Miss Camden pressed a hand to her heart as he came back to her desk. "I'm so sorry. I never brought in the coffee for your visitor."

"You make some fresh coffee while I go across to the mill. Then we'll start the day all over again."

She smiled gratefully and held out a folded piece of Lido Premium stationery. "Here it is."

Leaving the office building, Owen took the path that wound between the office building and the mill itself, an enormous rectangle bigger than a battleship, with black iron-framed windows. Two great smokestacks belched greasy vapor into the blue sky, announcing to the world that this was the biggest mill in the Northeast. Lido Premium churned out acres of copper sheeting and miles of copper wire every week, with its own railroad spur to move ore in and finished product out. One-tenth of all copper used in American manufacturing came out of that building. The city fathers had even erected an electric sign over the Bell Road bridge to that effect.

Halfway along the path, where he was out of sight of both buildings, Owen read the note.

Dear Karol,
I hope you remember me. Luca and I planned to get married today but he got arrested instead. The police came and took him to jail. I will hire an attorney this morning to get him out of this jam.
He told me to contact you for help. Please meet me at the courthouse this afternoon.
Tess Kennedy

Owen could hardly believe his luck. Dombrowski's friend Luca Lombardo, whom the newspapers dubbed

"Lucky" when he survived an attempted murder, was in trouble.

If the man was in jail, appealing to Dombrowski for help, then he was hardly in a position to blackmail Owen over the murder of the late Al Genovese.

His partner Benny Rotolo and Benny's squad of Polish thugs had been the only witnesses there the night Owen shot Al Genovese. That's what Owen thought, right up to the moment Dombrowski, Lombardo and an Irishman named Toby Gleason accosted him in the Lido Premium parking lot. They knew everything, including the blackmail scheme Benny and Genovese had run that cost Lombardo's boss, the owner of the Galliano Club, his life savings and more besides.

The only way to ensure their silence was to promise Owen's share of beer profits from Benny Rotolo's bootlegging operation. They claimed the money would be used to get Lombardo's boss out of debt.

But that money was better used to buy grapefruit spoons and mink jackets and contributions to charitable causes so Cynthia would call her husband *darling*.

Owen tore the note into tiny scraps and scattered them to the wind.

CHAPTER 4

Jailbirds

Luca Lombardo was nearly frozen by the time the paddy wagon stopped and the back hatch swung open. The two cops had to help him stumble out. They'd snatched him off the sidewalk in front of the Galliano Club before he could even get his coat. He blinked in the sudden brightness after the near-total darkness of the closed vehicle.

The cops shoved him unceremoniously into the courthouse, down a hall and through a heavy metal door into a dank basement space. Despite a small casement window set near the ceiling at the far end, the place was gloomy. And cold.

Luca tried to suppress a bone-deep shiver and failed.

"Got another one for you, Sestito." The cop gave Luca a push between the shoulder blades. Luca stumbled forward; his hands still manacled in front of him. "Gianluca Lombardo. One of yours. Under arrest for attempted murder and kidnapping."

The man in the uniform of a county Deputy Sheriff gave a curt nod of recognition and swung around the desk with a jangle of keys. He unlocked one of two jail cells facing the desk separated by a cinderblock wall. "In here."

One of the paddy wagon cops unlocked the handcuffs and the other flung Luca into the cell with a violent shove. The bars clanged shut.

"How the mighty have fallen." The first cop put a paper on the desk and wandered over to an electric percolator. "This for anybody?"

"Help yourself." Sestito sat down behind the desk and opened a book. "What's he charged with?"

"Attempted murder and kidnapping. No doubt more to come." The second cop similarly helped himself to coffee. "A couple of weeks ago he was everybody's hero. Lucky Lombardo. Now he's headed for Sing Sing."

"Or Old Sparky," the other cop added.

The first cop snorted. "Teach them to keep their hands off our women."

Sestito entered Luca's information into a big log book that lay open on the desk and made both cops sign it. The transaction reminded Luca of signing for bread deliveries.

He looked around, arms crossed over his chest to stay warm. The cell was marginally warmer than the paddy wagon but not by much.

The jail was run by the county, which hadn't bothered to make it into a garden spot. The walls were a bilious yellow and the floor was simple gray cement. The cell contained an iron cot topped with a ticking mattress, a flat pillow, and a woolen army surplus blanket folded at the foot, the words *U.S. Army* stenciled in white along the edge. A lidded bucket served as a toilet.

The cops finished their coffee and left, clanging the heavy metal door shut. The sound reverberated off the cement block walls of the cell with indescribable finality. Luca tried not to panic.

Joe Sestito wasn't a member of the Galliano Club, but they knew each other by name. Luca played first base for the Galliano Club baseball team and Sestito played saxophone in the Lido Civic Band, so was always on hand to start Lido Industrial League games with the *Star-Spangled Banner* and play *Take Me out to the Ball Game* at halftime.

The only Italian in law enforcement in the entire county, Sestito had been appointed to his position by the sheriff himself and had the reputation of being the toughest man in the entire department. He had dark blonde hair and a big-bladed Calabrian beak of a nose. As tall as Luca, it was rumored that he could twist a horseshoe. Luca had never seen it done, but if anyone could do it, his money was on the deputy sheriff.

Sestito leaned back in the desk chair and studied Luca through the cell bars. "Kidnapping and attempted murder? That's big trouble."

"I had a fight with a rich man who's after my girl." Another involuntary shiver shook Luca. "We were supposed to get married today."

"Looks like it was a pretty good fight." Sestito considered the bruises on Luca's face. "Who won?"

"I put both him and his brother down in the second round."

Sestito gave a snort. "You want some hot coffee?"

"Thanks," Luca said.

A percolator and a box of doughnuts sat on a low wooden filing credenza behind the desk. Sestito passed a steaming tin cup and a plain cake doughnut through the bars. Luca carried them to the cot, grateful for the hot coffee but also for the gesture.

The severity of his situation was beginning to take hold. Luca hunched himself around the warmth of the tin mug, wolfed down the doughnut, and thought about Tess. His *Tessa*.

Less than an hour ago, he'd revealed his deepest secret. It had shocked her, as Luca knew it would. Now he was in jail and he had no idea what was going to happen. What would happen once her strong-willed

Aunt Evelyn Thompson knew? Tess had walked away from an arranged marriage to a wealthy man. He had to hope that Tess was strong enough to defy her aunt yet again.

"What happens next?" Luca asked Sestito.

"You'll be arraigned." Seeing Luca's confusion, the deputy explained. "You'll talk to your lawyer, decide how you want to plead and get to tell the judge. He'll set bail. If you've got the money, you can get out in time to have dinner with your girl."

Luca understood the *dinner with your girl* part and none of the rest.

The metal door leading into the jail clanged open. Three Lido policemen barreled into the jail. The one in the middle, with his police coat unbuttoned and his hands cuffed in front of him, was Officer Sean O'Malley. Luca was so surprised he nearly dropped the tin mug.

Sestito passed in front of Luca and opened the door to the cell on the other side of the cinderblock wall. O'Malley's lips twisted as he recognized his fellow prisoner. Luca heard the metallic jingle as O'Malley's handcuffs were unlocked. "There you go, O'Malley," someone said.

Bolts of blue and brown went past Luca's cell as O'Malley made a run for it. Sestito reacted fast and grabbed O'Malley by the shoulder. O'Malley spun around and aimed a kick at Sestito's shin that landed like a thunderbolt. The deputy sheriff's leg buckled, sending both men cascading across the desk. O'Malley's arms windmilled but Sestito kept his grip on the disgraced cop with one hand and drove an uppercut into his jaw with the other.

Amid a flurry of papers, O'Malley crumpled unconscious to the ground. The big log book teetered over the edge of the desk and landed with a heavy thud.

"Pick him up," Sestito said through gritted teeth to the two cops. Both were standing like they'd been stuffed. "Put him in the cell."

The two cops dragged O'Malley by the arms and dumped him in the cell. Luca heard the door slam shut.

Limping badly, Sestito picked up the papers and the log book. When the desk was back in working order, he and the cops completed the handover transaction.

"Would you believe it?" Now that the excitement was over, this new brace of cops was even more ready to gossip than the first. "Blackmail. Sent a blackmail letter to Henry Blick, the operations manager at Lido Premium. Blick took it to the mayor and the mayor called in Chief Doyle."

"Made him arrest O'Malley himself," the second cop added.

"You want we should arrest him for assaulting an officer of the law?"

"Sounds like he's in enough trouble."

The two policemen left. Luca watched as Sestito carefully rolled up his pants leg to examine his shin. The bone was dented like a baseball bat with a notch cut into it. A purple bruise was spreading across the front of his leg.

Luca finished his coffee. If a cop as well-known as O'Malley could land in jail, what hope did a nobody like Luca have of getting out?

CHAPTER 5

Positive identification

It was early afternoon when the train rolled into the station in Lido. Hanna stepped off and followed the handful of people who seemed to know where they were going. Someone from the mayor's office was supposed to meet her in the baggage claim area.

The porter quickly found her suitcase. Hanna tipped him a dime. She lit a cigarette and decided that the entire Lido train station could fit inside the ladies' lounge in Chicago's Union Station.

It made a nice first impression for Lido, with polished wooden benches under a tremendous vaulted ceiling and a sweeping staircase with a Greek key design for a banister. Matching mosaic tile trim on the walls called attention to the semi-circular ticket booth and the spacious baggage area.

"Mrs. Vitello?" A man in a brown overcoat and a brown fedora bobbed his head at her. "I'm Stewart Quinn, from the mayor's office. We have a car waiting outside for you. It'll be my pleasure to escort you into Lido and see that arrangements are made during this difficult time."

"Gorski," Hanna said. "I use my maiden name. Gorski. Hanna Gorski."

"Mayor Peabody has asked that I bring you directly to his office so he can offer his personal condolences."

Instead of accepting his invitation, if one could charitably call it that and not an order, Hanna stubbed out her cigarette in a sand-filled ashtray at the end of a bench. She was tired and sticky from the overnight journey and would pursue her agenda and no one else's.

"My first priority is to view the body of this unidentified woman and decide if she's my sister Marta or not," she said. "You can either take me directly to wherever this woman's body is or I'll take a taxi."

"Yes, well, of course," Quinn said uncertainly. When Hanna didn't budge, he indicated the stationmaster's office. "I'm sure new arrangements can be made with a telephone call or two."

Thirty minutes later, Hanna was in the back seat next to Quinn as a police officer drove them to a blocky brick four-story building set against a gently sloping hill. Snow-dappled lawns, an iced-over pond and leafless willow trees made for a quiet, white landscape.

Inside, the hospital was also quiet and white. Nurses in starched aprons and white kerchiefs glided past, carrying pitchers of water or important-looking clipboards. A phalanx of orderlies in canvas jackets buttoned to the throat stood ready for the reviewing stand.

"Mrs. Vitello?" A silver-haired gentleman greeted her. "I'm Horace Saunders, the head doctor here. May I offer my deepest condolences on your loss."

"I use my maiden name." Hanna wondered how many times she would have to repeat herself. "Gorski. Hanna Gorski."

"Of course. Miss Gorski." Saunders had a droning, professorial voice that matched his goatee and fancy suit. "I trust you had a pleasant journey from Chicago?"

"It was long." Hanna wondered which door hid the body. "I'd like to view the body now."

"Yes, of course." Saunders pursed his lips. "If you'll just step this way."

He walked her through the first floor of the hospital, which was smaller than it looked from the outside, or maybe he was just keeping her away from the patient rooms. Quinn followed behind, along with two nurses in case Hanna fainted. Two uniformed policemen met them at the bottom of a short flight of stairs and accompanied them to a door guarded by more orderlies in their stiff white jackets buttoned to the throat.

Everything in the hall was clean and shiny and white. Walls, ceiling, lights, soft-soled shoes, medical people.

Dr. Saunders gestured for the orderlies to open the door. The group filed into a stark, unheated room. Hanna blinked at the cloying smell. Her empty stomach gave a lurch.

A tall wooden table draped in white sheeting occupied a third of the room. Hanna recognized the contours of a woman's body.

With Hanna, Saunders, Quinn, and the orderlies and nurses, the room felt suffocating. Only the policemen remained outside. The two orderlies positioned themselves on either side of the table. One of the nurses hovered at Hanna's elbow with a bottle of smelling salts.

"I'm fine," Hanna snapped and willed her stomach to behave.

Saunders cleared his throat. "Miss Gorski, you must understand that the body has been treated with care but was submerged for quite some time. Without family permission, only a partial autopsy was performed. No alcohol or illegal drugs were found in her system."

"All right."

"However, my point is that the body has been out of the water for enough time for--."

"I'm not going to faint," Hanna said brusquely. "Let's get on with it."

The two attendants peeled back the cloth covering the woman's face.

The walls closed in. Hanna went completely still.

Marta's face was white marble, skin stretched over high cheekbones and strong chin. Blonde hair, once curly, was lank and drab. Her eyes were sewn shut with thick black blanket stitches. Feathery eyebrows held that familiar arch, just like Hanna's.

Hanna pulled the hem of the sheet down to Marta's armpits, exposing her throat. Saunders made some inane remark about propriety but Hanna wasn't listening.

Deep lines scored into her sister's neck told the story better than any newspaper. Marta had been strangled.

"The newspapers say she was found with a necktie," Hanna heard herself say. "A red striped necktie."

"That's correct."

"Was she raped?"

Saunders cleared his throat. "She was not a virgin."

"But was it rape?" Hanna challenged the doctor.

"There was no indication of forced copulation."

In Hanna's imagination her sister's pale blue eyes were wide open, staring in terror at a man choking the life out of her. Hanna willed the image to widen like the view on a movie screen so the flickering image in her head would reveal the face of the man with his hands on her sister's throat.

"Miss Gorski?" Saunders broke into her thoughts, his voice a static-filled long distance telephone call. "Miss Gorski?"

Blocking out the crackle and buzz, Hanna saw her sister choke and gag, saw her flail against her killer's strength.

"Miss Gorski?"

Hanna found herself back in the sterile confines of the room staring at Marta's supine body, the hem of the sheet clenched in her fist. The cloying air was worse than in any post office booth with a sticky receiver in her hand. "I'd like to be alone with my sister," she said.

"Do you identify her as your sister, Marta Gorski from Chicago?" Quinn asked softly.

"Yes." Hanna bit the inside of her mouth to keep from weeping. "Yes, this is my sister Marta Gorski. Please leave."

Quinn shepherded everyone out. In the sudden silence, Hanna was very aware of her own breathing.

She broke the spell by shutting the door, catching a glimpse of the knot of people in the corridor whispering to each other as it closed. Then, steeling herself for the worst, Hanna pulled the cloth entirely off Marta's naked body and immediately wished she hadn't.

Flesh had melted off in some spots or maybe fish

had nibbled her. Bones were exposed here and there. The skin was pale and ugly. One hand was turned so that Hanna could see the burn mark from Marta's first days at the Harvey House when she brushed by a hot stove.

"What were you doing to end up like this?" Hanna whispered. "I wanted so much for you."

What was left of her sister didn't answer.

Hanna walked all the way around the body on the table, holding the balled-up sheet. As much as she wanted to run out of the room and never come back, she examined every visible inch of Marta's damaged body. Her eyes lingered on the red lines scoring the throat.

Now more than ever, Hanna was determined to know who had killed her sister. A new friend, obviously. Someone to whom Marta had given her virginity; someone who had the same dazzling effect on Marta that Sam had had on Hanna the day they met in Marshall Field's.

"I will find who did this," Hanna swore aloud. "I will make him pay."

Her words hung in the thickening air.

Hanna shook out the sheet and gently covered her sister's body again.

A tap sounded at the door. "Miss Gorski? Are you all right?"

"I'm finished," Hanna made herself say.

Saunders and Quinn came back into the room, the nurses hovering anxiously just outside the door with smelling salts.

"I'd like Marta's clothes," Hanna said. "Anything, really, that was found with her."

He gave her a package wrapped in brown paper. Someone had written the contents on the outside. *Silk camisole, man's tie, cotton bedsheet, black shoelaces.*

From the salacious news reports, Hanna knew that Marta was found wrapped in the sheet, wearing only the camisole and tie. The shoelaces were used to tie the sheet closed.

"Would you like to go now?" Quinn asked.

There was no life left to keep company, yet Hanna couldn't simply abandon Marta to this strange sterile place.

"Miss Gorski?"

"I want a priest to bless her," Hanna said. "A Polish-speaking priest."

"Of course," Quinn said. "The mayor's office will find someone to help you make arrangements with your church. The new foreman at Lido Premium is Polish and quite suitable. Perhaps he can be made available to assist you."

Hanna didn't move until Saunders slid a hand under

her elbow and eased her out of the room.

Identifying Marta's disintegrating body was nothing like Sam's wake in Cicero with Frank Nitti and the rest of Al Capone's boys milling around. This was not the way life was supposed to be. Hanna had never felt more alone.

The ride from the hospital to the courthouse was both too long and not long enough as guilt stabbed Hanna with a sharp, steely pain. She'd been so preoccupied with her own life that she'd failed Marta. First with Sam, then saving herself from Sam, and then trying to remake herself as a fashion model. Was actually relieved when Marta became a Harvey Girl and moved into the Harvey House dormitory. Marta was making her own way, earning a good salary and living with her co-workers, with a curfew and rules against men in their rooms. Hanna had actually thought Marta would be protected in the dormitory from making poor choices, the kind of choices Hanna had made and regretted.

"Here we are," Quinn said with false heartiness.

The courthouse was a hefty collection of red brick, fronted by creamy Doric columns and topped with a circular cupola. Quinn pointed out City Hall across the way and blathered on about a famous Revolutionary War hero whose statue overlooked a swath of snow-spotted grass. The afternoon sky was a glorious blue.

The universe had already forgotten Marta.

Inside the courthouse, the good people of Lido had moved on, too. Carrying the thick file she'd lugged all the way from Chicago, Hanna was escorted to an interview room, Quinn trailing behind. Nicer than a place to question suspects, which Hanna knew about from bailing Sam out of the pokey more than once, but not as nice as somebody's dining room. There was a table and chairs and a plaster cast of the city seal.

Mayor John Peabody came in to express his condolences and assure her that the police were working diligently to catch her sister's killer. He was a handsome man with a pleasant manner who doubtless spent much of his time perched on the moral high ground.

Hanna told him that her last name was Gorski.

Next, two detectives named Schultz and Dooley came in to take her statement. They were accompanied by Doctor Lanigan, the police department's physician who exuded a handsome smugness that made Hanna want to slap him. No doubt he was there in case she fainted.

Schultz was a tall dark-haired man with a wide chin and small eyes. He wore his police badge clipped to his belt so that Hanna could appreciate the front of his trousers. Dooley was a short Irishman with hair the color of a ripe peach and a smatter of freckles that made him look younger than he probably was. He wore his badge affixed to the breast pocket of his vest.

"Please accept the police department's condolences—" Dooley began.

"Yes, thank you." Hanna brushed his false piety away with the back of her hand. "Tell me who killed my sister."

"Now that we know who she is, we can move ahead with the investigation," Dooley said. "Let's start with your statement."

"Here are the police reports from Chicago. I brought a full account of what the police did, as well as the private investigator I hired." Hanna pushed the thick file to the police side of the table.

"This will be extremely helpful." Dooley wrote the date at the top of his pad of paper as Doctor Lanigan began leafing through the file with nicely manicured fingers. "Let's start with the last time you saw your sister."

Hanna answered question after question about Marta's life in Chicago. Her friends, the job at the Harvey House restaurant, the dormitory for the waitresses. Questions strayed into family matters. Hanna recounted losing both parents when she was fourteen, leaving her to raise 8-year-old Marta with the help of their uncle and cousins.

When the detectives touched on Hanna's marriage, she lied and said that the late Samuel Vitello had been in the import-export business.

Dooley kept his questions brief and professional. Schultz nodded along but let his partner do the talking. Lanigan continued to pore over the file, lips pinched in disapproval.

When Dooley ran out of questions, Hanna had one of her own. "Who is your chief suspect?"

Dooley put down his pen. Schultz crossed his arms over his chest. Lanigan closed the file folder.

Their hesitation was palpable. "You do have a suspect, don't you?" Hanna pressed.

"As Detective Dooley said," Lanigan said. "The investigation could hardly make headway when our victim remained unidentified, but the manner of your sister's death is similar to another crime here in Lido not so long ago."

"Go on," Hanna said tersely.

"Nick Procopio was the deputy foreman at the Lido Premium mill. He killed his supervisor and put the body in the river, in much the same way as your sister."

Hanna came halfway out of her chair. "Then why are we wasting time here? Let me talk to him."

"Unfortunately, he was apprehended by a police officer while attempting to strangle another citizen and died of his injuries."

"This man was a serial strangler?" Hanna lowered herself back into her seat and failed to understand how Marta could have been caught up in some raving lunatic's strangling spree in Lido, New York.

"Can we provide Miss Gorski with some back issues of the *Lido Daily Clipper*?" Lanigan asked the two detectives. Schultz nodded and left the room.

Dooley clasped his hands. "Jimmy Zambrano was the foreman of the Lido Premium mill, Lido's biggest employer. He went missing but it wasn't until his deputy Nick Procopio tried to kill the manager of the Galliano Club that we found out that Procopio strangled him to get the top job and put the body in the river."

"The manager of the Galliano Club?"

"Luca Lombardo," Dooley supplied. "Procopio apparently nursed a grievance about having his membership revoked a few months before. During their altercation, Procopio confessed to the killing and said where he dumped the body. Boasted about it, sounds like. When we went looking for the body, we found your sister. Same place along the river, same manner of death. It's possible that Procopio killed them both."

To Hanna's knowledge, no one in Chicago had

asked Marta's fellow waitresses if any customers asked for Marta or if she talked about a particular frequent traveler. But it made sense.

Perhaps Nick Procopio had met Marta at the Harvey House inside Union Station. Procopio must have been a salesman-type with all the flash and charm of Sam Vitello, regularly traveling between Lido and Chicago on the train. Hanna imagined that he always ate at the Harvey House before boarding the train back to Lido. Pockets bulging with cash, he wore tailored suits, pearl gray fedoras, striped ties and promised women the moon and the stars, just like Sam.

"Tell me about him, please," Hanna murmured.

Dooley consulted a notebook. "Nicola Procopio was 43 years of age. Married, four children. Roman Catholic, member of St. Rocco's Roman Catholic Church. Born in New York City but lived in Lido all of his adult life. Worked at Lido Premium since he was 20 years old. Was deputy foreman for about three years, working under Jimmy Zambrano."

"He was old. Twice as old as Marta."

Lanigan produced a photograph. "Now, Miss Gorski, we can show you his picture but only if you have a strong stomach."

"I won't faint if that's what you're worried about."

"I have smelling salts," Lanigan said.

Hanna decided that she disliked the doctor intensely. She reached for the photograph.

A man lay flat on a white sheet just like Marta. His eyes were closed but not sewn shut. Dark hair flecked with white, a once-broken prominent nose, fleshy and chapped lips, a loose-skinned jaw. Below a bristly chin, a slight Adam's apple was visible, along with the neck and shoulders of a middle-aged man with the heavy musculature of a manual laborer and enthusiastic eater.

Hanna's newfound understanding of her sister's killer popped like a bubble. Even in a pinstriped suit with a carnation in his buttonhole, this man would not have been young or handsome or charming.

"Was he a frequent visitor to Chicago?" Hanna asked in bewilderment as she handed back the photograph.

"Doubtful," Dooley admitted. "The Lido Premium mill keeps track of their workers. He clocked in six days a week until the day he died."

"Then how would Marta have met him?"

Neither Lanigan nor Dooley answered. Schultz came back into the room with a bundle of newspapers.

The room was silent except for the rustle of the pages as Hanna went through the weeks-old newspapers. Headlines leaped out that made her head pound and her throat burn.

CORONER SAYS UNKNOWN WOMAN FROM RIVER WAS STRANGLED

"LUCKY" LOMBARDO SAYS PROCOPIO DIDN'T CONFESS TO KILLING WOMAN

PUBLIC HELP SOUGHT TO IDENTIFY DEAD WOMAN

The name Lombardo jumped out, of course, being the same name on the letter in Hanna's purse. She combed through stories about the missing Jimmy Zambrano, Procopio's assault on Luca Lombardo behind the Galliano Club, Lombardo's rescue by Officer Sean O'Malley, and Procopio's dying confession. The discovery of Zambrano's body led to the discovery of Marta's body the same day.

Lombardo's photograph was in almost every news story. Hanna could see why. Replace his wavy hair with a patent leather helmet and the man could be the late Rudolph Valentino's twin brother.

"This makes no sense," Hanna said after she'd scoured every scrap of newspaper. She was even more determined than before to seek out this Lombardo and make him tell her everything he knew. "Marta was a waitress in Chicago. This man was twice her age, working in a mill hundreds of miles away. She didn't know him."

"You said she didn't live with you, but in a dormitory with other high-spirited girls." Lanigan opened the file from Chicago again. "It's an unfortunate fact that young women without parents often go wrong."

Hanna jabbed a finger at the newspaper with Marta's portrait in death on the front page. "Marta would have told me if she had met a man who was so wonderful she was going to run off with him. But how would she have met him in the first place if he never came to Chicago?"

"See here, Miss Gorski." Quinn had been silent during the exchange with the three men from the police department, but now he came to life. "Everyone is doing the best they can under very trying circumstances."

"Answer my question," Hanna snapped. Her head pounded but she kept her eyes locked on Lanigan.

"Unfortunately, we may never know," Dr. Lanigan said piously. "Keeping secrets is simply another bad habit of young women who aren't properly overseen. Modern young women smoke and drink in a permissive manner. Obviously that type of behavior leads to tragic results, as in this case."

"Marta was a good girl," Hanna exclaimed, her patience completely gone.

The doctor gave her an extra-oily smile. "Perhaps in time you'll appreciate that your sister can serve as a cautionary tale to other young women who may be tempted to go down the same road."

Hanna stood up, the room painted over with a red glaze. If she didn't leave right now she was going to hurl herself across the table and scratch Lanigan's eyes right out of his swollen, smug head.

"Miss Gorski?" Quinn's voice came from very far away.

"Where is the ladies' lounge?" Hanna asked loudly.

CHAPTER 6

Not guilty

"I'm Randall Freshman." He was a slight man in a dark gray suit with a gold chain looped across the vest for his pocket watch. "I've been retained to represent you."

Seated at the scarred wooden table in the small interview room inside the jail, Luca could only shake his head in confusion. "I don't know you."

"That is about to change, Mr. Lombardo." Freshman sat across from him and adjusted round tortoise shell glasses. "Miss Tess Kennedy made a very convincing case for my services. So here we are."

"Tess? Is she all right?"

"Apart from the bruise on her face and concern for you, she is fine."

Freshman uncapped a gold fountain pen and poised it over a sheaf of paper. "Now then, shall we get started?"

"I can't afford to pay you," Luca said.

"I was a friend of Miss Kennedy's late father. My fee will be determined at a later date." Freshman put down the pen. "In order to help you, Mr. Lombardo, I need to know exactly what happened last night. The charges against you are extremely serious. Kidnapping, attempted murder, assault with a deadly weapon, reckless endangerment, and assault and battery. If found guilty you could face life in prison."

"I didn't do any of those things," Luca protested.

"I assume you plan to plead not guilty."

Luca nodded, his spirits rising. Tess, his *Tessa*, had not abandoned him.

"Then let's get started." The lawyer picked up the pen again. "Now then. Now, Miss Kennedy recounted her version of events, but I'd like you to tell me in your own words exactly what happened last evening."

Luca took a deep breath. "I was at work like always. At the Galliano Club on Hamilton Street."

"The Galliano Club at 601 Hamilton Street? Owned by Vito Spinelli?"

"Yes."

"Was he there?"

"No, Vito went home already."

"Who else works there?"

"Guido Serra. He's the doorman. Sonny Zambrano helps after school. Washes the dishes and sweeps, whatever I need him to do."

"They were both there?"

"Yes."

"And you had customers?"

"A good crowd. There were also 42 members in the front and six playing pool in the back room. There was 12 dollars and 86 cents in the till."

"You're very precise."

"I like numbers."

Freshman regarded Luca in a thoughtful way. "Go on."

"I was reading the lady letters." Luca squirmed a bit in his chair. "Ladies write me letters because my picture was in the newspapers. Guido came in and said a lady wanted to talk to me. When I went outside, there was Tess."

"Miss Kennedy."

"Yes, Tess. She said she was done with Howland and asked if I wanted to marry her."

"Just to verify, you're speaking about James Howland?"

"Yes, her boss at the bank. It was in the newspaper that they were going to get married but Tess never wanted to. Her aunt arranged it with Howland's father."

Freshman nodded. "So Miss Kennedy came to the club and while standing outside, informed you that she'd renounced her engagement to James Howland and would marry you."

"Yes." Luca's head pounded with tension. "We decided to find a justice of the peace right away."

"But you didn't."

"Howland and another man drove up and shouted at Tess."

"What did they shout?"

"Howland still wanted her to marry him."

"What did Miss Kennedy do?"

"She shouted right back at him." Luca couldn't help but smile at the memory. *I dislike you intensely,* she'd yelled, loud enough to be heard all the way to Saint Rocco's church six blocks away.

"And then what happened?"

"He hit her. Almost knocked her down."

"Is that why you hit him?"

"Yes."

"Did you believe he was going to strike her again?"

"He was going to grab her. Take her away and she didn't want to go." Luca knew that he'd reacted automatically. "I had to fight his brother, too, before they would go."

"Sustaining injuries yourself." Freshman made a circular motion in the air at the level of Luca's face. "So you successfully defended Miss Kennedy from being forcibly taken by the Howland brothers?"

"Yes." Luca liked the way the lawyer talked with

such precision. "I made them get in their car and leave. Tess stayed with me."

"Of her own free will?" Freshman paused with his fountain pen poised over the paper. "Would you have let her get in the car with the Howland brothers if she so desired?"

"She didn't want to be with them," Luca said.

"But did you restrain her?"

Luca blinked. "I didn't have to. She didn't want to go."

"Did you kidnap Miss Kennedy or did she remain with you of her own free will?"

"Tess stayed with me. We were going to get married."

"Did you intend to kill either of the Howland brothers?"

An old quote came to mind. "How much more grievous are the consequences of anger than the causes of it."

"Marcus Aurelius," Freshman acknowledged.

"I was angry that he'd hurt Tess. But no, I have no wish to kill anyone."

Freshman picked up his pen again. "Did anyone besides Miss Kennedy see this fight between you and the Howland brothers?"

"Sure. Everyone came outside to watch. Guido,

Sonny, everybody who was in the club."

"Did they all see Howland hit Miss Kennedy?"

"No," Luca admitted. "I don't think so. Only Guido was outside with us."

"Us being you, Miss Kennedy, and the Howland brothers."

"Yes." Luca thought back. The sidewalk had been all but deserted at that point. "Only Guido saw that. Maybe Sonny saw through the window. I don't know. Everyone came outside after."

"Considering the number of eyewitnesses, including Tess Kennedy, it's possible that the case is over before it even gets started. I'll request bail of one thousand dollars."

"I can pay that."

"If I may make a suggestion, as soon as you're out on bail, marry Miss Kennedy exactly the way you planned. Howland can hardly accuse you of kidnapping your own wife. All he'll be left with is trying to prove he's not a lousy fistfighter."

Luca smiled. "I like that idea."

"In any event, we'll plead not guilty. When the judge calls out the charges and asks how you plead, you'll say not guilty."

"Not guilty," Luca echoed.

A small smile lifted the corner of Freshman's

mouth. "It helps that you are an American citizen and have no record of being in trouble with the law. But be prepared to answer more questions, Mr. Lombardo. Many more."

A tap sounded at the door. Sestito told them it was time.

Luca had only been in a courtroom once before, when he held up his hand and became an American citizen. Then he'd been buoyed by the majesty and excitement of the day, a day shared with two dozen others who were taking the oath of citizenship. This was different.

Tess was sitting in the first row of seats behind a sort of wooden gate separating spectators from the court officials. Luca saw her as soon as he entered the courtroom from a side door, following Mr. Freshman. He met her eyes. Tess nodded encouragingly; the purple bruise prominent on her cheek.

Waking up next to her that morning seemed like a lifetime ago.

Freshman showed Luca where to sit, next to the lawyer behind a table on the right side facing the judge's massive desk mounted on a dais. Luca didn't have time to see who else was in the courtroom or at the other table on the opposite side of the courtroom before a man in a uniform like Sestito's shouted.

"All rise! Judge William Pepper, now presiding."

The judge walked into the courtroom and took his seat behind the massive desk. He had silver hair carefully parted on the side and oiled flat to his head. He looped spectacles over his ears and gestured to the uniform. Luca and Freshman remained standing.

"In the matter of Howland versus Lombardo," the uniform trumpeted. "Mr. Gianluca Lombardo is accused of kidnapping, attempted murder, assault with a deadly weapon, reckless endangerment, and assault and battery."

Judge Pepper lowered his spectacles and blinked at Freshman. "Well, Rand, how does your client plead?"

"My client pleads Not Guilty to all charges, Your Honor."

"Hmmm." The judge pursed his lips. Shuffled some pages in front of him as everyone waited. "I gather your client is from the Italian colony," he said at length. "Does he know sufficient English to stand trial without an interpreter?"

"My client is an American citizen with full command of the English language."

"Well, that's too bad. I thought we might be able to deport him to Rome and have done with this nonsense."

Someone on the other side of the courtroom tittered. Luca craned his neck to look past Mr. Freshman and saw James Howland at the other table. He had two black eyes, heavy bruising below the sockets, and a bandage swathed across the middle of his face to keep his nose in place.

Luca was pretty pleased.

Freshman addressed the judge. "Your Honor, in light of the fact that this entire altercation is a misunderstanding over the affections of Miss Tess Kennedy, we move to dismiss the charge of kidnapping. Miss Kennedy is here now and ready to make a statement to the court that no kidnapping occurred, that she was not coerced in any way, and voluntarily stayed with Mr. Lombardo with the intention of marrying him."

"How old is this Miss Kennedy?"

"Twenty-four, Your Honor. She is not a minor child and would like to make a statement."

"The court is not interested in silly and misbehaving females," Judge Pepper said waspishly. "The motion is denied. The charge will stay and be addressed at the proper time."

Howland's lawyer spoke up. "The plaintiff requests that bail be denied. Let him out of jail and his kind will be on the first boat back to Italy.

"My client is an American citizen," Freshman said. "Bail is requested in the same amount as for any other citizen charged with these offenses."

Judge Pepper peered down at Luca. "As I've not seen proof of citizenship, I'm inclined to agree with the plaintiff in this case." He banged his gavel. "Bail is denied. Remanded for criminal trial in 10 days."

"All rise!"

Chairs scraped noisily as everyone stood. Judge Pepper stomped out of the courtroom.

Everyone started talking. Mr. Freshman turned to say something to Luca but was immediately cut off by a scrum of reporters who'd been in the back of the courtroom.

"Hey Lucky! Lucky Lombardo!" It was Gifford, the reporter from the *Lido Daily Clipper* who'd pestered Luca nonstop after he survived Nick Procopio's murderous assault, dubbing him Lucky for good measure. "Did you think you'd be back in the news so soon?"

Luca couldn't reply even if he wanted to. He got a last look at Tess's horror-stricken face before being bundled out of the courtroom.

"Back so soon, Lucky?" O'Malley mocked as Sestito opened the cell door.

Shut up, Luca wanted to say but he was too stunned to make a sound.

CHAPTER 7

A disgrace

Scarcely able to breathe, Tess Kennedy watched as the bailiff tugged on Luca's arm. An electric jolt of sadness and regret passed from him to her. Tess wanted to say something, anything.

And then Luca was gone.

As soon as the door closed behind bailiff and prisoner, there was a scramble for the double doors at the rear. Tess belatedly realized that reporters could file stories in time for the evening edition of the *Lido Daily Clipper*. Her life was going to unravel tonight on the front page.

It made the choice between going home to Aunt Evelyn or taking refuge in the apartment above the Galliano Club again that much harder.

Yesterday was supposed to be her wedding day. The day she signed her name on the marriage license, said "I do" before a justice of the peace, and embarked on a new career of wedded bliss with the man she loved.

Today was not supposed to be the day she watched Luca arrested, handcuffed and charged with attempted murder and kidnapping. Not the day Luca revealed the terrible secret he kept hidden in the past, a secret Tess never dreamed she would ever hear from the man she loved.

She'd barely come to grips with his shocking revelation when the police pounded on the door and arrested him.

As the courtroom emptied out, James and his lawyer passed the row of chairs where Tess sat, both resolutely avoiding a glance in her direction. Up close, James looked even worse; two black eyes and a metal cup over his nose held in place by a belt of white gauze. His brother Richard looked minimally better, with a single black eye and a swollen lip ornamented by a wreath of tiny cuts and bruises. Their parents followed.

"Swell bitch," Richard snarled. The slur was accompanied by a slobbery air kiss toward Tess.

"Don't speak to her," Muriel Howland trumpeted. Tess's would-be mother-in-law came to a stop with the size and grace of a battleship ramming a wharf. "This girl is a disgrace to her family name and no longer a member of polite society."

Furious, Tess leaped to her feet and turned her face to show the palm-sized bruise on her cheek. "Your son did that," she retorted. "He hit me! Is that the sort of man you raised him to be?"

"The impertinence--" Muriel was cut off when her husband grabbed her by the elbow.

As president of the First National Bank of Lido, Preston Howland had been Tess's employer for more than two years. He appeared not to recognize her but guided his wife out of the courtroom.

Tess felt weak and wobbly as Mr. Freshman came down the aisle. Hiring him was the only smart thing she'd done all day.

"No talking to the opposition, Miss Kennedy," he cautioned. "They have a weak case and no doubt will use anything against Luca, and you, by extension."

"It won't happen again," Tess said and felt a glimmer of hope. "You really think they have a weak case?"

"Which means they'll be desperate." Freshman shifted his briefcase to the other hand. "I hope you're prepared to be a star witness."

"Of course."

"You understand that your reputation will be called into question. Your morals, your honesty, your intentions toward both Mr. Howland and Mr. Lombardo."

"This is all my fault, isn't it? I let the farce with James go on too long, trying to please Aunt Evelyn, when I wanted to be with Luca. Now he's in jail because of it." Tess felt the weight of responsibility for not only what had happened but for getting Luca out of this mess.

"The charges are serious, but not insurmountable," Freshman said. "Although if there is any chance you will change your mind about James Howland, please let me know now."

"Absolutely not," Tess said firmly.

"I'd like you to have a picture made so that the bruises you sustained can be entered as evidence." They left the courtroom and emerged into the big center vault of the courthouse. The floor was dappled with streaks of the setting sun filtered through the windows set into the cupola high above.

Tess nodded. "What else?"

"I'll be talking to Mr. Lombardo in the morning, of course, but if there's anything in his background the prosecution can exploit, I'd like to know about it sooner rather than later."

"His wife died. And their baby. During the Spanish influenza epidemic."

"Useful to gain the jury's sympathy," Freshman said. "Anything else I should know?"

Tess slowed as they crossed the floor. "When Luca first came to America and he didn't have a job, he was a fighter. For money. In the back of an Irish saloon."

"Mr. Lombardo is already one of my most interesting clients. He quoted Marcus Aurelius to me." Freshman paused. "You do know that you won't be able to visit him in jail. You're a witness."

Tess blinked away an unexpected prick of tears. "What about a note?"

Mr. Freshman nodded. "I'll pass it to him but keep in mind that it could be read by the deputy in charge of the jail."

Tess scribbled three numbers on a piece of paper she found in her purse. *26 13 97*.

"Thank you for doing this." She handed the folded slip to the attorney. "I know it was short notice . . . and, well, not many attorneys will take an Italian client. Thank you."

"Your father was a good friend," Freshman said. "May I see you out of the courthouse? Do you need a ride home?"

"No, thank you," Tess said. "I have my car here."

She watched the lawyer pass through the wooden gate next to the semi-circular reception desk. When he left the building, she whirled around and rushed back into the courthouse. A custodian was the only person there, plying a broom just below the judge's dais.

"Hello," Tess said breathlessly. She skirted the table where Luca and Mr. Freshman had sat and pulled open the same door the bailiff had taken Luca through.

She was brought up short by a policeman behind a metal reception desk. "Can I help you?"

"Hello," Tess said. "I'd like to see Luca Lombardo. He was just in the courtroom."

The policeman gave her a curt nod. "He got took to the jail."

"Yes, I know," Tess replied. "So if you'd just direct me."

"Direct you where?"

"To the jail."

"No women allowed in the jail."

"No women allowed in the jail," Tess repeated. She saw the officer's name on the brass tag on his uniform. "Officer Flanagan, I don't want to take up your time. All I need is to speak to one prisoner. Very quickly. Just to know that he's all right."

"He'll be in the jail."

"Yes." Tess tried to edge past the corner of the desk. "That's where I want to go. So if you'll just let me pass."

"No women in the jail."

"What about women who commit a crime?"

"What crime?" The policeman narrowed his eyes at her.

"I am speaking hypothetically."

"Ho there, miss." Flanagan held up his hand. "You've got no cause to talk like that. The law's the law."

"Dear Lord." Tess clenched her fists. "Honestly, Officer. All I want to do is see a gentleman who was arrested this morning and is being held, very unfairly I might add, without bail. One prisoner. I promise not to do a can-can dance or anything else to excite the inmates."

"No women in the jail," Flanagan repeated stonily.

A second policeman joined him. "What's the trouble, Flanagan?"

"Lady here wants to go to jail."

"I do not want to go to jail," Tess exclaimed. "I wish to visit someone who was arrested on totally false charges and is being held without bail."

"Lucky Lombardo," Flanagan supplied.

"Not so lucky now," the second policeman said. "Did you hear what Judge Pepper said? That dago's in big trouble."

"May I pass?" Tess said, her voice trembling.

"No women allowed in the jail."

"So your thickheaded colleague has said, which is a ridiculous excuse--."

She never got to finish. One policeman on either side, with iron grips on her arms, Tess was summarily escorted through the courtroom and deposited on a bench in the lobby.

It truly was the worst day of her life, even worse than the day her father died and she went to live with Aunt Evelyn. If only Karol Dombrowski had come to help. Tess couldn't understand why he never showed up or at least dispatched a message in return. Not only had Karol forsaken her, but Luca's boss had been less than useless. After arranging things with Mr. Freshman, she had stopped at the Galliano Club. Barely noon and Luca's boss was already drunk.

It was getting late and Tess knew there was nothing more she could do for Luca right now. Her head was swimming, her entire body ached from tension, and she hadn't eaten all day. And to make matters worse, she had to confess to Aunt Evelyn before the evening edition of the newspaper was delivered to the big house on West Park Circle. The coming scandal was hardly what her aunt needed as the cancer in her lungs weakened her more every day.

Moreover, Annie Harper, Aunt Evelyn's housekeeper was going to crow in triumph.

Annie had begged Tess not to break it off with James and elope with Luca. Tess had sailed out of the house, suitcase in hand, loftily taking responsibility for making her own decisions. James Howland had prevented Tess and Luca from finding a justice of the peace to marry them right away, but nothing had stopped them from spending the night together.

Tess refused to regret that decision. She mustered the last shreds of her dignity, heaved herself off the bench and found the ladies' lounge.

A splash of cold water restored her equilibrium even as the bruise on her cheek stung. Hot food, a fresh cup of coffee, and then she'd face the lions of West Park Circle. Surely Aunt Evelyn would not champion James after she knew he hit Tess.

"You're a Vassar grad," she said stoutly to her reflection. "You can handle it."

"Might take a little more lipstick," a voice suggested.

Tess spun around. An elegant blonde woman was seated in the little lounge area beyond the stalls and sinks. A suitcase rested on the floor next to her.

The woman raised the cigarette in her hand in a languid salute. "Bad day?"

"You have no idea," Tess replied.

"Cigarette?" The woman held out a box of Lucky Strikes. "Or lipstick?"

"I'll take the cigarette." Tess rarely smoked but a gasper seemed like just the ticket. She tapped out a cigarette, returned the box and leaned forward when the woman offered a lighter.

"Thanks." Tess puffed the cigarette into life and inhaled. "Today was supposed to have been my wedding day."

"He punched you and left?" The woman was only a few years older than Tess but held her cigarette with a glamorous world-weary languor that made her seem much more sophisticated. Fashionable short blonde curls, blue eyes, and a strong chin. Long legs crossed at the knee under a pale blue skirt showcased slender ankles and patent leather Mary Jane shoes.

"No, he got arrested for fighting the man who did." Tess took another upholstered chair. "I'm Tess Kennedy."

"Hanna Gorski."

Tess blinked. "Oh my goodness. Your name was in the *Clipper*. Your sister, um." There was no good way to put it. "Was it your sister?"

"Yes."

"I'm so sorry," Tess breathed. "What a terrible thing to happen."

"Thank you." Hanna stabbed her cigarette butt into the standing ashtray and gave it a savage twist. "It's been a hell of a day and now I'm supposed to make polite small talk at a dinner party instead of finding out who killed my sister. I'm to stay with some people named Rutherford."

"I hope you find whoever did it," Tess said earnestly. "Everyone wanted to know who she was but the police never found out anything."

"I will." Hanna leaned forward. "I've got something they don't."

Tess leaned forward, too, consumed with curiosity and happy for any distraction from the rotten day. "What is it?"

"A letter from the man who found my picture and connected it to Marta."

"Really?"

"His name is Gianluca Lombardo and he has something to do with a place called the Galliano Club."

Tess nearly dropped the cigarette. "But that's my Luca!"

"The one in jail?"

"Yes, Luca. He runs the Galliano Club. Mr. Spinelli owns it but Luca runs it."

"You're sure?"

A folded piece of school notebook paper was thrust under Tess's nose. She read the letter and looked up. "I can take you there later, if you want. I have to pick up my suitcase from the apartment upstairs."

"Can you get me out of this damn dinner thing, too?"

"You could come to McSweeney's with me instead. My car is around the corner."

"What do we say if anyone asks?" Hanna tapped a cheek as she raised one delicately arched eyebrow. "I won, obviously, but were we fighting over a man or the last bottle of booze?"

Tess laughed for the first time all day. "Hanna Gorski, I think we're going to be friends."

CHAPTER 8

Plan in place

"How much are we talking about?" Karol Dombrowski asked.

"As much as two thousand." Broz Siwak gulped some beer.

"Two thousand a week?" This was an insane amount of money to Karol. He was the foreman of the biggest copper and brass mill in the Northeast and only made seventy-five a week. Less than his predecessor, too, because Karol was unmarried and had no children.

"Rotolo rakes in at least four thousand," Broz went on. "Sometimes five. Half of the week's profits."

Karol swore softly in Polish. "What does he spend it on?"

"Clothes. Booze. His girl." Broz shrugged. "Always has a big wad in his pocket."

"But he gets twice what Fisher gets?"

"Looks like it. Fisher gets a quarter. Rotolo gives me a quarter, too, to pay the crew. There's a dozen of us. Still, it's good money."

Karol mentally calculated what Rotolo was paying

his foot soldiers. Triple what they could get as even the most skilled line workers at Lido Premium.

"Enough to make a man forget what he's doing to earn it?" he asked quietly.

"Almost." Broz didn't meet his eye. "Almost but not quite."

They were in the back room of the Warsaw Club, the watering hole that all Polish men in Lido drifted through at one time or another. The place was small and dark, nothing like the big Galliano Club across the city where Karol's friend Luca Lombardo worked. Nor did it require dues or have a baseball team that played in the Lido Industrial League. The only requirements for drinking at the Warsaw Club were the Polish language and tolerance for the occasional bloody brawl.

"Twenty thousand," Karol reminded Broz. "Twenty thousand and we're done. "Then we walk away. The crew chief job is yours if you want it."

Broz drained his glass. "I'm not helping you because I want to get back at Rotolo. He's treated me fair. I'm doing it because Fisher is a murdering shit who thinks everybody else is dirt. Killed that farmer, Genovese. Point blank. Shot him six times."

From a hidden spot in the cemetery overlooking Rotolo's illegal brewery operation, Karol witnessed the murder. So had Luca and Toby Gleason, an Irish rumrunner who was friends with Luca. It gave them the ammunition to squeeze Owen Fisher out of his bootlegging earnings and recoup the money that Luca's boss paid when he was blackmailed by Fisher, Rotolo, and the late Al Genovese.

Broz had agreed to help after Karol had dangled both a stick and a carrot. The stick was possible arrest as an accessory to murder. The carrot was a crew chief job at Lido premium that would get his friend out of Rotolo's clutches.

"Twenty thousand from Fisher." Karol mimed dusting off his hands. "Ten weeks."

"It's not the same every week. Rotolo doesn't charge everybody the same for beer." Broz inclined his head toward the front room where Anton presided over the bar. "Sixty a barrel here. Seventy for the Galliano Club across town."

"Why?"

Broz shrugged; the empty glass trapped between large, calloused hands. "Rotolo's mad for the place. Thinks he's gonna buy it when the owner can't pay his tab."

Karol knew that Luca had tangled with Rotolo before, but he tucked the bit of information away to share over their usual Sunday evening chess game in Mrs. Esposito's boarding house where they both rented rooms.

A burst of angry Polish erupted from the front room. Both Karol and Broz tensed, but the voices moved away. A few shouts and sounds of the street door opening and closing let them know that the argument had moved outside.

Everyone except Broz wore the stained dungarees and tired expression of those who toiled in the mills. That included Karol, except the one afternoon a week when he was in the Lido Premium offices, learning the business side of the company. He was the first business apprentice, as the company's operations manager Henry Blick called the role. If all went well, Karol would eventually become Blick's assistant operations manager.

Broz made the Sign of the Cross and stood up. Karol watched him go, wondering how long before Broz cracked up. Once upon a time Broz had been Karol's right-hand man on Lido Premium's dipping crew, the team that cured sheets of copper in chemical baths. Now he was restless, eyes darting, drinking too much and too often. Angry at himself for throwing in with Rotolo's bootlegging outfit and angry at the world for putting temptation in his way. Angry at Karol, too, for being the first Polish crew chief at Lido Premium and then the first Polish foreman, as well as the youngest.

Karol returned empty glasses to Anton and got a nod of thanks. The newspaper was in the wire rack at the end of the bar. He unfolded it and skimmed the front page. The wedding of Prince Leopold of Belgium and Princess Astrid of Sweden earned a fair number of inches. Two hundred thousand turned out for the occasion. Leopold "walked rather awkwardly up the main aisle of the cathedral," according to the report. Karol grinned to himself. No doubt the young prince was drunk.

His grin faded as he saw the next column's headline.

"LUCKY" LOMBARDO ARRESTED, DENIED BAIL

He skimmed the article, flung the newspaper on the bar, and ran out of the club.

CHAPTER 9

First impression

Hanna didn't know what she expected, but it wasn't this. The Galliano Club wasn't a glamorous lounge or a swell Michigan Avenue-style hotspot. Nor was it one of those cellar-type Italian restaurants that Sam had favored with checkered tablecloths, wicker-wrapped chianti bottles, and food that permanently stained silk dresses.

This place was more like a community center for Italian men.

The building was nothing exceptional, just a two-story brick front duplex jammed right up to the wide sidewalk. A pediment decorated the roofline above five windows marking the second floor. Striped awnings protected dual front doors. Between them, gold letters painted onto a big plate glass window proclaimed *GALLIANO CLUB EST. 1912.*

A small crowd of men in rough clothes milled in front of the door on the right side, clustering around a tall blonde man.

"Oh my goodness," Tess trilled as she set the

parking brake. "That's Karol!"

"Who?" Hanna asked but Tess was already out of the car.

Hanna got out, too. She leaned against the fender and lit a cigarette.

"Anyone who was here last night needs to step forward as a witness," she heard the blonde man say. His voice held the remnants of a Polish accent. "Which means you can't talk to Gifford or any other reporter who comes around."

"Karol!" Tess rushed up to the group.

"Tess!" He took her hands. "I just found out about Luca's arrest."

"Now? Didn't you get my note?"

"Note? What note?"

"I left a note for you this morning with the secretary in the Lido Premium offices. She promised to give it to you."

"I'm sorry. I didn't get it. What happened?"

Hanna finished her cigarette, ignoring the looks that came her way, as Tess recounted the same story she'd told over a plate of chicken and dumplings at McSweeney's two hours ago. As before, it sounded like something out of a Norma Talmadge tearjerker.

The meal and conversation had restored Hanna's flagging energies. More than that, she found that she genuinely liked Tess Kennedy. Four years younger than Hanna, Tess had a determined attitude and a forthright way of looking at things through those spectacles of hers. She was also as sharp as a tack.

When Tess extended the invitation to stay with her at her aunt's home, instead of strangers named Rutherford, Hanna had readily accepted. "Having company will be a nice distraction for Aunt Evelyn," Tess had said. "She's ill. Cancer. Nothing contagious."

Hanna saw right through Tess's convincing tone. "What you really mean to say is that she's too polite to throw a fit in front of a guest. You know, about you breaking off your engagement and spending last night with a fella who is now in jail."

"That, too," Tess had admitted with a crooked smile.

Now, the tall blonde man named Karol edged Tess away from the group of men. "They'll search Luca's room at Mrs. Esposito's," he said to her. "It would be better if some of his things weren't found."

"You mean the ledger," Tess replied.

"Can I give it to you?"

Hanna watched out of the corner of her eye, fascinated. Clearly, Tess had not told her everything about the handsome Mr. Lombardo.

Karol put his head closer to Tess's ear. Tess nodded, evidently in agreement with his plan.

A young man came through the crowd. Unlike the others, he wore no coat over trousers and a band-collar shirt. A snowy white apron was tied around his waist. "You're Hanna Gorski," he said breathlessly. "I knew you'd come!"

"Hello." Hanna flicked away the stub of her cigarette. "Who are you?"

"Sonny Zambrano. I work here. At the Galliano Club, I mean." He shook her hand with real zeal. "You look just like the cover of *The Red Book*!"

"Thanks, I guess."

"Do you and Tess want to come inside?" Sonny asked eagerly. "Women aren't allowed but seeing as it's you, it should be all right for a few minutes. I mean, you're famous!"

Tess came over to Hanna as the tall blonde man loped off. "I'm sorry, I should have introduced you. That was Luca's friend, Karol Dombrowski."

Sonny pumped Tess's hand as well. "Oh, Miss Tessa, can you believe that Luca got arrested?"

"Not really, Sonny," Tess said. "You were here last night. You saw what happened. They'll call you as a witness, too."

"Do you want to come in?" Sonny asked. "I want to show Miss Gorski the magazine."

"It'll be all right?"

"Just this once," he said.

It was warm inside, with a welcoming cloud of tobacco smoke drifting toward a pressed-tin ceiling. Hanna's eye was immediately drawn to an enormously tall and thin bottle of golden liquor rising almost to the ceiling above the mahogany bar. Against its backdrop of a mirrored wall, the contents seemed to glow.

Empty bottles sat on glass shelves flanking it. Hanna saw labels for whiskey, gin, grappa, anisette, and limoncello, as well as other liqueurs she didn't recognize.

A copy of the October edition of *The Red Book* was there as well.

For a few minutes she was the toast of the place, with men shoving past each other to shake her hand and tell her that she looked just like the magazine cover.

"Did you tell her?" an old man croaked at Sonny after pulling Hanna down so he could kiss her on both cheeks. "About the letters?"

"Sit down, Tony," a worker in rough work clothes chided the old man.

"I'm Gio Tulipano." Someone else pumped Hanna's hand before lifting his chin toward the bar. "Sonny, give her some of Luca's electric coffee."

Hanna and Tess were seated at a table, one of a dozen in the big saloon, and supplied with mugs of hot coffee. Green paneling on the lower half of the walls warmed the big space. Baseball pennants and framed photographs of sports teams decorated white plaster above.

With frequent interruptions from the crowd, Sonny told the tale of the letter in Hanna's purse. As a result of his picture in the newspaper, Luca had received dozens of letters from female admirers.

"Lady letters," Sonny said. He gave an embarrassed bob of the head at Tess. "They asked for him to come visit. Promised him, um, relationships. He turned them all down, too."

"I know all about the lady letters," Tess said with a rueful grin.

"One claimed that she looked like you, Miss Gorski," Sonny went on. "Well, like the cover of the October edition of *The Red Book*. So we all trooped down to the newsstand to get a copy."

He pointed to the magazine in its place of honor on a shelf near the tall golden bottle. Hanna's portrait presided over the saloon with a slightly tilted, slightly mocking smile.

"It was the same night the newspaper printed photographs of your sister." The man named Gio Tulipano took up the story. "Luca put the magazine and the newspaper side by side and we all saw it. They looked just the same."

"I wrote a letter to the magazine editor and Luca signed it," Sonny finished. "And now, well, here you are."

"Yes, here I am," Hanna said, looking around the room. Thirty, forty men there and every one of them agog at seeing her. "What a story."

She didn't believe a word of it.

CHAPTER 10

Shock and shock again

Tess steered her green Ford coupe along West Park Circle. Hanna had been silent since they left the Galliano Club. "Are you all right?" she asked. "Apart from the obvious, that is."

She'd only met Hanna Gorski that morning but it felt like they'd known each other forever. Funny how intense situations could turn strangers into best friends.

"It's been a long day," Hanna replied.

"For both of us," Tess agreed. She slowed the coupe.

"You said the house was big, but damn," Hanna said, looking out the passenger window.

Tess parked the coupe in its usual spot. A huge black Franklin touring car was parked along the curb in front of her aunt's house. A chauffeur waited behind the wheel. Either Aunt Evelyn's doctor had acquired a new car and driver or an unexpected visitor was there.

Light shone cheerfully in the living room windows. Both women took out their suitcases and went in the front door.

"Hello," Tess called as they removed hats and coats.

"I'm home."

No one responded. Tess put a hand on the stairway banister and called up. "Hello? Annie? Anyone home?"

"Miss Tess?" Annie Harper appeared in the entrance to the living room, the housekeeper's face pinched in disapproval. "Well, if it isn't Miss Decisionmaker. Better late than never."

"Hello, Annie." Tess wasn't about to wither under the housekeeper's stare. "This is Hanna. Hanna Gorski. I've invited her to stay for a few nights. Hanna, this is Annie Harper, our housekeeper."

"Nice to meet you," Hanna said.

"Well, you couldn't have picked a worse time to show up." Annie made no attempt to be gracious.

"We'll just go upstairs to see Aunt Evelyn," Tess said. "Tell Cook we've already eaten."

"Mr. Bradshaw is here," Annie said stonily. "You better talk to him first."

"Mr. Bradshaw," Tess echoed. Homer Bradshaw was the owner of the Adirondack and Western Railroad and the business partner of Aunt Evelyn's late husband Benedict Thompson. The West Park Circle house belonged to the railroad.

A sixth sense told Tess that the day was going to get even worse than it had been already.

She and Hanna followed Annie into the living room.

Bradshaw stood by the fireplace mantle, a well-fed man in his mid-fifties with a silver toothbrush mustache, hair like a slick of mercury, and a subtly expensive windowpane check suit and vest. A gold chain looped across the matching vest and disappeared into a watch pocket.

The last time Tess had encountered the railroad mogul was at her engagement party. Muriel Howland had handpicked the guests, the food, and Tess's dress for the occasion. Already seriously ill, Aunt Evelyn had done little more than receive guests while seated in an armchair. At the event, Bradshaw had made no effort to hide his open assessment of the woman's health.

"Hello, Mr. Bradshaw," Tess said.

"Miss Kennedy." His eye passed over Tess and settled on Hanna. "Please introduce us."

"This is my friend, Hanna Gorski," Tess said swiftly. "Hanna, this is Mr. Homer Bradshaw of the Adirondack and Western Railroad."

"A pleasure to meet you." Bradshaw gave Hanna the same hungry look a man might give a steak after a month-long diet of turnips.

To Tess's delight, Hanna ignored him and lit a cigarette.

"To what do we owe the honor of a call so late in the evening?" Tess asked.

"Evelyn has passed," Bradshaw said without preamble. "I've made the proper arrangements."

"What?" Tess gasped.

"Miss Evelyn never woke up this morning." Annie's lips trembled even as her eyes accused Tess of neglect. "You should have been here."

"She's dead?" Tess groped for a chair and sat down heavily as tears threatened. "Oh, God."

"My condolences," Bradshaw said without sincerity.

Hanna passed the cigarette to Tess. She took it and drew in a lungful of smoke.

It was just a matter of weeks, the doctor had said when they came back from Saratoga. Instead of helping, taking the cure in Saratoga had only weakened Aunt Evelyn. Still, finding out that she had passed in the night came as a shock. It was supposed to happen when Tess was there to hold Evelyn and pray with her, and see the priest give her the Last Rites.

"What happened?" Tess asked Annie.

"The doctor said she just slipped away in her sleep. No pain at all. She's at Proctor's Funeral Home, just like she wanted."

"Oh, Annie. I'm so sorry I wasn't here."

"I guess you had better things to do," the housekeeper accused.

The arrow found its target. Tess's eyes filled with tears.

Bradshaw cleared his throat. "Now that Evelyn has passed, legal occupancy of this house passes to the railroad. I wanted to inform you and the staff personally."

"Just what does that mean?" Hanna spoke for the first time. "You're kicking Tess out of her home?"

"This is a longstanding arrangement stipulated in Evelyn Thompson's late husband's will." Bradshaw said. "Mrs. Thompson had the lifetime right to remain in this house for as long as she wished. That right does not extend to her survivors, including her niece."

Tess stood up. "I'm not the only one who lives here. There's Cook and Annie, too. How long do we have before we have to be out?"

"I would think that 48 hours should be sufficient. That should give you ample time to assemble personal possessions before the inventory."

"Inventory?" Hanna echoed.

"We'll need to make sure that railroad property remains with the house."

"Do you have a property list?" Hanna was taller than Bradshaw, which Tess hadn't noticed before.

"Pardon me, Miss--?"

"Gorski, Hanna Gorski. If there's no existing

property list, how will you know what belongs to Tess and what belongs to your railroad? You could claim every pair of Tess's silk stockings."

"Are you a lawyer, Miss Gorski?"

"No, but Mabel Walker Willebrand is my aunt," Hanna said, surprising Tess with the name of the federal Assistant Attorney General in charge of Prohibition enforcement. "One picks up on these things around the Sunday supper table."

"I will have a list prepared," Bradshaw said icily and turned to Tess. "My condolences, Miss Kennedy, on the passing of Mrs. Thompson. I know she was highly pleased with your engagement to James Howland." He nodded at Annie. "Miss Harper."

Tess didn't move until she heard the front door open and close, then she rounded on Annie. "Last night, did you call James and tell him I was going to the Galliano Club?"

Annie's chin lifted in defiance. "You were wrong to go off like that, Miss Tess. Mr. James had to know what you were up to and stop you."

"It was not your decision, Annie."

"Miss Evelyn picked Mr. James for you."

Tess was dimly aware of Hanna opening drawers and doors and studying the china figurines in the glass-fronted cabinet above Aunt Evelyn's mahogany secretary. "I thought we were friends, Annie."

"I worked for Miss Evelyn, not for you." Annie dabbed at her eyes. "Now you come home after a whole night away. Did you soil yourself with that Eye-talian? Did he hit you?"

"James hit me. Luca hit him back and went to jail for it. All because of you." Tess spat the words, grief wiping away all restraint. "This is all your fault, Annie. You had no right to interfere. No right at all."

"This is not what Miss Evelyn wanted for you," Annie retorted. "That's why the good Lord took her last night. So she wouldn't have to see what a tramp you've become."

"How dare you!" Tess shouted, shaking in rage and sorrow. "How dare you!"

"Tramp!" Annie screamed and fled the room.

The sofa and chairs blurred as Tess blundered out of the living room and went into Aunt Evelyn's library. The cabinet where her aunt kept so-called medicinal brandy yielded a half-empty bottle of cognac. Tess dumped an inch of liquor into a tumbler and gulped it down.

"Got any more of that?" Hanna came into the room, looking around appreciatively at the refined desk and plush chairs.

"Here." Tess sloshed a tot into another glass and

refilled her own. "Aunt Evelyn's medicinal brandy."

Hanna accepted a glass. "Go easy. That's real French cognac."

Tess blinked back tears and held out her glass. "A toast. To Marta Gorski and Evelyn Kennedy Thompson. Both gone too soon."

"Gone too soon," Hanna echoed and touched her glass to the one in Tess's hand.

The chime of lead crystal reminded Tess of happier times in the cozy library with the overflowing bookcases. She and Aunt Evelyn had sat by the window and celebrated her graduation from Vassar. Planned the big trip to Europe. Toasted her new job at the bank, the job that Aunt Evelyn had arranged behind Tess's back, the same way her aunt arranged the marriage to James Howland.

"The two of us are really on our own, aren't we?" Tess asked.

"Nobody else's rules," Hanna replied.

They sipped in silence. The house was quiet. Outside the window framed in cheerful yellow drapes, night pressed against the wooden sandwich boards erected to protect shrubbery against the snow.

"Mabel Walker Willebrand isn't really your aunt, is she?" Tess asked at length.

"Only now and then," Hanna said.

Tess gave a laugh that turned into a sob.

CHAPTER 11

Escort service

"I'm sorry about your sister," Karol said. Behind the wheel, he was acutely aware of the woman on the bench seat next to him.

"Of course you are," Hanna Gorski said. "Everybody's fucking sorry except the bastard who killed her. Was it you?"

"Are you asking if I killed your sister?" Karol was so surprised he nearly drove his Ford into the curb.

"Yes. Did you?"

"No, of course not. Why would you ask that?"

"I'm going to ask every man in Lido that question."

Karol decided there was no point in trying to make small talk.

He'd arrived at the mill that morning to hear the surprising news that he'd been volunteered to accompany Miss Gorski to Holy Angels Church and make arrangements with Father Nowicki. The second piece of surprising news was that Mr. Blick, Lido Premium's operations manager who'd championed Karol's selection as foreman, had gotten married. Karol had offered a brief congratulations before being sent on his way to change into a suit and collect Miss Gorski from the mayor's office.

"What's your name again?" she asked as she lit a cigarette.

"Karol," he said, unoffended at her faulty memory. "Karol Dombrowski. We met last night at the Galliano Club."

She blew out smoke. "The most prominent Polish person in all of Lido gets to escort me to a church."

"I'm not prominent," he told her. "But I'm happy to help."

"You're sorry or you're happy. Which is it?"

"Both," Karol said.

"Huh." She took a long drag on the cigarette. "So what's Lido Premium?"

"The biggest copper and brass rolling mill in the Northeast."

"What happens at a rolling mill?"

"We roll out copper for telephone wire and ship hulls and plumbing pipes," he said proudly. "Anything else you can imagine. One-tenth of all copper in American manufacturing comes from Lido."

"Bully for you."

Karol wondered if all women from Chicago were like this or maybe it was just that he was meeting her under difficult circumstances. Hanna Gorski was stunning but bristly and coarse.

Never very comfortable around women, Karol's brain slowed as he groped again for something to say. He could rap out instructions to teams of men, solve a dozen problems in a minute, but only if it had to do with running a wire roller, maneuvering a crane, or swinging a crucible of molten copper into or out of a furnace.

"Have you spoken to the police?" he asked at length. "I'm sure now that your sister has been identified, they'll be able to find whoever is responsible."

Hanna rounded on him. "Who do you think did it?"

"I don't know," Karol said in surprise. "But the police will find out now that they know her name."

She gave a raw laugh.

"That's what the police do." He desperately wanted the conversation to be over. "They investigate and they find out things."

"What do you know about the police?" Hanna took out another cigarette.

Karol didn't like the way she brushed him off. "I wanted to be a policeman. A pillar of America, like it says on the courthouse wall."

"A pillar of America," she echoed, her voice larded with contempt. "In Chicago men become police officers because the Chicago Outfit and the North Side gang pay them to look the other way. That's what being a policeman means. A uniform, a billy club, and living in somebody else's deep pockets."

"Not in Lido. The police help people. Law and order." Karol took a left turn. The difference in wealth between downtown Lido and the neighborhood around Holy Angels was soon apparent.

"So why do you work in a factory?" Hanna flicked her lighter and inhaled as soon as the tobacco caught. "Why aren't you a pillar of America in a blue uniform? You're big enough."

"It's a mill, not a factory."

She exhaled smoke toward the windshield. "Whatever. Answer my question."

"It didn't work out," Karol said uncomfortably. "Turned out to be good news. I got promoted to foreman at Lido Premium, with the chance to learn the business."

"You get to boss people around?"

"Five hundred," Karol said. "Lido Premium is the biggest mill in the northeast."

Hanna took a long drag on her cigarette, staring at him with an expression that said she didn't believe him. Karol focused on driving.

He could handle every last man at Lido Premium, but everything about Hanna Gorski made him want to run away as fast as his legs could carry him. She looked just like the glamorous blonde who graced the magazine cover, which was the pivotal clue to her sister's identity, but acted tougher than any man on the boiler crew. Barely even looked at him, just smoked one cigarette after another as she fired off questions and apparently didn't care for his answers.

At Holy Angels, Father Nowicki took them into the rectory and spoke gently to Hanna. Yes, he would go to the hospital to bless Marta Gorski's body. The funeral was on hold until the police released the body but they could make the decisions about the eventual Mass and burial. Karol sat on a wooden folding chair and hoped it wouldn't disintegrate under him.

Hanna spoke to Father Nowicki in the same terse way she had addressed Karol in the car. The priest didn't seem to mind. Karol agreed to be a pallbearer. Hanna didn't thank him.

Father Nowicki insisted that they join him for lunch in the musty rectory dining room. The priest's housekeeper served bowls of cabbage soup and pumpernickel bread, followed by boiled potatoes and juicy pork schnitzel infused with the sharp bite of paprika. Good, homemade Polish fare that was better than the food at Mrs. Esposito's boarding house.

Karol inhaled everything within reach. Hanna

picked at her food.

After the meal, as they made their way down the freshly-shoveled sidewalk outside the church, Hanna put her hand on Karol's arm. "Can you take me to where they found Marta? Where they pulled her out of the water?"

Karol stared at her hand, momentarily taken aback. "If you want."

Despite the cold, when he opened the car door for her, a bead of sweat tracked down his back, making his shirt stick to his skin under layers of suit jacket and wool overcoat.

He drove to the old city dock. This late in November, the Mohawk River was swollen with melted snow. Across the river, scrubby branches and fallen trees created a curtain that hid the land beyond. The banks on either side of the old dock were slushy. By January the river would be frozen over, the ice thick enough to skate on.

"This is where they pulled her out of the water?" Hanna asked, her voice tight.

Karol nodded. "The divers had all their equipment here, looking for the body of Jimmy Zambrano. He was the previous foreman at Lido Premium. Strangled and his body thrown into the river."

"I saw the newspapers," Hanna said. "A man named

Nick Procopio did it because he wanted the foreman job. Same job you have now?"

"Yes."

She gave a funny laugh. "Trust your deputy?"

Karol thought of Frank Conti. Solid. Reliable. Italian. "Yes."

"No one expected to find Marta, did they?"

"No."

The wind scudded over the worn planking. Their coats flapped noisily around their legs. Karol kept a hand on his hat to prevent it from sailing away. Hanna wore a gray ensemble with a cloche to match and seemed impervious to the weather.

Beyond the edge of the dock, the river slid past, foamy ridges on the leading edges of the current. The sky was the color of old pewter and the air carried the twin scents of rotting foliage and coming snow.

"Were there many people here?" Hanna asked. "How many people saw Marta when she came out of the water?"

"I wasn't there."

"She was naked except for a camisole and the necktie used to choke her." Hanna stared at the opaque water as it licked at the dock. "How many people saw her like that? Defiled and degraded, with everyone trying to get a good look."

"I'm sorry," Karol said. "I don't know."

"All the things I told her. Things that a big sister is supposed to say." Hanna wasn't talking to him anymore. She walked to the very end of the dock. "I said it all but I was too busy making my own mistakes and it didn't matter."

Before Karol could reach her, Hanna fell to her knees.

"Miss Gorski," Karol said in alarm. She was too close to the edge of the dock.

"It was my fault. I should have taken care of her." She rocked back and forth, sorrow spreading like a real thing around her.

An errant gust of wind pushed at them. Hanna gasped and turned toward him even as she teetered off balance. Karol caught her arm and they fell backward onto the hard wooden planks together.

Hanna buried her face in his coat, her entire body shaking as she wept.

Karol wrapped his arms around Hanna. The river was made of tears, he thought as inky water gurgled past the dock. Tree branches creaked in the winter breeze. The cold from the wooden dock seeped through his clothes, icy fingers moving past his socks and up his legs, but he didn't move.

He felt rather than heard her tears subside. Hanna's

body slowly relaxed inside the circle of his embrace. Eventually the only sound was the wind rattling the trees and the water lapping at the icy shore.

Karol looked down at her crystal blue eyes and wind-tossed blonde hair and had no idea what to say. Hanna blinked at him, both sadness and hunger in her eyes.

Then she stretched up and pressed her lips against his.

It was the hardest, most bruising and insistent kiss of his life, not that he'd had many. Hanna gripped the collar of his overcoat and Karol held her tightly as the moment went on and on, as wild and heady as a ride in an airplane as it barnstormed across the sky.

Hanna abruptly pulled away, scrambled to her feet, and walked away.

Dizzy with desire, Karol peeled himself off the dock. He found his hat and brushed off the dirt. She was waiting by the car, another cigarette already lit.

He opened the passenger side door for her, then eased himself behind the wheel, his head still swimming with the intensity of their embrace. Hanna smoked and stared out the window as the scenery changed from the rural outskirts of Lido to the downtown district.

"I need to go to 112 West Park Circle," she said

abruptly as the courthouse came into view.

"Not back to the mayor's office?"

"Do you know where West Park Circle is?"

"I can get you there."

Karol recognized Tess Kennedy's green coupe parked on the curving street before he saw the house number. Two big moving trucks were in the drive. Karol pulled in behind the coupe, cut the engine and went around the side to open Hanna's door. She got out, flashing slim legs in the process.

"This is Tess's house, isn't it?" Karol watched burly men carry out a rolled-up rug. "What's going on?"

"Her aunt died. Tess has to move out. I'm helping her." Hanna started toward the house, then paused and looked over her shoulder. "Thank you for accompanying me today, Mr. Dombrowski. And for agreeing to be my sister's pallbearer. I'm sure there were other things you would prefer to have done with your time. Run your factory and so forth."

She walked swiftly toward the house, the hem of her skirt swinging around those slim legs. Karol unconsciously mashed his hat in both hands as he watched her ignore the trucks and glide in the front door.

He headed for the mill in a foul mood, promising himself he'd do his bit at her sister's funeral, then forget he ever met Miss Hanna Gorski of Chicago.

And then he realized he'd completely forgotten to ask where Tess planned to live now. Where should he bring the items from Luca's room at the boarding house to keep the police from finding everything?

CHAPTER 12

A new place to live

"Mr. Spinelli?" Tess hovered in the doorway, waiting for the owner of the Galliano Club to raise his head.

When he did, Vito Spinelli gave a start. He obviously wasn't expecting to see a woman in his place of business as he got to his feet and lumbered around the side of the desk. "You're Tessa, aren't you? Luca's Tessa."

"Yes, I'm Tess Kennedy." It felt strange to say that she was engaged, but she'd already be married if it wasn't for Annie. "I'm Luca's, er, Luca's fiancé."

Mr. Spinelli blinked at her. He had a luxuriant mustache; big basset hound eyes and the general look of a collapsing barrel held together by a wrinkled wool check suit. "Luca's in jail."

"Yes, I know." Tess took a step into the office. It was a nice, big space, with a tawny leather Chesterfield sofa, lovely bookcases that were mostly empty and a desk the size of her Ford coupe. Pictures on the walls and baseball pennants created an inviting space, with a candlestick telephone, too. The office was far more welcoming than any of the starchy offices at the First National Bank of Lido.

Unfortunately the effect was ruined by the half-empty bottle of Old Bushmills and a glass full of amber fluid on top of the pile of account ledgers.

Mr. Spinelli saw where she was looking. "First one today," he said as if noticing the bottle for the first time.

"Yes, well," Tess said uncertainly. "I wanted to speak with you because, well, it appears that I've moved into the apartment on the second floor."

"Upstairs?"

"Yes, where Miss Cross used to live." She tried to give a reassuring smile but it was dawning on her that once again, it wasn't even noon and he was already drunk. "Luca had the key so now I've got the key and I moved in a few things because my aunt passed, you see, and I had to find a new place to live in rather a hurry and Luca said Miss Cross wasn't coming back."

"Luca's still in jail, no?"

"Yes, he showed me the apartment before he got arrested." Tess thought *showed* was a better choice of words than *stayed with me*. She opened her purse determined to get the issue of the apartment settled before Aunt Evelyn's funeral. "I can pay rent, of course. Would twenty-five dollars a month be acceptable?"

He ran a shaky hand over the drooping mustache. "I lost my boy in the war, you know. Now I'm gonna lose Luca, too."

"No, you won't," Tess said with more confidence than she felt. "Neither of us will."

"*Madonna santa.*"

"He has a very good lawyer," Tess went on. "Randall Freshman. He's coming here tomorrow to ask you some questions about Luca. About working here and if he's good at his job."

In the past three days she'd had her portrait made, answered hours of questions in Mr. Freshman's office, stripped the West Park Circle house of every personal item she could find, and ignored the increasingly salacious stories printed in the *Lido Daily Clipper*. Stories with headlines like **UNLUCKY LOVE TRIANGLE TRIPS UP LUCKY LOMBARDO.**

Both she and Hanna had become adept at avoiding the reporters who patrolled Hamilton Street, trying to get a quote.

"I had to hire David," Mr. Spinelli said. "Because Luca's not here."

"I met him when I came in." Tess had introduced herself to the young man behind the bar. David Ferlo had a maimed hand but a nice, quiet way about him. He didn't stare slack-jawed like the others in the saloon when she walked in, Guido practically sobbing with confusion over what to do about her determination to speak to his boss.

"Luca does the accounts."

"I can help with accounts until Luca gets back," Tess said. "I used to work at the bank."

"You're a good girl, Tessa." For the first time, Mr. Spinelli really focused on her. His eyes were watery.

Tess counted out twenty-five dollars and put the bills on the desk. "There. My first month's rent. Thank you for being so understanding." Without meaning to, Tess reached out and took Mr. Spinelli's hand. Gave it a squeeze. "I'll be upstairs if you need me."

The gesture seemed to wake him up. "Tell David to give you some sandwiches."

The apartment over the Galliano Club was stuffed to the gills with items salvaged from the house on West Park Circle. The door opened wide enough for a slim girl and two sandwiches wrapped in a dishcloth to pass through before the leading edge whacked into crates and cartons and rolled rugs.

Hanna came out of the kitchen with two mugs of coffee. She edged past a teetering pile of books and handed one to Tess. "Did you tell him you'd already moved in?"

"He didn't mind." Tess unwrapped two crusty rolls,

each loaded with fig jam and wafer-thin slices of prosciutto ham. "Even had his new barman make us lunch."

They ate standing up, the chairs barely visible under piles of table and bed linens.

Left to her own devices, Tess would have left the West Park Circle house with a single suitcase, her college diploma and a trunk full of books. But when Hanna walked through the house asking what belonged to the railroad and what didn't, Tess realized how much in the home didn't belong to the railroad. Clothing, jewelry, wedding china, personal stationery. Not those favorite chairs, items Aunt Evelyn inherited from her parents, nor the books that once belonged to Tess's father.

Not only that, but whatever Tess salvaged from the house on West Circle would be whatever she and Luca had to start their life together. Furniture. Books. Plates and silverware. Sheets and quilts.

Annie watched, radiating disapproval, but said nothing when Tess took Aunt Evelyn's clothing out of the closet by the armload. Nor did the housekeeper protest when the movers came. Tess didn't ask Annie if she wanted any mementos.

By the time Tess said her final goodbye to the house on West Park Circle, the trucks she'd hired were full to bursting.

The last items got crammed into the coupe, including four Persian rugs, a silver punchbowl with 12 matching cups, and 50 green leather-bound volumes of the Harvard Classics published by Collier's.

Bradshaw paid Cook and Annie their wages and a severance, too. Dixon, the chauffeur, had always been paid by the railroad so he went first, along with the boxy Nash.

"Thanks for coming with me," Tess said as they finished and got ready for the funeral.

"You'll be all right," Hanna replied.

"I know." Tess had cried her eyes out over losing Aunt Evelyn, but also found herself grappling with mixed feelings. Aunt Evelyn had taken her in when Tess lost her father and gave her the rare opportunity for a woman to go to college. Yet she'd also schemed behind Tess's back and tried to force her into an arranged marriage with James Howland. She'd given Luca permission to court Tess, then reneged. In many ways, Aunt Evelyn had not played fair.

The funeral was at Saint Brigid's church. Tess and Hanna walked up the steps. A cold and damp November wind pummeled them, threatening to steal men's fedoras and women's cloches as their overcoats flapped around their legs.

The man from Proctor's Funeral Home wore a purple sash as he directed ushers to escort guests to reserved pews. Tess and Hanna were led, not to the front pew on the right side normally reserved for close family members, but to a pew five rows behind.

Homer Bradshaw and his wife were already seated in front.

The pews between the first and fifth rows were filled with people Tess didn't know. No doubt, they were Bradshaw's hand-picked minions from the Adirondack and Western Railroad boardroom.

As the organ ground out a painfully slow version of *Amazing Grace*, Tess watched her would-be in-laws Preston and Muriel Howland take the front pew on the other side of the aisle. To her amazement, Annie sat immediately behind them.

At the front of the church, her aunt's casket rested on a stand draped with white linen. It was black, with silver fittings; definitely not the polished walnut Tess had picked out.

The urns on either end were filled with lilies, not pink roses.

Bradshaw's eulogy was all about Aunt Evelyn's support for her husband, Benedict Thomson, as he and Bradshaw conceived and built the Adirondack and Western Railroad.

Tess clenched her fists in her lap to keep from shouting out that Benedict Thompson had been a cruel husband and certainly not the love of Evelyn's life.

Among the items Tess had carried out of the West Park Circle house was a bronze box full of letters to Evelyn from a man named Max Lauder. Weeks ago, Annie had told Tess how Evelyn was already married for several years when she met Max and fell in love. Annie had acted as the go-between, facilitating an exchange of letters between the two lovers.

Max's last letter was to include a bearer bond giving Evelyn the means to leave her husband and join her lover in California but it was never sent. Crushed, Evelyn stayed in her miserable marriage. Yet she had loved Max enough to keep his letters for more than two decades.

Bradshaw and five strangers came out of the pew to act as pallbearers. The casket was duly loaded into the hearse for the trip to the cemetery's mausoleum. The ground in upstate New York was already frozen. Actual burials would happen in the spring.

A reception line formed outside to greet those coming out.

"It's not appropriate for you to be here," Bradshaw said to Tess as she stepped forward.

"Excuse me?"

"I won't have Evelyn's funeral spoiled by scandal," he said quietly.

"I'm expected to accept condolences at my aunt's funeral. I'm her last living relative."

"You've already caused enough damage to her reputation. The newspapers have been quite informative on that fact."

"I'm not going anywhere." Tess planted herself at the end of the receiving line.

Preston and Muriel Howland were the first to walk past, offering sympathy to Bradshaw and his railroad flunkies. They passed Tess without speaking, evidently having gotten the same legal advice Mr. Freshman gave to Tess about not jeopardizing the trial.

No one else spoke to Tess. They passed by, eyes averted and lips pursed in disapproval. Not even the priest acknowledged her presence.

She was a pariah.

CHAPTER 13

Agita

The food in the jail wasn't bad and Sestito gave him the newspaper every day, but Luca was a caged lion with a chronic case of *agita,* that classic Italian malady mix of restlessness, irritation, and worry. He paced the cell constantly, unless he had a visitor or stopped to eavesdrop on O'Malley in the next cell.

The cement block wall separated the two cells, so it was impossible to see the disgraced police officer, but they could carry on a conversation if they wanted to, which Luca mostly didn't. But today, he leaned against the dividing wall and listened to the quiet conversation between O'Malley and Mr. Dorsey, his lawyer, who stood with arms folded outside O'Malley's cell.

O'Malley and his lawyer weren't invited to use the small interview room where Luca had met with Mr. Freshman. Sestito sat behind the desk. Now and then Sestito looked at Luca who pretended he wasn't listening. Sestito pretended, too.

"The Bison Club should be the least of your worries," Dorsey said to O'Malley.

"Character witnesses, every one of them."

"Keep in mind that your intended blackmail victim is also a member," Dorsey said.

"Doc Lanigan will be enough," O'Malley said.

Dorsey shuffled his feet a bit. "If I call him as a character witness, the prosecution can ask him what he heard you say about Mrs. Blick at the Bison Club banquet. He was at your table, he tells me, along with Blick, Rutherford, and a few others."

"That bastard!" O'Malley's shout gave Luca a start.

From behind the desk, Sestito glared at O'Malley's cell. "Settle down," he called.

Luca edged closer to the front of his own cell, intrigued by the overheard conversation.

"Bastard," O'Malley said again, but this time in a low voice. "Blick is defending that whore."

"You don't have a defense," the lawyer said tiredly. "Your letter to Blick was a federal misuse of the mails. A blackmail attempt, pure and simple. There is absolutely no truth to what you claim about her background, which wouldn't entitle you to use the mail to extort money from him even if there was a shred of evidence. My best advice is to change your plea to guilty, apologize profusely, and say that you see the error of your ways."

"The woman is a whore," O'Malley insisted.

"Doesn't that count for anything?"

"So you say, but no one has produced any proof to say she's anything but a nice woman who is now married to Henry Blick, one of the richest men in Lido."

"Telling your client to plead guilty." O'Malley's voice was spiked with anger. "What kind of a lawyer are you?"

"An honest one."

"Well, maybe I need a new lawyer."

"I'll talk to Chief Doyle and let him know you won't change your plea."

Luca settled onto the cot in his cell as the lawyer strode past. Sestito got up from the desk to let the other man out and disappeared. The jail was quiet.

"You doing all right in there, O'Malley?" Luca got up and stood at the bars.

"Why wouldn't I be all right?" O'Malley's voice threw a snarl into the quiet.

Sestito came back with the evening newspaper, just as Luca caught the faint call of the steam whistle at the Lido Premium mill all the way on the east side of Lido. Dinner would arrive soon; a pail from the Black Kettle restaurant that Sestito served out on thick Syracuse China plates with green rims.

So far meals had been a lesson in barely edible American food. Beef stew, fried chicken, overcooked pork chops. Too many potatoes and not enough flavor. Luca longed for a slab of lasagna blanketed with parmesan cheese, *arancini* the size of an apple, eggplant drowning in spicy *arrabiatta* sauce. Garlic and parsley. Sharp, salty olives cured in oil. The signature sandwiches he made at the club.

Sometimes he would doze off thinking about salami, pepperoni and roasted red peppers layered with provolone cheese on a ciabatta roll and drizzled with balsamic vinegar. Or slices of chicken spread with basil pesto then topped with sun-dried tomato and soft hunks of mozzarella.

Sestito read the newspaper, then folded it and passed it through the bars of Luca's cell. "You're off the front page."

"That's a change," O'Malley interjected from his cell.

"Thanks, Joe." Luca read the newspaper slowly, trying to make it last. He'd never known time to pass so slowly.

Mr. Freshman had come twice, armed with pages of questions for Luca to answer. His cousin Enzo Russo visited, too, bringing his wife Rosaria's mouth-watering cooking. A dish of linguini, chicken cutlets and a slab of gingerbread the size of a dinner plate. Things at the farm had settled down, although Luca could tell from the catch in his cousin's voice that things were still strained with Rosaria.

As soon as Enzo left, Luca wished he hadn't eaten the food so quickly.

Karol and Toby came. The Irishman's sunny outlook was undaunted by the jail. With Joe Sestito within earshot, it had been a cryptic conversation, but Luca was able to learn that his box of valuables was now safely in Tess's possession. As Karol had anticipated, the police came to search Luca's room at the boarding house.

Along with his personal papers, the box contained not only the two thousand dollars he'd earned rumrunning with Toby but the pocket ledger kept by Owen Fisher, with its damning evidence of how the accountant had cheated Benny Rotolo's bootlegging operation.

Luca had other visitors, too. Vito and Sonny and many of the merchants who owned businesses on Hamilton Street, even the old-timers who spent their days drinking red wine in the club like Tony Bilotti. But the only person he wanted to see was Tess.

His *Tessa*.

She sent books and writing paper, which Sestito let him keep, but when Luca tried to read his attention invariably drifted. He recalled the night they'd spent together; each minute, each touch, every expression that crossed her face.

Unable to speak to her, Luca was plagued by the nightmare that Tess was done with him. The distance between West Park Circle and East Lido was too far to bridge. His secrets were too much for Tess to keep.

More than once he regretted telling her so much. All he'd done was hurt her. Make her doubt him.

Yet he'd wanted to be as honest with her as he could. Tess had a right to know the danger she was in with him.

Luca knew that the sins of his past would never be absolved. They would never leave him alone and because of that, anyone he loved was cursed. His wife Rafaella and their infant child died because Luca lived in a perpetual state of mortal sin. That would not change, because Luca did not regret his actions and could not atone for them.

His eye fell upon a picture under the obituary section. Evelyn Kennedy Thompson, widow of Benedict Thompson, co-founder of the Mohawk and Adirondack Railroad, was put to rest yesterday after a funeral at Saint Brigid's Catholic Church. Survived only by a niece, Miss Tess Kennedy, 24.

He studied the picture, trying to reconcile the striking woman with the disease-riddled crone he'd known, the woman who gave him permission to court Tess, then took it back, as if she'd only belatedly learned of the stain on Luca's soul.

O'Malley started talking, trying to engage Sestito.

Dinner came. Chicken with a pale yellow gravy. The coffee was the only thing with any flavor.

CHAPTER 14

Do you recognize this?

Either someone had told the Lido stationmaster not to answer Hanna's questions or he simply was too busy making the trains run on time to notice who rode them. Either way, he knew nothing about blonde girls arriving in Lido last autumn.

The next step was to wash Marta's camisole and the wretched striped tie and visit clothing stores.

According to Tess, Van Dyke's was the most expensive store in Lido. Hanna decided it was even fancier than Gossard's in Chicago merely on the basis of the window displays.

She walked into an opulent reception area furnished with a long counter to keep out the riffraff. Brocade chairs and swagged draperies invited new shoppers to relax while the correct escort was summoned. Tantalizing glimpses of actual merchandise could be seen on the other side of a grand archway.

Van Dyke's was the sixth store Hanna had visited so far that morning and by far the most elegant.

"May I help you?" The woman behind the counter

was also tall and slender but at least 20 years older, with a black silk dress and a coil of gray hair.

"I'd like to see your lingerie department," Hanna replied.

"Of course." The woman pressed a button that apparently would summon a clerk. "Shopping for anything in particular today, dear?"

"I need to know if your store sold this particular style of camisole." Hanna unfolded Marta's silk camisole on the counter. Now washed and ironed, it was no standard Munsingwear undershirt, but an obviously high-quality garment. The silk had heft. Satin ribbon outlined the straps. Handmade Belgian lace edged the neckline and bottom hem.

The woman behind the counter smoothed the camisole and checked for a label. When she found none, her expression changed from bland curiosity to troubled awareness. Her hands pulled back as if touching it would infect her with Marta's death. Every clerk in every other store had the same exact reaction.

"This is the camisole our unidentified young woman was found in," the woman said, making it into a question that didn't expect an answer. "You must be her sister."

"Hanna Gorski."

"I'm Mrs. Scott." She gave Hanna a small smile.

"May I speak for all of us at Van Dyke's and offer my condolences on your loss."

"Thank you."

The clerk from the lingerie department appeared as tall and slender as Mrs. Scott and similarly dressed in black. She introduced herself as Mrs. Cook and led Hanna through the arch and into the main part of the store. Both men's and women's clothing and shoe departments were staged around a central seating arrangement of gold satin sofas and chairs. Hanna followed her to Women's Foundations and once again spread Marta's camisole on a counter.

Mrs. Cook examined it closely and agreed that it was certainly a fine garment and yes, the lace was surely Belgian. She showed Hanna a similar camisole currently in stock, reverently wrapped in tissue paper and nestled in a flat lavender-colored box.

"The new Mrs. Blick purchased two of a similar quality just this morning," she said, as if Hanna knew the customer. "They're from Lavande of Paris. We don't usually carry that brand, it's very exclusive. But we could look through customer records to see if any others were sold recently."

Like Gossard's, VanDyke's was hardly the type of store where strangers did their shopping. Every customer had a personal account. Purchases were faithfully recorded, along with size, color preferences, alterations, and if the item was delivered or picked up in the store.

Hanna was served a cup of coffee while Mrs. Cook pressed a button under her counter and summoned Mrs. Scott. The two women pored over a collection of little blue folders and found no other purchases besides the two bought by the new Mrs. Blick.

"I see. Thank you for checking." Hanna replaced Marta's camisole in her purse and took out the red striped tie.

"Of course," said Mrs. Scott.

Mr. Dunlop presided over Men's Accessories, a portly older gentleman with a fringe of white hair and silver-framed spectacles. He wore a perfectly tailored suit and a discreet navy-blue tie.

Hanna showed him the red striped silk rag that had once been a man's necktie. The silk was twisted out of shape, as if some fibers had shrunk and others had not, while spots of rusty blood marred the simple design of red and white stripes separated by a thin line of charcoal.

"All of our ties are arranged by color," Mr. Dunlop said. He adjusted his spectacles, obviously uncomfortable with the situation. "Let me show you."

He opened a glass-fronted cabinet and took out

several long shallow boxes. Neckties of every design lay inside. None were the same design as the tattered rag that had been wrapped around Marta's throat.

Mrs. Scott walked Hanna back to the elegant foyer.

"Thank you for all your help," Hanna said.

"I'm very sorry we couldn't be more helpful," Mrs. Scott said. "What will you do next?"

"I'm not sure." Hanna wasn't sure she had the energy or the will to try any more stores.

"You've modeled before, haven't you?" Mrs. Scott asked. "Of course you have. Everyone knows about your portrait on the cover of *The Red Book*. The newspaper said you were at Gossard's."

"Yes, I was a floor model."

"I'll be frank, my dear," Mrs. Scott said. "If the women of Lido know that you're here, they'll come in droves to see you wear my fashions. You're somewhat of a celebrity, you know."

"Are you offering me a position?" Hanna needed the money but was she ready to tie herself to Lido?

"Why don't we go have a chat in the lounge?" Mrs. Scott said. "I'm positively gasping for a cigarette."

CHAPTER 15

A little situation

Benny was in Chief Doyle's office again, the weekly payment in the inside breast pocket of his jacket. He was wearing another new suit from a swank shop in Syracuse. Bold white stripe on gray, red lining and it came with two pairs of trousers. It was nearly as nice as the suit from Marshall Field's he was wearing when he had to skip Chicago.

"Chief Doyle will be back momentarily," the old crone of a secretary had said when she let Benny into the inner sanctum. He was invited to wait all by himself, a real gesture of trust.

Just one more way the universe was telling Benny that he had the Lido cops in the palm of his hand.

He'd been in the chief of police's office before, of course, although sometimes he sent Broz Siwak to deliver the weekly envelope. Give Broz a little taste of the big leagues while showing Doyle that Benny wasn't some two-bit operator. He had people to run errands.

Still, Benny knew to step carefully around Doyle. The chief was an Irishman as big as a trolley car with a bassoon for a voice and hands like grappling hooks. Devilishly greedy. Not even the Chicago cops could compare to Doyle in the money-grubbing department and Benny had run into quite a few back when he was a torpedo for Hymie Weiss's North Side gang.

Benny paced around the office as the minutes ticked by, starting to wonder if Doyle meant to make him sweat for some reason. Or just make him jealous.

The office was real swell, the sort of setup Benny would have when he owned the Galliano Club and could run his rackets from a proper office. Right now his choices were a sticky booth at Perk's Diner, or a freezing corner of the pumphouse with beer gurgling through the tanks and Broz's bunch of Polack thugs milling around.

A giant desk, leather armchairs, velvet draperies and a diploma the size of a bedsheet hung on a wall. Doyle was a member of the Loyal Order of the Bison, the framed scroll proclaimed. The paper was watermarked with the etching of some sorta lumpy cow and lousy with wax seals and signatures. Must be a big deal for Doyle to display it like this. Maybe Benny would investigate the Bisons. Get a big diploma himself to hang on the wall of his office in the Galliano Club.

The door swung open and Chief Doyle lumbered in, unbuttoning the top button of his uniform tunic to relieve his ample jowls. "Just the laddie I wanted to see," he boomed. "Mrs. Clancy, give us some privacy."

The door shut noiselessly behind him.

"Good to see you again, Chief," Benny said.

"Get away from my pride and joy." Doyle stabbed a sausage-sized finger in the general direction of the Bison Club diploma. "I wouldn't put it past you to carry it out and sell it on the street."

Benny pulled the envelope of money out of his pocket and casually dropped it on the desk. "Always a pleasure doing business with you."

Doyle scowled. "Not so fast, Rotolo. Seems we've got a little situation."

Benny had read the story in the *Lido Daily Clipper* with a smile plastered over his mug. "Officer O'Malley got himself in trouble. Attempted blackmail, was it?"

Quick as a wink, Doyle grabbed his wrist and twisted, pinning Benny's torso to the massive desk. "O'Malley's none of your business, you dago runt. I'm talking about a real situation."

Cheek pressed against the polished wood, Benny opened his mouth to protest before his arm snapped like a twig, but Doyle didn't give him the chance.

"That Gorski woman is asking questions. She talked to the stationmaster at the train station. Every clothing store in town, too, waving that flimsy camisole like a battle flag. My detectives tell me she thinks some slick fella talked her sister into running away with him all the way here to Lido. Planning to ask questions until she finds some link to Chicago."

"Nothing to do with me," Benny managed. The pain in his wrist radiated all the way to his shoulder. Stars danced through his vision.

"You're from Chicago."

"Coincidence."

"She's looking for a coincidence and I think you're it." Doyle let go.

Benny straightened up, wobbled a step back and sat in one of the leather armchairs. His vision slowly cleared.

Doyle lit a cigar, eyes on Benny as he struck the match and played the flame in a circle around the end of the stogie.

The shrewd old copper wasn't going to lose his weekly payola from Benny just because the Gorski woman was asking questions. No, Doyle wouldn't be raising the issue unless there was something in it for him.

"Doesn't she know that the Lido police are working night and day to catch her sister's killer?" Benny asked leadingly.

Doyle puffed on his cigar.

"She should be leaving the investigation to the professionals," Benny went on.

"Aye, that we are." Doyle blew a smoke ring toward the ceiling. "Too bad our resources are so slim."

Benny considered the envelope lying on the desk. A thousand dollars every week to keep his beer trucks running and the Lido police away from the pumphouse brewery. A sizable amount of so-called resources, but clearly not enough to cover the present situation.

"More resources would let us close the case." Doyle saw where Benny was looking and slid the envelope into a drawer. "Get the poor dead lass finally buried and soon forgotten. Miss Gorski can go back home and give our compliments to the devil the next time she sees him."

"As a concerned citizen, I'd like to help the department with its resource problem," Benny said carefully. "Would an extra five hundred take care of the situation?"

"No, not nearly, laddie." Doyle exhaled a wreath of smoke.

"Two thousand," Benny offered.

"Let's make it three," Doyle replied through the haze. "Three thousand a week might just be enough to find a solution."

Benny's mouth went dry at the thought of ponying

up three thousand a week, but it was better than the alternative named Old Sparky.

"Money well spent," he managed.

"Don't I know it, laddie." Doyle winked at him. "Don't I know it."

CHAPTER 16

Shortchanged

Inspector Finch hadn't called on Owen again. With every passing day, Owen convinced himself that the postal money order issue was not a problem. He'd covered his tracks just fine and besides, Benny was done with the so-called information racket now that Al Genovese was out of the picture, so to speak.

After Owen shot Genovese, that smelly farmer, no one ever came forward to ask about him. No Missing Persons investigation, no newspaper article about a missing Bell Road farmer. No connection between the manure-smelling nobody and Owen Forbes Fisher, scion of Lido high society and the newest addition to the Bison Club's Membership Committee.

Despite the looming meeting with Dombrowski, Owen felt optimistic. Lombardo was in jail, taking some of the power away from the threat of blackmail. Cynthia was happy with her new mink jacket from Van Dyke's. Hopefully the glow would last a few weeks before she needed more sterling silver flatware or another string of pearls.

He drove the Ford over the lip of the berm, his stomach rising into his throat as the Ford tipped down the other side. He braked as the tires slithered in the snow but got the vehicle halted alongside a big Cadillac.

The bootleg brewery was set up in the remnants of the original Lido Premium mill, known as the Packham Foundry, on the banks of the Mohawk River where the water churned hard enough to drive an electricity-generating paddlewheel. The place burned to the ground years ago, leaving just a stark brick chimney and a stone pumphouse. A natural berm and dip toward the river meant that the whole outfit could not be seen from any road. The only way to access it now was by driving a barely-there road that wound along the edge of the ancient Settlers Rest cemetery that topped the rise.

Yet somehow, three immigrants had seen an accountant kill a farmer. If Owen didn't pay them off, they'd go to the police. Or even worse, they'd show his pocket ledger with the leather corners to Benny and explain how Owen had skimmed beer racket profits off the top.

Of the two threats, the one involving Benny was the greater evil.

Owen went into the pumphouse, where Broz Siwak

had his crew filling barrels, and went into the small curtained-off space that was the office. It was unheated, of course, and Owen blew on his fingers before opening the lockbox where Broz left cash collected during the previous night's deliveries.

"Have you seen this, Fishy?" Benny barreled into the tight space brandishing a rolled-up newspaper. In the frosty air, steam coiled away from every word.

"What's that?"

Benny slapped the newspaper against Owen's chest, driving the buttons of his coat into his throat. "The Sheik got himself arrested," he crowed. "Attempted murder and kidnapping."

"Who?"

"Lombardo. Luca Lombardo from the Galliano Club." Benny shoved the cashbox and Owen's paperwork aside and spread out the newspaper. "Don't that beat all."

"Yes, I heard," Owen said and resumed counting.

"With Lombardo in jail, Spinelli is gonna crack." Benny rubbed his hands together. "He can't make it a day without Lombardo telling him what to do. Old man's got one foot in the grave and the other on a banana peel."

Owen pushed the newspaper aside to record amounts in the proper columns in his account book, the big one he used to show how transparent his accounting was. Fifty percent to Benny, twenty-five for him and the rest to Siwak to distribute to his hoods.

"Wait a minute." Benny yanked the account book away from Owen and swiveled it toward himself. "Gotta change the numbers, Fishy."

To Owen's horror, Benny thumbed through a stack of twenties, then pocketed the entire five thousand dollars.

Benny grinned at Owen's expression. "We got a new business expense."

"What sort of expense?" Owen gurgled.

"What kind do you think?" Benny patted Owen's cheek, the gesture verging on a bully's slap. "The big business kind."

With a sinking feeling in the pit of his stomach, Owen redid the divvy. His share was seven hundred dollars, a third of the usual amount.

"Looking nervous there, Fishy." Benny folded up the newspaper and took his fifty percent off the makeshift desk. Added it to the wad bulging in his coat pocket. "You think the ghosts are watching from the river? Or have the fish et their eyes yet?"

"Don't say things like that, Benny." Owen flinched at the memory of Al Genovese's face when the gun went off.

"What are you, a cream puff?" Benny gave Owen's shoulder a shove hard enough to knock off his hat and send him reeling into the wall.

Sharp stones kissed the back of Owen's head. His knees buckled and he slid partway down the wall, his coat snagging on rough texture and patches of ice.

"Hey, Fishy." Benny hauled him upright by the front of his coat. "You're a torpedo, remember? Toughen up."

Owen blinked away tears of humiliation. "It isn't enough, Benny. Seven hundred is nothing."

Benny gave him a little shake. "Hey, Fishy, we got a little unexpected business expense, all right? We'll make it up next week."

"It's always something, Benny," Owen heard himself say. "You take all the money and I take all the risk. Like money orders. The Post Office knows about them."

"I tell you what, Fishy." Benny grabbed Owen by the tie and pulled him close enough to see the outline of the gun in Benny's jacket pocket under the overcoat. "I'm gonna make you a partner in the Galliano Club. A twenty percent share. How does that sound?"

"I don't want shares in a speakeasy," Owen moaned.

"Sure you do, Fishy. Think about it. You and that hot tomato you call the missus in the best speakeasy this side of Chicago. Best place north of Manhattan. You could be right there at the table with me, Fishy. You and the little missus. You'll be a partner. All the best people in Lido will be yanking your sleeve, wanting to get in. Drink some real likker and watch the show. The mayor's gonna love you, Fishy."

"I want my money, Benny." Owen squirmed away. "You can't just waltz in and take an extra five thousand. You're already taking Nick's share. It's not fair."

"We'll make it twenty-five percent," Benny said grandly. "A twenty-five percent share of the Galliano Club. Gonna make you a rich man, Fishy, a man of respect. Capone is gonna cry when he hears about my place. Anybody who wants to find the fella who owns New York, they'll find him at the Galliano Club. And you'll be at the same table, how about that?"

He grabbed the rolled newspaper and thumped Owen's chest. "Twenty-five percent of the best speakeasy in New York state, Fishy. You're a lucky man."

Owen didn't move.

Benny grabbed the remaining cash and left the office area. His voice in the brewing area revved with excitement as he flipped Broz a little extra for keeping the beer flowing.

The stone wall radiated freezing damp but Owen

stayed where he was, the paltry seven hundred clutched in his hand, until he heard Benny's Cadillac start up and roar away.

CHAPTER 17

Outside the mill

Winter had settled on upstate New York in earnest, gleefully blowing snow flurries across roads and sidewalks. Every morning an army of men tackled the white stuff with shovels and plows before heading to the city's mills, offices, schools, and shops. At Lido Premium, the stokers were responsible for keeping the sidewalks and car lots around the mill clear.

The sun had set hours ago, when the workday was still in full swing. Snow or no snow, orders had to be filled. Sheets of copper had to be loaded onto rail cars behind the sprawling brick building. Spools of wire had to carry telephone conversations and electricity.

Karol left the mill. The night watchman threw him a salute, which Karol returned before turning up the collar of his mackinaw with one hand. His empty lunch pail swung in the biting wind as he plodded toward Hamilton Street.

The foreman's job at Lido Premium was a hundred decisions every day, but Karol relished the challenge. So far, operations manager Henry Blick had agreed to all the changes he had suggested. The new safety procedures were in place. Nobody had balked or complained. The anticipated protest by the Italian workers at having a Polish foreman had yet to materialize.

Frank Conti, his deputy, was a good man and they made a good team. Their first challenge had been to find a replacement for Conti, previously head of the crew that ran the big wire rollers, and for Karol as the dipping crew chief. If Broz ever did come back to the mill, Karol would shuffle the crew chief jobs again, maybe even create an additional position at that level.

He was doing good things at the mill. And it wasn't a factory.

Instead of continuing on toward Hamilton Street, Karol doubled back, staying inside the looming shadow of the mill. He trotted around the side of the building, his footfalls too loud in the quiet after hours of being battered by the roar of the boilers and the boom of heavy machinery. Soon the electric light over the front entrance was around the corner, forcing Karol to keep a hand on the bricks to find his way.

He considered himself an honest man. Certainly a law-abiding man. He'd even memorized the entire volume of *The Civil Government of the United States*.

But tonight he was committing blackmail. Karol

wondered what Hanna Gorski would think about that. Probably nothing. She was a beautiful model touched by tragedy who'd already forgotten him.

"Dombrowski." From the shelter of the night watchman's shed, the accountant blinked nervously at him.

"Hello, Mr. Fisher," Karol said.

"Your friend Lombardo's in jail," Fisher said. "Makes your threat somewhat weaker, I would think."

"Debts still have to be paid." Karol gestured for the money.

Fisher surrendered a thin envelope.

Karol rifled through the bills. "One hundred dollars? Is this a joke?"

"It's no joke."

"There should be two thousand in here," Karol said, trusting Broz's assessment of how much Fisher was getting from Rotolo's bootlegging operation.

"I don't have two thousand dollars." Fisher swallowed convulsively a few times. "Honestly, I don't have it."

"Why not?"

The nervous accountant seemed close to tears. "Benny said he had some unexpected expenses. He took almost all the profit from this week's deliveries."

"I don't care what's going on with Rotolo unless it

means I need to show him your ledger." Karol was tired and angry. His best friend was in jail and he couldn't stop thinking about Hanna Gorski. "Or maybe the police need to find out about what happened to Al Genovese."

"I tell you, I don't have the money."

"You've been getting two thousand a week from Rotolo's operation. What did you do, throw it all away?"

"You can't treat me like this," Fisher protested. "I'm a college man. A member of the Bison Club! You're nothing but a jumped-up Polish nobody that Henry Blick picked to be teacher's pet."

"Listen to me, little man." Karol grabbed Fisher by the coat lapels and actually raised him to his toes so that they were face to face. "Maybe you're telling the truth and maybe you're not. Next week you'd better come up with at least two thousand, understand? Or else the police are going to find out you killed Genovese."

Fisher's eyes bugged out. A little bubble of saliva formed between his lips.

"Two thousand," Karol reiterated. "Next week. Same time, same place. Anything less and we go to the police. Or Benny."

"I made a mistake," Fisher moaned. "One mistake and now my life is ruined."

"You killed a man," Karol said harshly.

He let go, disgusted by the accountant's pathetic protest and ashamed of himself for taking advantage of the man's crime. As Fisher scuttled away, Karol thought he might be sick.

CHAPTER 18

False start

"All rise."

Acutely aware of Tess seated several rows behind him, Luca stood up next to Mr. Freshman. Judge Pepper strode into the courtroom through the door that appeared to belong to him alone. With a flourish of black robes, he sat on the throne behind the giant desk raised on its dais.

"Court is now in session in the case of Howland versus Lombardo," the bailiff intoned. "You may be seated."

Judge Pepper banged his gavel, directing all eyes toward him. "This is a criminal proceeding," he announced. "I thank the jury for their time and scrupulous attention to the facts of the case and not the sensational tripe that has appeared in the newspapers. Mr. Cromwell, welcome to Lido. Are you prepared for your opening statement?"

A tall, elegant man with wavy brown hair and a gray tweed suit rose from the table across the courtroom where he sat with James Howland. The banker still had purple rings around his eyes but no longer wore his metal nose cap and bandages. The baseball mustache was gone, too, leaving him only slightly less pompous.

Luca felt a shiver of electricity run through the courtroom. In the past ten days, he'd gotten a rapid-fire education in American law, helped out in equal measure by Joe Sestito and a book Karol lent him. He was the defendant, the person accused of a crime. James Howland was the plaintiff, the person who was doing the accusing.

Cromwell ignored Luca as he walked past the defense table to address the twelve men of the jury. "The good citizens of Lido consider their fair city to be a safe place." His voice was a mellow baritone. "A place where a man and woman may walk down any street in safety and comfort at any time of day. Or night."

He spun on one heel in an abrupt, attention-getting move and pointed to Luca, his arm fully extended. "Yet there are those whose background and intentions deny us that God-given right!"

Luca tensed. Freshman put a restraining hand on his forearm.

With a smug flourish, Cromwell turned back to the jury. "Gentlemen, put yourself in James Howland's shoes. An Ivy League graduate. Vice president of the

First National Bank of Lido. A young man on the cusp of marriage. A fine upstanding citizen who attempted to rescue the woman he loves from the hands of a dangerous undesirable. An immigrant from southern Italy with the worst attributes of the criminals who breed there. Yes, I am talking about the defendant who bewitched a respectable young woman, creating a rift between her and the plaintiff. Like a pirate, the defendant was intent upon soiling her, stealing her virtue, and claiming his prize, to the point of attempting to murder her betrothed. In his attempt to rescue this poor, soiled young woman, James Howland was forced to fight for his life."

A loud sob interrupted the flow of his voice.

Judge Pepper banged his gavel. "Now Muriel, get ahold of yourself. We're just getting started." Another bang. "Go ahead, Mr. Cromwell."

The attorney unfolded himself from his stooped position holding the wooden railing that separated the jury box from the rest of the courtroom. "In the next few days, you will learn that the defendant Luca Lombardo is a violent man with a long history of assault. James Howland and his brother Richard were just his latest victims. You will see how a man like that has no business in Lido, nor in New York state, nor anywhere else in America. You will be afforded the opportunity to strike a blow for justice against this dangerous undesirable and cleanse your community of his presence. If you don't, his next victim may not be as brave or as lucky as James Howland."

He stalked across the courtroom back to his seat. The courtroom was silent.

Freshman moved around the side of the table, polishing his spectacles. "Gentlemen of the jury, thank you for being here today. My name is Randall Freshman. My client is Gianluca Lombardo, an American citizen with all the rights and privileges that you enjoy. He is an educated man who has a good job. He pays his taxes and supports his community. His batting average last season in the Lido Industrial League was the same as the New York Yankees' own Lou Gehrig. They both play first base."

A soft chuckle circled the courtroom.

The attorney adjusted the spectacles on his nose and clasped his hands behind his back. "Now, my colleague Mr. Cromwell is going to huff and puff and attempt to paint a picture of violent and salacious behavior. His words will create a gross distortion of the truth, which is that Mr. Lombardo fell in love. Yes, he fell in love and was loved in return. On the evening of this young couple's intended marriage, the plaintiff decided to intervene. You see, the young woman had spurned

James Howland. Yet he tried to lay claim to her, the same as he might claim a new suit or a pair of shoes."

Freshman crossed the courtroom and looked pointedly at James Howland. "The use of force is never a good basis for marriage. Yet that is precisely what the plaintiff attempted to do. Mr. Lombardo intervened to save the woman he loves. Now he stands accused and his good name attacked, because the plaintiff was humiliated by his failure to win the girl." The lawyer's voice rose, strong and stalwart. "This trial is as simple as that. As you hear testimony, keep asking yourself this question. Would you stand idly by and watch the woman you love be dragged away and forced to wed a man she'd already refused? Not once, not twice, but at least three times?"

He approached the jury box and placed his hands on the rail. "I ask you to listen carefully to the witnesses, carefully enough to hear what is in their hearts."

Judge Pepper banged his gavel again as Freshman returned to his seat. "The prosecution may proceed."

James Howland was the first witness. He carefully made his way up the two steps to the witness chair, turned to face the courtroom, placed his hand on the Bible and swore to tell the truth, the whole truth and nothing but the truth.

Cromwell stood next to James. "Mr. Howland,

thank you for coming today. I know you have been recovering from injuries. This must be very difficult for you."

"I'm nearly recovered," James said with a martyred air.

Cromwell went to a table with some papers spread on it, selected one and showed it to James. "Mr. Howland, do you recognize this newspaper clipping?"

"Yes," James said. "It's the announcement of my engagement to Tess Kennedy from the *Lido Daily Clipper*."

"Can you read the date of the announcement?"

James dutifully read the date of the newspaper.

Cromwell looked up at the judge. "Let the record show that the date of the announcement of the engagement between Mr. James Howland and Miss Tess Kennedy was two weeks before the events of the night we will now discuss."

The judge waved a hand. "So noted. Proceed."

Cromwell threw the jury a triumphant look, as if he'd won an early knockout. "Thank you, Your Honor." He replaced the newspaper clipping on the table, went to the witness box, and leaned against the wood paneling. "Now, Mr. Howland. Having established that you were engaged to be married to Miss Kennedy, could you please tell the court how you felt about her?"

"I envisioned a happy future with her as my wife," James said mechanically.

"And she reciprocated your affections?"

"So she led me to believe." James paused. "We celebrated our engagement at her home, with her late aunt, Evelyn Thompson, who was very pleased with the match."

"So you are engaged to Miss Kennedy, envisioning a happy future. How did Mr. Lombardo intervene to disrupt your relationship with Miss Kennedy?"

"He was a customer at the bank. Always trying to talk to Miss Kennedy, who worked as one of our account managers. Of course she left the position before the wedding. We agreed that my wife would have a social position to maintain. It wouldn't be right for her to go to work like a laundry woman."

A loud cluck of righteousness came from a large woman in a white dress, the same one who'd interrupted Cromwell's opening statement. From the family resemblance, Luca inferred that she was Howland's mother.

"So Mr. Lombardo made a pest of himself with Miss Kennedy?" Cromwell asked.

"I even caught him speaking to her outside the bank one day. It was freezing cold and he'd lured her outside without a coat. Whatever he'd said to her was very vexing, too. She looked like she wanted to cry. I assumed he'd said something vulgar."

Luca recalled that day. Tess had rushed out of the bank after he'd made a withdrawal. If only she had run away with him there and then. If only he'd asked.

"So the defendant was already known to you as someone with an unsavory attitude toward Miss Kennedy."

"Yes."

"What happened when you and your brother arrived at the Galliano Club? Did you see Miss Kennedy?"

"Yes." James licked his lips, readying himself for the dramatic portion of his performance. "Miss Kennedy and Mr. Lombardo were in front of the club. They were speaking in an animated way."

"For the court, can you point out the man you saw Miss Kennedy with that evening?"

James pointed at Luca. Their eyes met. James dropped his hand and shifted in his seat. Luca forced himself to remain perfectly still instead of leaping over the table and the paneled front of the witness box and choking James until he admitted that this was all a farce.

Cromwell nodded sagely at James. "So you recognized both Miss Kennedy and Mr. Lombardo standing in front of the Galliano Club. Was anyone else there?"

"A man I didn't recognize. I found out later he was the Galliano Club's doorman."

"Miss Kennedy and Mr. Lombardo were in conversation when you and your brother arrived. Did they greet you?"

"No."

"Why not?"

"They were arguing."

"Miss Kennedy and the defendant?"

"Yes."

"How could you tell?"

"He punched her in the face."

CHAPTER 19

Listening to lies

"That's a lie!" Tess shouted as she leaped to her feet. "A lie. He hit me!"

"Order! Order!" The judge hammered his gavel. "Sit down, young lady. There will be no outbursts in my courtroom."

Tess dropped into her chair, fuming. The room quieted but tension lingered, humming like electricity sparking inside a broken insulator.

Judge Pepper narrowed his eyes at Cromwell. "The plaintiff is reminded that he is under oath."

Cromwell pressed his hands together. "My client is well aware of his oath, Your Honor."

"Does the plaintiff wish to rephrase his answer?"

James licked his lips and shook his head.

"No, Your Honor," Cromwell said.

The judge sat back. "Then his answer stands. The jury will disregard the outburst from a spectator."

Tess clenched her fists in her lap, knowing she should be grateful that the judge hadn't kicked her out of the courtroom. Next to her, Hanna bumped her with an elbow.

Cromwell cleared his throat. "After Mr. Lombardo struck her, what happened?"

"He saw us," James said. "He must have known that we saw what he did because he charged at us like a rodeo bull."

"Were you aware that when Mr. Lombardo first came to America from Italy, he was a successful fistfighter in New York City?"

"I have since learned that, yes."

"Would you have confronted him if you were aware of that fact on the night in question?"

James lifted his chin in a heroic pose. "He struck Miss Kennedy. I had no choice but to confront him. If I had to do it over, I'd still confront him."

Tess hoped James could feel her eyes burning a hole right through his lies.

"Did anyone else there see the fight between you, your brother and Mr. Lombardo?"

"Dozens came out of the Galliano Club." James grew animated; they were on *terra firma* as far as the testimony he'd rehearsed. "They formed a semicircle around us. Shouting and hollering in a foreign language. All rooting for Lombardo, that much was clear."

"The crowd was against you?"

"Definitely."

"Would you say the crowd was a dangerous and frightening mob?"

"Yes," James insisted. "My life was in mortal danger. Richard's, too."

"How did the fight end?"

"I wanted to mix it up with Lombardo again, give him a knockout punch, but my brother was in a bad way. I thought he had sustained life-threatening injuries. We left to find a doctor."

"Were your injuries severe?"

"Both Richard and I were incapacitated for days. I was unable to go to my office at the bank. Richard delayed his return to Yale and was in bed for a week."

Tess clapped a hand over her mouth at this latest lie. In bed for a week! Richard had been in that very courtroom for Luca's arraignment the very next day.

Cromwell nodded gravely. "Turning back to the question of Miss Kennedy. Did she make an attempt to depart with you?"

"No, Lombardo was right there next to her."

"Did you believe that Miss Kennedy was too traumatized to leave the scene with you?"

"Objection!" Freshman rose to his feet. "Leading the witness."

Judge Pepper grimaced. "Sit down, Mr. Freshman.

This is eyewitness testimony."

James simpered a bit. "I left her with that brute. I'm not proud of that. I simply couldn't keep her from making a terrible mistake."

"So very easy to blame yourself," Cromwell said, reeking of false sympathy. "One last question, Mr. Howland. Are you still in pain?"

"Every day."

The judge called a recess for lunch.

Tess was exhausted with repressed fury as she and Hanna stood up. She wanted to say something to Luca, ask if he was all right, but of course he was led away. Arm-in-arm with Hanna, Tess shoved past a gaggle of reporters and left the courthouse. A bowl of chicken soup at the drugstore and then they were back in the courtroom for the cross-examination.

James was on the witness stand again; hands clenched on the arms of the witness chair.

Freshman shuffled through some papers in front of him. "Tell me, Mr. Howland. During your engagement to Miss Kennedy, did she ever kiss you?"

"Kiss me?"

"Objection!" Cromwell was on his feet. "No relevance to the proceedings."

Freshman looked at the judge. "Your Honor, I will prove that the nature of the relationship between Miss

Kennedy and Mr. Howland is at the root of Mr. Howland's altercation with Mr. Lombardo."

Judge Pepper pursed his lips and finally relented. "I'll allow it, Mr. Freshman, but I advise you not to stray into prurient details."

"Once again, Mr. Howland." Mr. Freshman drifted closer to the witness. "Did Miss Kennedy ever kiss you?"

"Of course. We were to be married."

"Once, twice?"

"I don't recall. A gentleman does not tally up such things."

"Isn't it true that Miss Kennedy kissed you a single time, which was at the engagement party at her aunt's house to celebrate your engagement and then only under duress from the assembled guests?"

"I don't recall."

"Did she ever allow you to take her hand?"

"I don't engage in public displays of affection."

"While courting Miss Kennedy did you take her to the theater? A restaurant? Perhaps a concert or a lecture?"

"I saw her every day at the bank. There was no need to engage in other entertainments."

"So you never took her out for a romantic evening. A walk in the park? Tell the court, did you pick out a china pattern together? Decide on sterling?"

James bristled. "I left that to Tess and her aunt."

"What about flowers," Mr. Freshman went on remorselessly. "No doubt you gave your fiancée flowers. What is Miss Kennedy's favorite?"

"I don't know." James glanced pleadingly at his attorney.

"Jewelry? Surely a man of your means would present his fiancée with a piece of jewelry."

"I gave her an engagement ring."

"Who picked it out?"

"My mother."

"No romantic courting, no flowers, no personal gifts." Mr. Freshman clicked his tongue in disapproval. "Perhaps this lack of visible affection was offset by a romantic proposal that swept her off her feet. Please tell us how you proposed marriage to Miss Kennedy."

"My father arranged it with her aunt," James said, his voice dropping. "I expect her aunt told her."

"You never made a direct proposal of marriage to Miss Kennedy?"

"It wasn't necessary."

"Did you have a conversation with Miss Kennedy about marriage? Was she pleased with the arrangement?"

"We had an engagement party," James said

doggedly. "The announcement was in the newspaper."

"An engagement party." Freshman drew out the phrase. "Instead of a proposal of marriage. What did you and Miss Kennedy discuss at the party? What questions did she ask you?"

James turned beet red. "Something silly about telling her secrets."

"How did you respond to her question?"

"I told her not to be a ninny."

"A ninny." Freshman moved toward the jury as if to remind them to seek what was in the heart of the witness. "Could you define the term, please?"

"Silly. Someone who talks about silly things."

"Yet Miss Kennedy was an account manager at the First National Bank of Lido and a graduate of Vassar College with a degree in economics. Summa cum laude. Can you reconcile those facts with your description of her as a ninny?"

"She's got an independent mind," James said.

"An independent mind," Freshman echoed loudly. "Meaning that she says and does things based on her own views of the situation?"

"I suppose."

Freshman positioned himself between the witness and the jury. "Shortly after the engagement party, Miss Kennedy notified you that she can no longer honor her aunt's wishes and will not marry you. Is that correct, Mr. Howland?"

"I thought she was joking."

"Yes or no, Mr. Howland?"

"Yes."

"She specifically said she would not marry you, in effect breaking off the engagement?"

"Objection!" Cromwell was on his feet again. "Badgering the witness."

"Sustained," the judge said. "I believe you have made the point, Mr. Freshman. The court understands that the engagement between Miss Kennedy and Mr. Howland was a business arrangement which Miss Kennedy sought to end."

Tess balled her fists in fury. Why had it taken nearly the entire day to make that clear?

Freshman changed tack. "Mr. Howland, did you believe that Miss Kennedy drove to the Galliano Club in her own distinctive green Ford coupe with a suitcase full of her clothing, of her own free will?"

James hesitated. Tess was conscious of everyone in the courtroom leaning forward, waiting to hear the answer.

"I don't know," James said. "Maybe he lured her."

"With what? Honest affection?"

"Objection!" Cromwell was on his feet.

"On what grounds?" the judge asked.

"Witness cannot presume to know the thoughts of a third party," Cromwell said smugly.

"Sustained."

Tess didn't think Mr. Freshman had won the point. The mood in the courtroom felt dense and uncertain.

"All right." Freshman paced a bit, hands clasped behind his back. "Miss Kennedy had already resigned from her position as an account manager at the bank and broken off your engagement. Would we be able to presume she no longer felt any attachment to you?"

"Objection!" Cromwell was on his feet.

"Sustained," Judge Pepper said. "Mr. Freshman, you are trying my patience. The witness cannot presume to know the young lady's thoughts."

"Understood, Your Honor."

Cromwell slowly sat down.

"Let's start again, Mr. Howland." Freshman now lingered next to the witness chair. "On the night in question, you went home and had dinner with your parents and your brother Richard."

"Yes."

"What prompted you and your brother to go to the Galliano Club?"

"Miss Annie Harper, housekeeper for Tess's aunt, telephoned the house." James straightened up, sure of himself again. "She said that Tess had gone to the Galliano Club and somebody better get over there right away before Tess did something we'd all regret."

Tess felt the blood pound in her head. She chanced a glance at Annie, seated in the second row behind Muriel and Preston Howland. The former housekeeper stared at the ceiling.

"Such as?"

"She said Tess wanted to elope with this Italian fellow who worked at the Galliano Club."

Freshman addressed the jury from his position near the witness. "So based on this tip from Miss Harper, you decided to go to the Galliano Club to, ah, intercept Miss Kennedy?"

"Yes, that's right."

"You brought along your brother, who recently won the Golden Gloves prize at Yale. Any particular reason you asked him to come along?"

"I'm a banker, not a fighter."

"Did you intend to engage in a fight with Mr. Lombardo?"

James gaped at the attorney.

"Answer the question, Mr. Howland," Judge Pepper said peevishly.

"It's the Italian colony," James said, recovering his aplomb. "Everybody knows it's a dangerous place."

Freshman came closer to James. "Now you have testified that the defendant struck Miss Kennedy and you attempted to defend her."

"I still considered her my fiancée." James beamed, a white knight on a charger full of lies.

"During the fight with Mr. Lombardo, in which he was battling both you and your brother, what was Miss Kennedy doing?"

James shrugged. "Standing there."

Freshman nodded. "So Miss Kennedy, having been struck, so you have testified, remained on the scene." He paused. "Was she very far from her automobile?"

"It was by the curb."

"So Miss Kennedy was how many feet away from it? Three, four?"

"Approximately."

"Would it have been a relatively simple maneuver for her to get into the vehicle while her alleged captor, Mr. Lombardo, was otherwise occupied?"

The courtroom was completely silent. Freshman waited. Tess held her breath.

"I suppose so," James conceded. "I mean, she knows how to drive."

"Yet she did not leave." Mr. Freshman stopped pacing and fixed James with a stony stare. "Wouldn't you say that was strange, considering your own contention that the defendant had struck her and that Miss Kennedy is a very independent-minded young woman?"

"Objection!"

"What is it this time, Lionel?" The judge frowned at Cromwell.

"The witness cannot presume to know what was in Miss Kennedy's thoughts."

"The question is directly related to the plaintiff's charge that Miss Kennedy was kidnapped by the defendant," Mr. Freshman retorted. "Despite the fact that she arrived at his place of employment of her own volition and had the means to depart the scene as well."

Tess and Hanna exchanged glances. Mr. Freshman was subtly brilliant, working James into a corner.

"Well, I think he's got you on that one," Judge Pepper said to Cromwell with a sigh. "Sit down and let the witness answer."

"What am I supposed to answer?" James was smart enough to sense a trap.

"Why didn't Miss Kennedy leave the Galliano Club when it was clear she had the opportunity and means to do so?"

But James was ready. "She was waiting for me," he asserted.

Tess sucked in air. Another lie!

"Yet she did not depart with you," Freshman pressed. "In fact, didn't she shout at you to go away when you first arrived?"

"I don't recall," James said stiffly.

"Where was Miss Kennedy when you and your brother left the Galliano Club?"

"Still on the sidewalk with him. Lombardo."

"Did you leave Miss Kennedy at the Galliano Club because you knew she preferred Mr. Lombardo to you, not because he was holding her captive as the charge of kidnapping implies?"

"My brother and I were in danger," James said stubbornly.

"And she was not?"

"Objection!" Cromwell bellowed. "Leading the witness."

"Sustained," the judge said.

Tess let out her breath.

CHAPTER 20

Golden Gloves

It was only the afternoon of the first day of his trial and Luca wasn't sure he could take much more. But he gritted his teeth and slid his hand into his trouser pocket. Touched the bit of paper with Tess's counting game numbers on it.

26 13 97. Add the digits and the solution was one. They were still one heart, just like when they were courting.

Richard Howland was sworn in as the prosecution's second witness.

This was Golden Gloves, the collegiate boxer who'd nailed Luca with a couple of good punches. Slimmer and better looking than his brother in a well-cut three-piece suit and fashionable oblong wristwatch, Richard exuded smug privilege. He showed no ill effects from their fight.

Even without the icy sidewalk and knee to the groin, Luca would have been able to take him down but the brawl would have lasted three times as long.

Cromwell took him through the events of the

evening in question. Richard parroted everything his older brother already said.

"James wanted to save Miss Kennedy," Richard declared. "I was really just along for moral support."

"Did you see the defendant strike Miss Kennedy?"

"Well." Richard shifted in his chair. "Not exactly. I was still getting out of the car when it happened."

The prosecuting attorney moved on to questions about the actual fight. Luca realized they were trying to show that not only had he struck Tess, giving James and Richard an excuse to come to her rescue, but that he was some sort of professional prizefighter who'd instigated the fight, then delivered near-lethal beatings to both of them.

"He didn't fight fair," Richard said indignantly at the end of Cromwell's questions. "He didn't fight like a gentleman. He didn't know the rules."

Freshman stood for the cross-examination. "Mr. Howland, thank you for coming today. Were you well acquainted with Miss Kennedy?"

"I met her at the engagement party. Swell girl. Kind of uppity, but James didn't seem to notice. Didn't matter to me. I wasn't going to marry her."

"Were you aware that she had severed her employment at your father's bank and the engagement to your brother?"

"Sure. My mother was apoplectic."

Muriel Howland gave a low wail. Once again, she was seated in the first row behind the plaintiff's table, absolutely unmissable in a tent-like orange dress and matching hat speared with a dyed ostrich feather.

"Muriel," Judge Pepper warned.

Muriel flapped a hand toward the judge and dabbed at her eyes with a handkerchief.

Cromwell focused on Richard again. "Was your brother aware of your mother's distress?"

"Sure. He was right there when she went on about it."

"Yet he testified that he still considered himself engaged to Miss Kennedy."

"Not after Lombardo broke his nose." Richard gave a braying laugh.

"But what about the night you and he went to the Galliano Club?" Freshman pressed. "Did he consider himself still engaged to her then?"

"I guess so. I mean, he was real steamed up after that phone call."

"The phone call from Annie Harper, the late Mrs. Evelyn Kennedy Thompson's housekeeper."

"Yeah, that's the one."

"What was your mood on the way to the Galliano Club? Angry? Nervous?"

"I was excited," Richard said.

"Excited? Why?"

"We were going to teach the dago a lesson about stealing American women."

"The dago being the defendant, Mr. Lombardo?"

"Yes." Richard avoided looking at Luca.

"Was your brother excited, too?"

Richard hesitated. "James was more nervous. No, maybe righteous would be a better way to describe him."

Freshman didn't rehash the fight the way Cromwell had done, but poked and prodded at the edges of the story, implying that Richard was young, excitable, dying for a scrap, and less than trustworthy.

The last two witnesses of the day were Preston and Muriel Howland, the parents of James and Richard.

Muriel alternately sobbed and fluttered her handkerchief as she said how she'd taken her son's flighty fiancée to her bosom. She was highly emotional, weeping into an embroidered handkerchief in between questions from both attorneys, and bemoaning the shame Tess Kennedy had brought to both their family and to the First National Bank of Lido. She cried over the pain and terror her sons had experienced, as if they were children and not grown men.

Tess was portrayed as an immoral woman who

didn't understand the honor her son James was ready to bestow upon her as his wife. No, they'd all been taken in by a deceptively bookish and sweet exterior that hid wanton immorality. Muriel praised the dearly departed Evelyn Kennedy Thompson, God rest her soul, who took the girl in when she was orphaned.

The implication was that if Tess hadn't been so immoral, her parents would still be alive. Apparently, they'd perished of heartbreak over their child's reckless and ungodly ways.

At some point during the woman's watery testimony, Luca found that he was actually grinding his teeth together. The noise inside his head sounded like rocks stirred in a bucket. He massaged his jaw to make it stop.

Freshman kept his cross-examination brief and Luca understood why. The woman was there to garner the jury's sympathy, although it was clear Judge Pepper was already in her corner, saying things like "Now, you take more time, Muriel," and "Now then, Muriel, don't you fret."

In contrast to his wife's antics, Preston Howland was stone-faced as he swore to tell the truth and took his seat on the witness stand. He deeply regretted agreeing to hire Miss Kennedy and the arrangements for his oldest son to marry her. In both instances, he was swayed by the late Mrs. Thompson and her connections to the Adirondack and Western Railroad, which he believed would help his son's social standing.

Cromwell led him through the events of the evening. The telephone call, his sons' departure from the family home, and their return covered in blood and half dead. The portrait he painted had the members of the jury sitting upright, their faces creased with worry. That could have been any father, any one of the jurors who had a family and wanted to keep them safe and away from a loose woman.

Howland deeply regretted the entire sordid situation but did not see how any red-blooded American father could see his sons harmed and not do something about it.

"Thank you, Preston," Judge Pepper boomed when the witness was done. The gavel slammed down. "This trial is adjourned until nine o'clock tomorrow morning."

Luca exchanged a look with Tess across the crowded courtroom before the bailiff led him back to the jail. She was with Hanna Gorski, a tall blonde whom he recognized not only from the newspaper but from Karol's description.

The cell door clanged behind him.

"Judge Pepper throw the book at you yet, Lucky?"

O'Malley called from the other cell.

Luca loosened his tie and took off his suit jacket before throwing himself onto the cot. He closed his eyes, still seeing the stricken expression on Tess's face.

This was all his fault. She didn't deserve this.

CHAPTER 21

Blaming the past

"Stop reading that," Hanna called from the kitchen as she plated the eggs. "You were there."

"The plaintiff's mother, Mrs. Preston Howland, made a great impression upon the jury," Tess read aloud. "Her distress was evident."

Hanna came out of the kitchen with two plates of scrambled eggs and toast. "You'll get your turn soon."

Tess threw down the newspaper. "It's how the newspaper portrays it. I'm a goose and all the Howlands are martyrs instead of a pack of liars."

Hanna sat and pronged a forkful of eggs. The little apartment, not quite so cluttered now that they'd organized things properly, had come to feel like a refuge. The tiny dining table was set for breakfast with vintage sterling silver and starched Russian linens. Tess said she planned to sell some of the extra items from Aunt Evelyn's house and buy some better dining chairs, but Hanna liked what was there well enough. In fact the living room, transformed with draperies, rugs and furniture from the West Park Circle house, reminded her of a particularly posh hotel suite that she and Sam had occupied for a few weeks at the beginning of their marriage, when there were still stars in her eyes.

"Nervous?" Tess asked after a moment.

"Hopeful," Hanna replied.

Yesterday, as they were leaving the courthouse, a messenger handed her a note summoning her to Chief Doyle's office in the morning. Quinn would pick her up.

"Maybe it means the police have arrested someone."

"I hope so, too."

Hanna drank some coffee and lit a post-breakfast cigarette to calm her nerves. She'd been awake most of the night, listening to Tess breathe and imagining confronting her sister's killer. In her mind's eye he looked like Sam. A literal ladykiller.

When Quinn arrived, Hanna was waiting at the base of the stairs. He opened the car door for her, with an air of repressed excitement that could only mean one thing. They'd found Marta's killer.

They mounted the big stairway to the second floor. Hanna saw small brass signs indicating the way to the chief's office, the usher's cloakroom, and the law library.

"After you," Quinn said as they headed down the hall in the correct direction.

He pushed open a paneled door to see a secretary with gray hair and thick tortoiseshell spectacles at a desk in a reception room with striped wallpaper and a big oil painting of the courthouse. A nameplate on her desk proclaimed her to be Mrs. Theodora Clancy.

Quinn doffed his hat. "Stewart Quinn and Hanna Gorski to see Chief Doyle."

"Of course, Mr. Quinn," the secretary said. "You're expected. The others are all here."

They passed into an inner office and were immediately greeted by a booming Irish voice.

"Ah, Quinn. And Mrs. Vitello."

"It's Gorski," Hanna said. "Hanna Gorski."

But Chief Doyle wasn't listening as he came forward and pumped Quinn's hand, then briefly held Hanna's fingers with an approximation of an old-fashioned bow over her hand.

Mayor Peabody was there, as were the two detectives she'd spoken to before, Schultz and Dooley. Several other men milled by a large framed certificate. Introductions were quickly made. Clive Brewster was a New York State Senator and Robert Montgomery was the owner and editor of the *Lido Daily Clipper*. As if the room wasn't crowded enough, Captain Watson of the New York State Troopers was in attendance.

Doyle waved a hand for everyone to sit. "Mrs.

Clancy will bring in the coffee."

Hanna perched on the edge of the proffered leather chair, her heart thundering. Surely with such an audience, Chief Doyle was going to make a big announcement.

He looked like a chief of police. Brass buttons strained over an ample belly and the stiff collar pinched loose jowls. A thicket of silver hair, shifty eyes, and a nose streaked with red veins that said he liked his Irish whiskey, Prohibition be damned.

The office trumpeted his power. Dark blue velvet curtains, polished wood paneling, leather armchairs and settees. Flagpoles in every corner with a collection of unfurling silk.

Her eye was drawn to a huge certificate mounted on the wall opposite the door. Gerald Francis Doyle was a member of the Loyal Order of the Bison and obviously damned proud of it.

The men talked among themselves. Train timetables, an expansion of the Franklin factory in Syracuse, and someone named Claude Harris who'd bagged a twelve-pointer on a hunting trip to the Adirondacks. Someone else was going dusk hunting. Hanna thought they meant duck hunting, but no, they were talking about shooting birds at dusk.

Mrs. Clancy wheeled in a tea cart. Coffee was

served. As soon as the secretary was gone, Chief Doyle slurped his cup dry and said he'd called them all there for a reason.

"Our brothers in blue in Chicago have sent their Missing Persons file on Miss Marta Gorski, recently identified by Mrs. Vitello, her sister."

He was rewarded by a round of head nodding. Hanna bit her lip to refrain from correcting him. Doyle was playing out his line, the better to build the anticipation before he reeled in his fish and stunned them with a rock.

The chief went on. "We've taken a good look at it. A good look, mind you. Putting it together with the results of our investigation, we feel confident that we can name who did wrong by your sister."

Chief Doyle regarded everyone in the room with supreme satisfaction. "Now, let me explain. The timing fits. The murder weapon fits. And the motive is an old, sordid story, begging your pardon, Mrs. Vitello. Now, Jimmy Zambrano went missing right at the beginning of October. The police in Chicago say Miss Gorski was already missing by then. By the time Zambrano got put into the Mohawk River by his killer, poor little Miss Gorski was already there."

He paused for effect, then puffed out his cheeks, blew out the air and threw out meaty hands, palms out like a preacher. "We all know by now that Nick Procopio killed Jimmy Zambrano to get the foreman job. Strangled him with a copper wire. Lombardo from the Galliano Club was supposed to be his next victim because Procopio got kicked out for cheating at cards."

He paused to make sure his audience was hanging on every word. "We suspected that Procopio practiced before he attacked Zambrano and now we know it for certain. Miss Gorski was his first victim, strangled after a lover's quarrel, then put into the river. A rehearsal, so to speak. All confirmed by the Chicago boys in blue."

The room erupted in manly congratulations all around, the chatter bubbling around Hanna's disbelieving ears. She stared in amazement around the room. Only Detective Dooley wasn't part of the chorus of self-congratulations.

A photographer came in. Hanna knew it would do no good to protest. Now that he'd solved a high-profile murder case and announced it to Lido's notables, Chief Doyle wasn't going to change his mind, no matter how many lapses of logic Hanna pointed out. He was right in saying the timing and means of murder fit, but that was all. A waitress in Chicago, Marta hadn't known some disgruntled factory worker in Lido who wanted a better job.

Hanna felt hollow inside as she stood for

photographs with Chief Doyle and the mayor.

Afterward, the man from the newspaper asked Hanna for her reaction.

"You must be very satisfied that your sister's murder was resolved so quickly by the police in Lido." He looked at her expectantly, pencil poised over a pad of paper.

"It was a miracle," Hanna heard herself say. "Simply a miracle."

CHAPTER 22

Trial by number

The snow piled on street curbs was speckled with dirt and exhaust. The air was still, almost silky. Instead of frost, dew glittered on enamel signs and the glass globes of the lampposts like showers of diamonds. The sky was an encouraging blue.

Tess walked into the courthouse alone, shoulders square and chin held high, the note from Luca in her pocket. Mr. Freshman had passed it to her when the trial adjourned yesterday.

The note said so little, yet so much.

63 22 13

The solution was eight. A number that was heavy and bulky, just like James. Easily divided in two.

It was Luca's way of saying that James's testimony was weak. Able to be broken in two.

Buoyed by the crisp brilliant sunshine that said winter was over when the season had barely begun, she wasn't going to let anyone provoke her today. As Mr.

Freshman had said to her after the trial adjourned yesterday, she would set the record straight when it was her turn to testify.

She ignored the cordon of reporters waiting on the courthouse steps, crossed the magnificent lobby and took a seat in the front row. When Luca was led in, their eyes met. He gave her a sad half-smile.

The second day of the trial was all about proving that James was the most honest man in Lido.

Every single employee of the First National Bank of Lido testified as a character witness. When questioned by Mr. Cromwell, all said virtually the same thing: Mr. Howland was an excellent, honest boss who was devoted to Miss Kennedy but careful not to display overt affection while they were together in the bank.

Tess struggled to stay silent as Cromwell asked each witness to express their opinions about her. As if they'd all been provided the same script, her former fellow account managers, the tellers, and even the secretaries said that Tess was flighty. Always suggesting improvements to banking procedures that were neither useful nor welcome.

Women were too emotional for the hard-nosed world of banking, one colleague declared. Mr. Howland had been overly generous in making her an account manager with all the responsibility that position carried.

He hoped Miss Kennedy could find a more suitable position as a teacher or secretary.

Tess imagined him falling down the courthouse steps and getting run over by a trolley.

Mr. Freshman asked all the bank employees the same questions. First, did Miss Kennedy display anything but an appropriate business-like attitude toward bank customers. All replied in the negative.

The last point was not lost on the jury, as Cromwell intended, given that James had already testified that Luca was one of those customers.

The second question to each character witness was if they'd been surprised to see the announcement of Miss Kennedy's engagement to Mr. James Howland in the newspaper.

Every answer was the same: "Yes." No one could recall any instance of affection between them.

The only character witness who departed from the script was Ralph Clark, Tess's favorite teller.

Cromwell began with the same questions he had posed to every other bank employee. Ralph gave the same answers as everyone else. Mr. Howland, the vice president, was honest and forthright and fair. The bank ran like clockwork.

Tess realized that by bringing his case against Luca, James and his father had put the First National Bank of

Lido on trial, too. Half of Lido did their banking there. The building itself was a downtown landmark.

The stakes were higher than Tess had imagined.

Then it was Mr. Freshman's turn to question the witness.

"Mr. Clark," he began with a friendly nod at the young man. "As a teller you must come into contact with bank customers on a regular basis. Correct?"

"Yes, sir."

"Know their schedules, their banking habits?"

"Yes."

"Was the defendant, Mr. Lombardo, one of those regular bank customers?"

"Yes."

A murmur, brief and barely audible, circled the courtroom. The judge reached for his gavel, but a hush fell over the courtroom again.

"In fact," Freshman began to pace. "Wasn't Mr. Lombardo a very regular customer? With regular deposits and withdrawals on a very reliable schedule?'

"Oh yes, sir," Ralph said, glancing toward Luca. "He deposited the same amount every week. I knew it was his salary from his job at the Galliano Club. Then once a month, always the first Monday of the month, he withdrew exactly half of what he'd deposited the previous month and sent a wire transfer to a bank in

Italy."

"Every month?"

"Yes, sir. And he always knew down to the penny how much interest his account earned. Never needed a scratch pad or an adding machine. He has a good head for figures."

"How long did Mr. Lombardo maintain this schedule of deposits and withdrawals?"

"Oh, as long as I've worked there."

"Which is?"

"Four years, sir."

"So for at least four years, Mr. Lombardo sent half of his income to Italy. Did something happen to change that?"

"The bank in Italy sent a telegram. It was in Italian and nobody knew what it said. His account went to Miss Kennedy to handle."

"Because she spoke Italian?"

"No, because she always handled the odd things that weren't routine."

"Not routine work," Freshman mused. "Accounts that required problem-solving skills, then?"

"Yes. The accounts no one else wanted to handle, at least that's how it seemed to me. She always found a way to fix problems. And she got things done so much faster than the others."

"Objection!" Cromwell glared at Ralph. "Hearsay."

"Sustained," Judge Pepper said in a rush.

Freshman gazed at the jury, silently making the point that Tess could hardly be flighty if she was a problem solver before his next question. "Were you working when the defendant, Mr. Lombardo, came into the bank after the telegram arrived and his account was assigned to Miss Kennedy?"

"Yes. It was the first Monday in October. He came up to my window with the form for a wire transfer. When I checked his account, I sent him to Miss Kennedy's desk."

"Was Mr. Lombardo already acquainted with Miss Kennedy?"

"I don't think so," Ralph said. "He seemed alarmed that the usual transaction wasn't happening."

"So what happened next?"

"Well, as I recall, he sat down with Miss Kennedy at her desk and she must have shown him the telegram from the bank in Italy. He looked real sad. Then she comes to me and makes out the forms to show that the money never left his account and instead should be paid to him. Next thing, she says she's going to help him send a telegram to Italy and she'll be back later. She got her coat and walked out of the bank with Mr. Lombardo."

"Did you ever find out who Mr. Lombardo was sending money to?"

"His late wife's parents. The telegram from the bank said that they had died and the account was closed."

Mr. Freshman raised his eyebrows, his gaze taking in the entire jury box. "Mr. Lombardo sounds like an uncommonly generous man."

"He's a real nice gentleman," Ralph offered.

"Since then, has Mr. Lombardo continued to deposit his salary into his account?"

"Yes, sir. Always comes to my window and we have a chat."

"So he remains financially responsible?"

"Yes, sir. He's got a real sharp mind for the numbers. Adds in his head like lightning."

Mr. Freshman paced a bit more. "So let's consider this. Mr. Lombardo has been a loyal customer of the First National Bank of Lido for years. He has a good head for numbers, keeps his account growing steadily. Why would he attempt to murder the vice president of the bank where he keeps his money?"

"Objection!" Cromwell was on his feet. "Leading the witness, Your Honor. This witness has no grounds to answer such a question."

"Question withdrawn," Freshman said mildly.

Tess couldn't resist a triumphant glance at James.

He was hunched in his seat next to Cromwell, staring at his clasped hands. Obviously, his mother hadn't told him what to do when the other side scored a home run.

With the supply of bank employees exhausted, Cromwell called Miss Annie Harper to the stand.

Annie sat demurely in the chair, gloved hands clasped, a few wisps of gray hair peeking out from under a beige wool cloche hat. A new hat, Tess couldn't help noticing. Cromwell stood near, one hand resting casually on the rail below the witness stand.

"Now, Miss Harper, is it correct that you served as the housekeeper to Mrs. Evelyn Kennedy Thompson for many years, residing with Mrs. Thompson on West Park Circle, here in Lido?"

"Yes."

"How many years were you with Mrs. Thompson?"

"Twenty-five," Annie said with a sniff. "Mr. Thompson was still alive then. I stayed with Miss Evelyn until the day she died."

"And during that time, she brought her niece, Miss Tess Kennedy to live with her?"

"Yes. About ten years ago."

"Please tell us about that."

"Well, the poor girl was the daughter of Miss Evelyn's brother. He was some sort of scientist, never had two nickels to rub together and raising the girl by himself. When he died, the girl came to live with us as Miss Evelyn's ward."

"How old was Miss Kennedy at that time?"

"Fourteen and wild and angry as the day is long. Her father let her do anything she wanted, even wear trousers like a boy. She didn't know the things young ladies of quality are supposed to know. How to set a table or embroider or even play the piano. Miss Evelyn had her hands full from the start."

"Not an easy transition, then."

"A willful child. But Miss Evelyn kept her, even sold her own jewelry to send her to that fancy college for women and take her to Europe."

"Thank you, Miss Harper. Given that you lived in the same household with Miss Kennedy for ten years, how would you describe her. Headstrong? Stubborn? Unreliable?"

"Flighty," Annie said.

Every bank employee, as well as James and Richard had used the same term. Tess clenched her fists in her lap.

"Flighty, yes. Flighty." Cromwell let his gaze seep over the jury as he intoned the word. "Now, please tell the court how you met the defendant, Mr. Lombardo."

"Miss Tess invited him for Sunday supper. She wanted Miss Evelyn to meet him."

"In what capacity? It is hard to imagine Mrs. Thompson having anything to do with the Galliano Club."

"Miss Tess considered him a suitor. She wanted him to ask Miss Evelyn if he could court her. Court Miss Tess, that is."

"How did the evening go?"

"Well, he came in, making a fine impression. Nice overcoat. Fine suit. Brought Miss Evelyn a dozen roses, too, from Fulton Florist. After they had supper, Miss Evelyn took him into her little sitting room and they had a little talk."

"Were you aware of what was said?"

"I don't like to say I eavesdropped but Miss Evelyn being so sick, I tried to stay nearby." Annie had the good grace to color a little. "Miss Evelyn told him he wasn't the sort of fellow she had in mind for Miss Tess but he wore her down, talking real smooth in that accent of his, until she said yes."

"Were you surprised that Mrs. Thompson allowed Mr. Lombardo to court Miss Kennedy?"

"She regretted it right away."

"Objection!" Mr. Freshman rose from his chair. "Speculation."

"Sustained." Judge Pepper sniffed in the general direction of the jury. "The jury is to disregard the witness's last statement."

Mr. Cromwell cleared his throat. "How long did Mr. Lombardo's courtship of Miss Kennedy last?"

"A few weeks. Miss Evelyn took a turn for the worse and Miss Tess went to Saratoga with her so Miss Evelyn could take the cure. It was there that Miss Evelyn told Miss Tess about the arrangement with Mr. Howland. I was relieved. Mr. Howland was just the sort of husband that Miss Tess needed. A fine, upstanding man from a good family. Well off, too. That's what Miss Evelyn was most worried about. She wanted Miss Tess to make a good marriage. She talked about financial security all the time, because her own husband had left her with nothing except charity from the railroad he founded. She didn't want Miss Tess to ever be in the same situation. Worried about money all the time."

"Presumably Mr. Lombardo did not have sufficient wealth to satisfy Mrs. Thompson."

"He's a poor man from Italy. Miss Evelyn didn't want Miss Tess to marry poor."

"Did the defendant return to see Mrs. Thompson after it was announced that Miss Kennedy was engaged to Mr. Howland?"

"He came to the house to see Miss Evelyn. She was real sick by that time but she agreed to see him. Right in her bedroom. I didn't think it was proper for her to talk to a gentleman, much less a man like him, while she was so sick in bed, but she insisted. I think she felt bad that she'd ever given him permission to court Miss Tess in the first place."

"Were you present during his conversation with Mrs. Thompson?"

"No. She made me go downstairs, not even wait by the door."

"Did you see Mr. Lombardo after his conversation with Miss Evelyn?"

"Yes. He came down the stairs with a box. I recognized it as one of her jewelry boxes."

"One of her jewelry boxes? Had he stolen it?"

"No, he said she gave it to him but that he didn't want it. Left it with me to give to Miss Tess."

"Was that all?"

"No, he said he wasn't going to allow Miss Tess to marry Mr. Howland."

"Did he say how he was going to prevent the marriage?"

"I didn't ask," Annie said grimly. "And he didn't say."

"So now we come to the night in question." Cromwell's forehead creased in concern. "Mrs. Thompson was mortally ill and confined to her bed.

Where was Miss Kennedy?"

"When the doctor left, Miss Tess packed her suitcase and said she wouldn't be home that evening. I asked if she was going to meet him." Annie cut her eyes to Luca.

"Let the record show that the witness indicated the defendant," Cromwell said. "Please continue, Miss Harper."

"We had words and she left."

"Did she surprise you?"

"Well, being so flighty and all, I guess we should have expected something like this to happen."

"What did you do? Did you tell Mrs. Thompson?"

"Oh no, she was too ill for a nasty shock like this." Annie lifted her chin proudly. "I telephoned Mr. Howland and told him that Miss Tess was probably at the Galliano Club with Mr. Lombardo and he should hurry there right away before something bad happened."

"Did he seem grateful?"

"Oh, yes. Very grateful."

Cromwell asked a few more questions calculated to portray Annie as the faithful family retainer who acted out of a deep sense of loyalty to Evelyn Thompson, her long-term employer. Tess's stomach was a mass of angry knots as she listened to Annie, a woman she'd once counted as a friend and confidante.

At last, it was Mr. Freshman's turn to question Annie. His demeanor was starkly different from Mr. Cromwell's friendly, almost brotherly way of posing questions. Mr. Freshman approached the witness stand with a scrap of paper in his hand.

"Miss Harper, you are 63 years of age, is that correct?"

"Yes." Annie had not been expecting the first salvo to be about her age and shrank against the back of the witness chair.

"Are you now or have you ever been married?"

"No."

"And as you testified, you were employed as a housekeeper to Mrs. Evelyn Kennedy Thompson for twenty-five years. Any suitors during that time?"

"Gracious, no." Annie gave an embarrassed little laugh."

"Moving on. You were an employee during the time Miss Kennedy came to live with Mrs. Thompson and grew up. You watched her evolve from an orphaned child in a new and unaccustomed atmosphere, which took away many of the freedoms she enjoyed while being raised by her father, into a young woman who graduated summa cum laude with a degree in economics from a prestigious college to pursue a

204

position in the First National Bank of Lido. Is that a fair description of her progression while you were an employee of the house?”

“Well, yes, but--.”

“Excellent. Can you tell the court how Miss Kennedy reacted to being told she had to sever her relationship with Mr. Lombardo and marry Mr. Howland?”

“She carried on for quite a bit.”

“Because she did not want to end her relationship with the defendant and marry the plaintiff?”

“I suppose,” Annie admitted. Her eyes flicked toward Tess and then down to her hands.

“Did she say she wanted to marry Mr. Howland?”

“Not at first,” Annie mumbled. “She . . . said things like he wasn’t smart. But Miss Evelyn wouldn’t hear of it. She said that Mr. Howland was a good choice. That it was all arranged. Miss Tess could cry about it, but Miss Evelyn said she needed to be mature and settle down. Make a good match. Not be so flighty.”

Freshman frowned. “As an employee of the house, why did you take it upon yourself to telephone Mr. Howland?”

Tess suppressed a grin. She could tell that Annie disliked being called an “employee of the house.” The housekeeper had never regarded herself as a servant.

Now she was being reminded in public that she was.

"It was what Miss Evelyn would have wanted me to. And she was too sick to do it herself."

"Surely managing your employer's relationships was not part of your job description."

"I knew what Miss Evelyn wanted," Annie said doggedly.

"Did she approve of notifying Mr. Howland that Miss Kennedy had gone to the Galliano Club to elope with Mr. Lombardo?"

"She never knew." Annie sniffed. "She passed that night."

"Miss Harper, where are you employed at present?"

"I'm the housekeeper for Mr. and Mrs. Norman Duncan."

"Mrs. Duncan is the sister of Mrs. Howland, mother of James and Richard Howland, is she not?"

"Yes, I believe so." Annie's voice was little more than a whisper."

"Ah." Freshman walked back to the defendant's table, in effect turning his back on the witness. "One last question, Miss Harper. Were you instructed to use the word 'flighty' when referring to Miss Kennedy?"

Annie mumbled; a gloved fist pressed against her mouth.

"Could you repeat that?" Freshman closed in on her.

"Loud enough for the court to hear, please."
    "Yes," Annie whispered.

CHAPTER 23

Look for the weak link

"What's your name?" Benny asked.

"Guido. Guido Serra." The doorman had always been friendly enough and today was no exception.

"Well, Guido Serra." Benny poked yesterday's rolled-up newspaper into Guido's porky gut, right between two rows of straining coat buttons. "In about ten minutes I'm going to own this place, lock, stock, and barrel. That means you, too. You want to lose your job or you want to let me go talk to old man Spinelli?"

Guido gaped at him. Benny could almost hear the gears trying to turn. Jesus, what a useful idiot.

He shoved past the now-motionless doorman, yanked open the door and swaggered into the club.

Every time he saw the club, it got a little bigger and his plans for the speakeasy grew. Bronze light fixtures punctuated the pressed tin ceiling and warmed the paneling on the lower half of the walls. He'd keep all that but dump the pictures and sports pennants. Too much Yankees, not any Chicago Cubs.

The crowning glory of the place was the huge

mahogany bar running the entire length of the wall on the right side. The damn thing was a long skinny stage. When Benny took over, he'd put some dancing girls on it.

The wall behind the bar was mirrored and striped with shelves of liquor bottles. Empty, every last one, which was a real windfall. Benny could fill them with wood alcohol and charge 20 bucks for a teaspoonful and after two drinks nobody would know they weren't drinking top-shelf stuff.

But he wouldn't touch the prized bottle of Liquore Galliano that rose through the middle of the mirrored display like a pointed yellow spear. The bottle was nearly as tall as Benny himself. Still full to the brim, with the import sticker from Italy, too.

All the possibilities of what this place could become somersaulted through Benny's thoughts. Add some velvet curtains, a stage for the shows, and get rid of so many tables. In Chicago, people drank more when they were standing up.

Benny had come at the right time to make the deal with Spinelli. It was still an hour before the end of the work day and the whistle that governed everybody's life. He'd use it to signal speakeasy customers. They'd know to start coming when the last whistle blew. Benny slapped the newspaper into the open palm of his left hand, congratulating himself on getting a head start on plans for the new and improved Galliano Club.

A couple of fellas in mackinaws and dungarees leaned on the bar, chewing sandwiches like cud, mugs of coffee at their elbows. A couple of old-timers were bent over a card game. Probably grannies who didn't speak English and didn't have two nickels to rub together. Well, starting today they could find someplace else to cheat at cards and eat free pickled eggs.

A young kid in an apron watched Benny with real thoughtful eyes. "Can I help you?" he asked, both hands on the bar top like he thought he was in charge.

Another kid in an apron was there as well but clearly not in charge. Had a crippled hand, too.

"What's your name, kid?"

"Sonny Zambrano."

"Well, kid. I'm here to see Vito Spinelli. Got a business proposition for him."

"Mr. Spinelli is in his office." The kid started to move toward the end of the bar. "I can show you."

"No need." Benny gave him a wink. "I know Vito real good."

He set off down the hall, whistling loudly. The pool room to the right was empty. He'd get rid of those two elephant-sized tables and create a gambling parlor.

Roulette and blackjack. This place was going to be world-famous, punters from New York City like Arthur Rothstein would beat a path to Benny's door.

The Galliano Club was going to mint him enough money to go back to Chicago and slaughter every Chicago Outfit goon for what they done to Hymie Weiss and Dean O'Banion. Sometimes, Benny played imaginary conversations with Al Capone in his head. They always ended with Capone all confused and begging Benny to leave him alone.

Spinelli was behind his desk but stood up shakily when Benny came in. The office reeked of whiskey. There was a glass on the desk, with about an inch of the stuff in it. Probably had a bottle rolling around in one of the desk drawers.

"What do you want?" Spinelli was glassy-eyed. Sure hadn't expected nobody to walk in on him.

"Hey, Spinelli. Came by to see how you were with Lombardo in jail and all." Benny advanced on him, hand out for a friendly shake. "Bygones, eh?"

The old man's hand trembled against his. When the handshake ended, Benny didn't let go.

"What's this funny business?" Spinelli demanded, trying unsuccessfully to pull his hand free.

Benny grinned at his discomfort. "You know how they killed Dean O'Banion in Chicago, Vito? Frankie

Yale shook his hand but didn't let go so his buddies could pump Dean full of lead. Have to admire Frankie. Musta took guts of iron to stand there and not let go."

"Are you here to kill me?" Spinelli asked, too sozzled to be scared.

"Just setting the tone." Benny released the man's hand and took a gander around the office. Desk, bookshelves, a nice comfy sofa as big as a bed, and a hefty black Liberty safe. Benny decided to keep it all when the office was his. He threw himself onto the big Chesterfield. "Your boy Lombardo went and got himself arrested. Kind of changes the landscape around here, don't it?"

Spinelli looked at him blankly, hand stealing toward the tumbler full of whiskey.

"Lombardo's got the whole First National Bank of Lido against him," Benny went on. "What's he got to fight with? Pickled eggs and coffee? Nah, it never does to get on the wrong side of the money. He'll be lucky if he don't get the electric chair for attempted murder."

"You came to tell me this?"

"The whole mess happened here, right in front of your place. Attempted murder and kidnappings are bad news for any business. Bet the cops have been nosing around already, seeing what kind of establishment you run. Puts you in kinda a delicate situation, no? You want to keep the beer flowing, you got a real problem."

Spinelli closed his eyes and took a gulp from the glass.

"You understand what I'm saying to you, old man?" Benny asked in exasperation. "Thanks to Lombardo, you got big problems. Better get out of this mess now, before it gets worse."

The glass drained, Spinelli wiped his mouth and mustache with the back of a trembling hand. "Is that why you come now? To tell me about my problems?"

"I'm willing to help out a pal." Benny leaned back, real casual-like. "I got a new business proposition for you. Twenty-five thousand for this place, lock, stock, and barrel. Cash sale. Right now. That's three grand more than I offered you before. Sign over the deed to the building and the cash is all yours. Buy the wife something new. Get your boy a lawyer who knows the judge's soft spot, if you take my meaning."

He reached inside his coat, drew out a brick of cash and threw it on the desk. It made a dull, chunky sound as it landed on the wood. "Twenty-five thousand. I give you the cash, you sign over the deed."

"The Galliano Club isn't for sale," Spinelli said slowly but his eyes locked onto the cash.

"Everything is for sale," Benny said. "Women, cars, clubs. All a matter of price."

Spinelli shook his head. "I need to talk to Luca first."

"That's your problem, old man." Benny was getting angry at the stubborn attitude. "Everyone knows you're a stinking lush who can't do nothing without Lombardo. You can't keep the plates spinning by yourself, never could. He's going to be in the slammer for a long time. Sell to me now while there's still something to sell. Without him, this place is going under and we both know it."

"Luca's a good man," Spinelli said, hand hovering near the cash.

"I ain't going nowhere until I see that deed." Benny loomed over the desk. "You're a drunk and this place is too much for you without Lombardo. So let's settle on a price. Twenty-five big ones."

"No, no." Spinelli hunched into himself like a nervous turtle. "I can't sell now."

"Hey," Benny exclaimed. "I'm offering you cash. Take it now or I'll run you dry. No more beer."

Spinelli blinked at him. "Maybe I don't need your beer."

"You think the men around here are going to pay for Gleason's whiskey? Think you'll be able to get any more for yourself?"

The old man slowly got to his feet. "You don't show

respect."

"Respect!" Benny hooted. "You're an old drunk standing in the way of real money. I don't got to give you nothing."

"Get out," Spinelli said with more vigor than Benny would have thought the old man had in a month of Sundays. "Get out."

Benny reached inside his coat for the Colt Pocket Hammerless but a loud thump made him stop and spin around. Sonny Zambrano, the kid from the bar, stood there with a baseball bat in his right hand. "You need anything, Mr. Spinelli?" he asked.

"Mr. Rotolo is going now." Spinelli stayed standing.

Benny could hardly believe what was happening. Some runty kid was running him out of a place that by all rights should belong to him? Without a chance to draw on Spinelli?

"You think about my offer, old man," he snarled. "It's the last one I'm gonna make. Take it or there'll be trouble. The kind of trouble you don't want to have."

He strode out of the office, fedora tilted over one eye like he was still on top of the world.

Sonny followed him down the hall and through the saloon to the little half-wall that guarded the vestibule, nodding to the claw-handed kid behind the bar. Jesus, a snot-nose and a cripple. Spinelli was dreaming if he thought he could hold on to the club.

When they got to the door, Benny decided to dispense some advice. Sort of like when Hymie Weiss took Benny under his wing. "You're on the wrong side of things, kid. Spinelli ain't gonna hold out much longer. A week, tops. Lombardo's going down and taking this place with him."

"What you read in the newspaper was wrong," Sonny said stubbornly. "I know. I saw what happened."

Benny thought about yanking the baseball bat out of the kid's hands and beating some sense into him but something in the kid's stance said that he'd learned a few tricks from Lombardo. "You got moxie, kid, but you're betting on the wrong horse."

Sonny narrowed his eyes. "Guido was there, too. We're both going to testify. Luca will be back."

Benny forced a laugh and pushed past him.

Guido was at his post in the vestibule, watching the sidewalk through the window in the outer door. Benny tipped the fella a dollar and was rewarded with slobbering gratitude.

Parked half a block away on Hamilton Street, the Cadillac offered warmth and a direct line of sight to the Galliano Club. Benny sat and watched the doorman.

CHAPTER 24

Woman to woman

"This is it?" Hanna asked dubiously. The two-story clapboard house looked similar to all the other houses in this part of East Lido where the streets were narrow and crammed with people. Bedsheets flapped from clotheslines strung across both upper and lower porches. A side garden of sticks poked up from the snow, suggesting a summer crop of tomatoes or pole beans.

The neighborhood wasn't much different from where she'd grown up in Chicago, where kids played stickball in vacant lots as trains rattled through the sky and Hanna learned to use her fists.

"It's that door." Sonny was with her on the skinny sidewalk in front of the house, shoulders hunched and hands thrust into the pockets of his navy pea coat. He lifted his chin at the right side of the house. "Mr. Procopio killed my dad, too. I'm not going in."

Hanna resisted the urge to light a cigarette to calm her nerves. "I don't blame you. Does anyone talk to her?"

Hanna had spent the middle of the day in the apartment over the Galliano Club by herself, smoking like a chimney and rehashing all the reasons why Chief Doyle's conclusion made no sense. Yet she had no alternative theory of her sister's murder to investigate.

"Ma talks to Mrs. Procopio sometimes." Sonny kicked at a clump of frozen snow. "Says she didn't know."

"Do you think that's true? That she didn't know?"

"Not really."

"Anyway, thanks for showing me where she lives."

"She's not nice," Sonny warned, taking a couple of steps backward.

Hanna shrugged. "Doesn't matter. Go on, get back to the club."

Sonny trotted off. Hanna climbed the steps and rapped on the door.

Shouting erupted from the other side. She heard a machine gun burst of Italian, childish wailing, and the smack of a hand hitting a cheek.

The door flew open. A slight woman with dark hair and a tasteful caramel-colored dress under a stained white apron glowered at Hanna until her eyes widened in recognition. "What are you doing here?"

"I'm--."

Maria Teresa Procopio wiped her hands on the

apron. "I know who you are."

"Good," Hanna said evenly. "We need to talk about your husband. May I come in?"

"No speak English," Maria Teresa said. "Go away."

"Don't try that crap on me." Hanna shoved the door open all the way and stepped over the threshold. "I don't think your husband killed my sister, Mrs. Procopio. But I think we should talk about it."

"Why don't you believe my Nick killed the girl?" Maria Teresa spat. "Everyone else does."

Hanna produced the striped tie. "Did this belong to your husband?"

"What's this, a necktie for a baby?" Maria Teresa regarded the rag with contempt. "Nick owned one necktie. Black, for funerals and baptisms."

"Is that what you told the police?"

"When? I never seen that before."

"The police never showed you this tie? They didn't ask if this belonged to your husband?"

Maria Teresa's eyes narrowed in suspicion. "No, why should they?"

"This was wrapped around my sister's throat when they brought her out of the river."

"It didn't belong to my Nick."

Hanna stuffed the tie back into her purse, furious with the Lido police department, furious with herself for not coming here sooner, and furious at Marta for having gotten herself killed.

"Did your husband ever go to Chicago?" she heard herself ask. "Take the train there?"

"No."

"Did he ever write letters to someone in Chicago?"

"Letters! My Nick write letters?" Maria Teresa gave a short laugh but there was no humor in it and her expression quickly became thoughtful. "Why are you asking questions about Chicago?"

"That's where my sister lived."

"So why did she come to Lido?"

"That's what I'm trying to find out."

Somewhere in the house, a child screeched loud enough to make Hanna flinch. A raucous argument ensued, childish voices hollering in both Italian and English.

"Go ask Lucky Lombardo," Maria Teresa scowled. "I hear that everyone writes him letters."

She closed the door, forcing Hanna to take a step away from the threshold. A lock turned. Children continued to scream.

CHAPTER 25

Take a vote

"Shall we come to order?" Doc Lanigan asked, his voice rising over the murmur of private conversations.

Owen took a sip from his heavy cut glass tumbler as the waiter discreetly slipped out, closing the double doors behind him. The seven men around the long conference table settled down under the watchful eye of a dozen portraits of past Bison Club presidents. This was Owen's first meeting as a member of the Bison Club's Membership Committee, and he was suitably impressed.

There were seven seats on the committee, including Doc who was the current chairman. The president of the Bison Club was automatically on the Committee, so Jack Rutherford was there, looking damnably wealthy and at ease in equal measure. Henry Blick sat on Rutherford's left, seemingly a little less sharp-edged since his unexpected marriage.

The other three around the table were Bison Club stalwarts. Edgar Bailey owned Bailey Wire and Tubing. Jasper Coe was synonymous with the Candyland

Supper Club. Alfred Sowell had something to do with railroads including the lucrative Adirondack and Western.

Each man around the table was fortified for what was sure to be a lively discussion with a tumbler of medicinal brandy and a Cuban cigar. Crystal ashtrays rested at each elbow, next to an agenda printed on embossed Bison Club letterhead.

NOMINATIONS TO CONSIDER
Dr. Ezra Feinman
Edward Sherman Everett

NEW BUSINESS
Membership status of Sean O'Malley

The last item was going to be the most contentious. Like everyone else around the table, Owen had read the newspaper reports of O'Malley's arrest by Inspector Finch from the Post Office. Charged with misuse of the Postal Service by sending a blackmail letter to Henry Blick. Whispers going around the smoking room at the club said O'Malley made lewd accusations against Blick's new wife, although that never appeared in the *Lido Daily Clipper*.

Owen faced the discussion with a great deal of

trepidation. He owed Doc Lanigan for getting him on the Membership Committee. Lanigan and O'Malley were brothers-in-law, so it was clear how Lanigan would vote. Of course, he'd expect Owen to vote with him.

But on the other hand, Owen worked with Blick, who was the very pinnacle of Lido society. Moreover, Owen couldn't escape the fear that Blick's single blue eye and ramrod-straight posture gave the man some superhuman power to poke into men's souls and learn their secrets. Owen simply couldn't afford to alienate the man, especially if things went badly with Dombrowski.

The thought of what might happen when Owen didn't produce the money made his hands shake. He nearly jumped out of his skin when Doc Lanigan rapped on the table to bring the meeting to order.

"We have two applications for membership to discuss this evening," Lanigan announced. "And one motion to remove a member from the club's rolls."

After reviewing the minutes of the last meeting and formally welcoming Owen as replacement for the late Judge Smoot, Lanigan presented the membership nominations for Dr. Ezra Feinman and Edward Sherman Everett.

Ezra Feinman was a Princeton graduate, a doctor

specializing in gastrointestinal problems. Everyone around the table knew the name because six months ago the doctor operated on a child struck by a car on Liberty Street. The *Lido Daily Clipper* had reported that Feinman used a ground-breaking surgical technique to save the youngster's life. Repeatedly clearing his throat, Lanigan reeled off a long list of professional certifications, awards, and post-graduate study at both Oxford and the Sorbonne in Paris, France.

As Doc Lanigan proceeded to read the second nomination, Owen wondered if he hadn't detected a hint of professional jealousy when it came to the other doctor's qualifications. Lanigan had never pursued any fancy specializations, seemingly content to be a general practitioner spending most of his time on the health of the police department. But perhaps he was feeling a bit as if he'd been left at the starting block.

Feinman was nominated by a fellow medical man whose family roots traced back to the first Dutch settlers in the Mohawk Valley. His nomination carried the required five signatures, one of which belonged to Henry Blick. An endorsement from a member of the Membership Committee virtually guaranteed acceptance into the Bison Club.

The second nomination for Edward Sherman Everett was more modest. A graduate of Carlisle

Commercial College in Pennsylvania, Everett was the new General Secretary of the Y.M.C.A., coming to Lido after a stint at the national level for that worthy organization. He was a member of the New York State Physical Directors' Society, a Mason, and attended Holy Trinity Episcopal Church. His nomination was also endorsed with the required number of signatures, although none from the seven around the Committee table.

When the nominations were read, Lanigan opened the meeting for general comments.

"Well, Everett sounds like our kind," Jasper Coe said right off and was met with murmurs of approval.

"I agree," Owen said. "He's a member of our church and seems a fine, upstanding sort."

Bailey gave a sniff. "Pity we can't say the same about Feinman. He may not feel comfortable here. Not his kind, so to speak."

Jack Rutherford tapped ash from his cigar into an ashtray. "True, we only have a handful of doctors."

"That's not what I meant," Bailey said stiffly.

"Don't we already have a Jew?" Alfred Sowell asked.

"Randall Freshman, the lawyer," Lanigan murmured.

Owen was shocked. He never dreamed that the

Bison Club would welcome a Jew. He blamed it on Jack Rutherford and his society wife, who was continually embracing social causes and ensnaring Cynthia in Women's Institute activities. The Rutherfords were terrifically popular but far too progressive.

"Well, I should think one is more than enough." Bailey picked up his brandy glass.

"Perhaps more than enough," Sowell said. "Freshman is defending that Italian who tried to kill Preston Howland's boys. Imagine, plucking your clients from the gutter and representing them in court. Shows how low they'll go."

"I hear he has a strong case." Blick broke his silence in a voice that wasn't loud but carried an authority that made Owen want to shrink away. "The defendant, Mr. Lombardo is a friend of Mrs. Blick's."

The room grew deathly quiet.

"Hear, hear, Henry." Coe lifted his glass. "A belated congratulations on your recent nuptials. Better late than never, eh? Good luck, old man, and much happiness."

An impromptu round of toasts to Blick and his new wife helped ease the tension.

"Perhaps we can come back to the nominations later," Lanigan said smoothly. "After we discuss the last item on the agenda. A motion has been made to strip Sean O'Malley of his membership in the Bison

Club."

Owen wasn't the only one who squirmed a bit as Lanigan spoke. It was not so long ago that the club held a banquet in O'Malley's honor for thwarting one murder and solving another. The club had lavished awards and accolades on him.

His subsequent arrest gave every club member a proverbial black eye. The move to strip him of membership was predictable vengeance, yet hard to argue against.

Jack Rutherford spoke up. "I move to strip Sean O'Malley of his membership on the grounds of his duplicitous and rancorous behavior toward another member of the Bison Club. He is under arrest for the attempted blackmail of a member of this very committee."

Blick stood up. "I recuse myself from this discussion and any decision the committee makes."

"Yes, that seems appropriate," Lanigan said with a tight smile.

As Blick walked out, Owen wondered if Doc shouldn't recuse himself as well, given that he and O'Malley were related by ties of marriage. But Lanigan didn't seem to make that connection for himself.

"The *Clipper* has leaked dribs and drabs," Bailey lamented. "Whatever possessed O'Malley to do such a thing?"

"O'Malley appears obsessed with the new Mrs. Blick," Rutherford said. "Very distressing for all concerned."

"Appalling behavior," Coe said. "A postal inspector had to come to Lido to clean up our mess."

"Why hasn't there been more action from Doyle?" Sowell demanded.

Lanigan cleared his throat. "I believe that Chief Doyle has said he'll conduct an internal investigation."

"An internal investigation?" Sowell snorted. "When there is clear evidence of blackmail?"

Owen suppressed a shiver and sipped his brandy to steady his nerves. He was the only man in the room who knew that blackmail lapped beneath Lido like a river of darkness.

Benny Rotolo had tried to blackmail at least two people. Russo, that farmer on Bell Road, plus the owner of the Galliano Club. Three men were blackmailing Owen because they knew he'd killed Benny's partner Al Genovese.

Owen's thoughts twisted in on themselves, bringing him back to the burning situation with Dombrowski and his equally brawny and detestable friends. Benny had the money Owen needed to pay them off. All that malarkey about shares in a nonexistent speakeasy meant Benny was frittering away Owen's cash on cheap women and expensive suits.

"Has O'Malley been suspended from the police department?" Coe asked.

"Chief Doyle has so far resisted the mayor's calls to do so," Rutherford replied. "Nor has he seen fit to issue a statement regarding O'Malley's arrest."

"Too busy with that Gorski matter," Sowell lamented. "And the unsolved murder of one of his own officers. Officer Scully gunned down on the side of the road and still no arrest."

There was a general discussion about the array of problems confronting Chief Doyle. Lanigan eventually got the meeting back on track.

"Gentlemen," Rutherford said, leaving his cigar balanced in the divot on the edge of his ashtray. "I believe the Bison Club, by stripping the man of his membership, can and should send a message where currently a vacuum exists."

"A vacuum?" Lanigan gave an awkward chuckle. "You mean in reference to Chief Doyle? That's rather harsh language, don't you think?"

Rutherford took up his cigar again. "The club's mission is the betterment of Lido's citizens. If the police are not in step with that, perhaps the Bison Club needs to review its guidelines regarding police membership."

"I should say so!" Coe had been quiet throughout this portion of the meeting but it was clear he was troubled. "If the police have this type of scoundrels in their ranks, perhaps the Bison Club is not a suitable venue for police participation."

Lanigan bristled. "Surely you are not thinking of stripping Chief Doyle of his membership."

"I think there's a concern," Owen ventured, trying to play peacemaker. "That Chief Doyle is protecting his officer but--."

"Exactly," Sowell interrupted, punctuating the word with a jab of his cigar into the air. "Has Doyle got something to hide?"

"That's an excellent question." Across the table, Bailey took up the thread. "Was Doyle part of a scheme against Henry? A simply appalling thing to do, by the way. The Blick family goes back generations! The Bison Club does not tolerate criminal behavior and right now neither Doyle nor O'Malley are showing clean hands. I'm with Coe. Maybe the police aren't fit for the Bison Club."

Lanigan stiffened. "Gentlemen, let's not leap to conclusions.

Owen felt his face redden. "Wait, yes, that's not what I meant to--"

Sowell cut him off. "We are completely dedicated to the health, welfare and morality of the citizens of Lido."

"I believe Dr. Feinman meets and even exceeds such criteria," Rutherford observed.

"An excellent point, Jack," Coe said. "I'd rather have a medical man, no matter what his religion, than a blackmailing policeman."

"Hear, hear," said Bailey. "Perhaps Feinman can fix my dyspepsia."

After another hour of lively discussion, Henry Blick was asked back into the room for the vote on new members. Both nominations were unanimously accepted.

Blick refrained from casting a vote on the last agenda item.

Sean O'Malley was stripped of his membership by a vote of 5-1.

An agenda item was proposed for the next meeting of the Membership Committee: Nominating procedures for police officers and if current police officers would be allowed to retain their club membership. This time Lanigan abstained.

The motion was carried with another vote of 6-0.

Doc Lanigan found Owen in the parking lot after the meeting, face suffused with anger. "I counted on you,

Owen," he snarled. "You're supposed to vote with me! I got you on the committee!"

"I know, I know." Owen raised both hands, ready to surrender or apologize or both. "But this was about Blick. If it had been anyone else, I would have voted with you. But Blick, well, I can't afford not to be seen as on his side."

Doc was hardly mollified. "I've got to tell Chief Doyle that the entire issue of policemen becoming members is under review. He's going to slay me."

Owen opened his mouth to apologize again but Doc simply stormed off.

CHAPTER 26

Disease of the mind

Tess and Hanna had stayed up late the previous evening. There was so much to talk about. Why the police decided to blame a man Marta Gorski couldn't possibly have known. Why Maria Teresa Procopio, the man's widow, was so believable.

When they exhausted that topic, they discussed the trial. Why did Annie Harper feel entitled to ruin Tess's life? And, as Hanna put it, why was she such a vengeful old bitch?

"Her whole life was Aunt Evelyn," Tess mused as they sat at opposite ends of the bed with cups of hot cocoa. It was nearly midnight. Both wore pajamas and robes. Outside, a gentle snow was falling, turning the apartment into a cozy winter nest. "Housekeeper to a co-founder of the Adirondack and Western Railroad. Without that, Annie's nobody."

"Like the rest of the world."

Tess grimaced, recalling the testimony in the courtroom. "I'd like to be a nobody again."

"If I'd known you were so flighty, I'd never have

agreed to live here." Hanna poked Tess with a bare toe. "Stop reading the newspaper."

"What are you going to do now?" Tess asked, hoping Hanna wasn't going to go back to Chicago.

Hanna took a deep breath. "I'm going to give Marta a hell of a funeral."

The next morning, while Hanna went to make arrangements with the priest at Holy Angels Church, Tess went back to the courthouse.

Cromwell called the next witness, a man named Finn Conover. Tess recognized the name, although besides Luca it was clear no one else in the courtroom knew who the man was. Conover had owned the saloon in New York City's Bowery neighborhood where Luca fought for money after arriving in America. No ring, no neutral corners, no rules, just a shouting circle of men cheering and drinking and betting on their favored bare-knuckle fighter.

She watched the weather-beaten Irishman take the stand. A big man wearing a mismatched tweed suit, with a rumpled tie, Conover had a bend in his nose and a scar over one eyebrow.

"Mr. Conover, please state your name and place of residence for the court, if you please." Cromwell approached the witness stand.

"Finn Conover," the man boomed out. "Aye, all the

way from New York City."

"And do you recognize the defendant?"

"Aye, sure. Luke Lombardo, we called him. A grand slugger of a boy from Calabria. Knew about ten words of English. Of course, it's been some time. He's quite the gentleman now, I see. This'll be one for the lads back home, so it will. Bet he speaks proper English now, too."

"How did you become acquainted with the defendant?"

"Well, as I say, it was some time ago, mebbe 1919 or so? Before Prohibition, when the beer and spirits trade was grand. Aye, musta been 1919, the year of the big influenza in New York City. I was running my own saloon. Conover's Saloon in The Bowery. We had fights there. Bare-knuckle boxing. Strictly amateur." Conover raised both hands. "Nothing illegal of course, just a wee bit of betting on the side. Even the coppers came by to watch."

"Bare-knuckle boxing is quite dangerous, isn't it? Fighting until your opponent is knocked out?"

"We had one or two cracked heads," Conover agreed cheerfully.

"How did the defendant come to be a fighter in your establishment?"

"Well, like I says, we had fights there on Saturday

nights so I was always looking for fighters who could stay standing after a few punches, give the crowd something to get excited about. The more fights a fella won, the bigger his winnings of course, and the higher the stakes, the more the customers drink. Good for business if you catch my drift."

"Yes." Cromwell managed a weak but encouraging smile.

Conover rubbed his hands together, relishing the attention. "Mostly I picked Irish fellas but one day I'm walking along and a fella runs past and tries to grab a lady's purse. A real pregnant lady, too. Well, her man catches the thief and lays him out with one punch and gets her bag back. Wasn't even a big punch. Just a good clip on the chin and the next thing this thief is laying on the sidewalk like he's pushing up daisies. I catch up to the fella with the big swing and tell him to come to the saloon on Saturday if he wants to make twenty dollars. He doesn't know too much English but he understood me all right."

"You're referring to Mr. Lombardo, the defendant?"

"Sure was. Just arrived from Naples or Genoa, wherever the Italians come from. A real handsome face, too. I figured the ladies would like that."

"Did he take you up on your offer?"

"Turned up the next Saturday night. I put him in and

he won the fight without even trying. Same thing the next weekend."

"How many fights did Mr. Lombardo win at your establishment?"

"All of them." Conover grinned, showing a gap between his front teeth. "Every time he was in the ring, he won. Even when I put him in against Plugger Horan. Twice his size and undefeated, too."

Tess started to feel sick to her stomach.

Cromwell rolled his shoulders, almost like a fighter warming up. "Did Mr. Lombardo knock out this Mr. Horan?"

"Oh, aye. It was a grand fight. Folks still talk about it. Lombardo left poor old Plugger looking like a train wreck. Threw him down on the ground and battered him black and blue. Busted ribs, busted head, the works."

"Would you say that Mr. Lombardo left Mr. Horan in a serious state?"

"Och, aye. Beat him to a pulp," Conover said cheerfully.

"And his other opponents? Were they similarly beat to a pulp?"

"Every one of 'em."

Tess stopped watching Conover and watched Luca instead. She was behind him but close enough to read his mood in the set of his shoulders and the way he'd lean toward or away from Mr. Freshman. Right now his shoulders were rigid, all of his attention on the witness.

Mr. Cromwell cleared his throat. "If Mr. Lombardo was an undefeated bare-knuckle fighter, winning big purses, he must have been very good. A very good fighter."

"The boy was good. Tall for an Italian. Fast hands, good reflexes, good muscle."

"Thank you." Cromwell hesitated, then returned to his table where James sat, looking bored. "Your witness, Mr. Freshman."

Mr. Freshman approached the witness box. "Mr. Conover, thank you for coming all the way to Lido from New York City. Let's clarify a few details."

"Aye, go ahead."

"The last time you spoke to Mr. Lombardo was seven years ago?"

"Aye, that's right."

"Since that time, were you aware of his move to Lido?"

"No."

"His employment at the Galliano Club here?"

"No?"

"His relationship with Miss Tess Kennedy?"

"No."

"What is your assessment of the current state of his pugilistic skills?"

"Well, I ain't seen him fight in seven years, like I said."

"Ah." Mr. Freshman stood by the witness stand, his brow furrowed in thought.

Conover's enthusiasm for being the center of attention faded.

"Do you know the plaintiff or his brother?" Mr. Freshman asked, his voice harsher than before. "Mr. James Howland or Mr. Richard Howland?"

"No." Conover shifted in his chair.

"Can you provide an assessment of the current state of either man's pugilistic skills?"

"No, never seen either of them fight," Conover said. His eyes went to Cromwell who was bent over a pad of paper and studiously writing. James sat like a lump next to him, mouth slightly open as he watched the witness.

"So your only purpose in coming here was to recount a brief acquaintanceship with the defendant that took place seven years ago."

"I was invited," Conover said stubbornly.

"And in the intervening seven years, you had no contact with the defendant?"

"No."

"No idea about his present life situation,

relationships, employment?"

"No."

"Seven years' worth of a blank slate, then?"

"I suppose," Conover said slowly.

"No further questions," Mr. Freshman said and crossed to his seat behind the table.

Before Judge Pepper could tell Conover that he could go, Cromwell shot to his feet. "Your Honor," he said to the judge, "Permission to cross-examine the witness. Counsel's line of questioning has opened a new line of inquiry."

Tess blinked, not sure she understood.

Mr. Freshman rose. "Your Honor, there was no new line of inquiry."

Cromwell approached the judge. "The absence of interaction between the witness and the defendant does not diminish their prior relationship."

"I'll allow it." Judge Pepper pointed to Cromwell. "Make it brief, Mr. Cromwell."

Cromwell nodded and spoke directly to the jury. "Mr. Conover, you have established that the defendant was a skilled amateur prizefighter. Would you say he had the potential to become a professional prizefighter?"

"In a real ring, you mean?"

"Objection!" Freshman was on his feet again. "The

witness is not a professional boxing judge nor a boxing trainer. He merely provided a venue for illegal backroom brawling a number of years ago. It is unclear to the defense how this is a new line of inquiry."

"The witness mentored a number of amateur fighters, including the defendant," Cromwell snapped back.

Judge Pepper sniffed. "Proceed, Mr. Cromwell."

"Was the defendant good enough to be a professional fighter?" Cromwell repeated.

"Aye, a regular John L. Sullivan. A real cool customer, always calculating it seemed like. Not like the others. Most of the fighters were just wild sluggers, no real skills, just lots of courage and drink in them. Not him."

"Given his prowess, in your opinion, did Mr. Lombardo have the skill and prowess to beat a man to death?"

In the first row behind James, Muriel Howland actually screamed.

"Objection!" Freshman snapped.

"Objection denied," Judge Pepper bellowed. "Witness is directed to answer."

Conover heaved a theatrical sigh. "Sure, yes, yes. Laid them right out, nearly ready for the mortuary they was. Even Plugger Horan, who made two of him."

"In other words, a dangerous man."

"Oh, aye. Sure."

"Thank you, Mr. Conover," Cromwell again addressed the jury, his mouth turned down in an expression of regret that he'd been the instrument of such shocking news.

And it was shocking news. When the judge adjourned the trial for lunch and left the courtroom, the buzz of gossip was deafening. Muriel Howland's voice could be heard above the hubbub, declaring that only God above had saved her sons. Of course, when the doors at the back of the courtroom opened and spectators streamed out to find lunch, the reporters descended like vultures.

Tess braved the chaos and met Hanna at the drugstore but Conover's testimony had shaken her. Not that she learned anything new, but the way Cromwell had managed to twist the past promised trouble ahead.

The last witness of the day was Donald Montgomery, a physician all the way from Princeton University in New Jersey who specialized in diseases of the brain.

After a lengthy series of questions designed to impress the jury with Montgomery's credentials and expertise, Cromwell finally got to the point. "Based on your review of the case, do you have a diagnosis of disease for the defendant?"

"Indeed I do." Montgomery was a large confident man in his late fifties who reminded Tess of Homer Bradshaw. Same empire-builder attitude, same overpriced suit, lacquered hair and polished brogues. Putting him on the stand after Conover gave the jury the impression that the danger had been contained. Sanity and stability presided over the courtroom once again.

"Based on an in-depth study of the defendant's case history," Montgomery said. "In my professional opinion he suffers from an acute case of immigrant psychosis."

Conover made a sweeping motion with one arm to indicate an uneducated audience. "Could you explain the disease to the court?"

"With pleasure." Montgomery exuded confidence. "This is a mentally repressive compulsive disorder that immigrants from locations which lack proper education and refinement suffer from when they are placed in more advanced civilizations such as the United States."

"A sort of homesickness?"

"Nostalgia to be precise," Montgomery corrected the attorney. "The word nostalgia is a combination of the Greek words *hostos*, meaning homecoming, and *algos*, meaning pain. The definition is thus an excessive and damaging longing for a past home which is viewed through a sentimental lens. It's a disease of the mind."

"And what are the symptoms of immigrant psychosis?"

"Violent behavior," Montgomery said. "Uncontrolled violent behavior."

Tess felt her breath turn into little angry gasps.

"The kind of violent behavior that could lead to an assault severe enough to be classified as attempted murder?"

"Certainly," Montgomery said.

Freshman stood up when it was his turn to question the witness and walked toward the jury box with a sheaf of papers in his hand. "Dr. Montgomery, how long did you spend with the defendant, Mr. Lombardo?"

Montgomery frowned. "I don't understand the question."

"How much time did you spend speaking to the defendant prior to your medical diagnosis of immigrant psychosis?"

"I didn't speak to him."

"You didn't ever speak directly to him? No examination, no consultation?"

"I am a research and teaching physician." Color crept from Montgomery's collar to his forehead. "My conclusions are based on scientific observation and literature."

"When did you observe the defendant prior to seeing him in court today?"

Montgomery blinked. "In this case, my diagnosis was based on case files."

"In fact, you have not seen him before today, isn't that correct?"

"Yes."

"And where did the case files you say you have reviewed come from?"

"The case files were provided by Mr. Cromwell."

"This file?" Freshman showed the doctor the papers in his hand.

"Yes."

"Let the record show that the doctor positively identified the police report of the defendant's arrest to be the basis for his testimony."

Montgomery was positively puce.

A murmur rose from the courtroom. Judge Pepper pounded it into silence with his gavel.

"No further questions, Your Honor." Freshman took his seat.

Tess silently applauded Mr. Freshman's effort to discredit Dr. Montgomery's methodology but wondered if it had much effect. Cromwell had succeeded in planting the idea that Luca was a dangerous, violent man who shouldn't be allowed to roam Lido's streets.

Judge Pepper banged his gavel again. "This trial is adjourned until next Wednesday," he announced. "Randall, will you be ready to present your defense?"

"We're ready today," Mr. Freshman said.

"Well, my gout is gifting you a few extra days," the judge growled. "Had the cream sauce at lunch and now I've got an attack coming on."

CHAPTER 27

O'Malley changes his plea

Five days full of nothing but *agita* loomed ahead of Luca.

The trial had become a two-edged agony. The first agony was knowing that Tess was suffering. The second agony was the constant expectation that Howland's lawyer would accuse Luca of the murder of Humberto Orsini in the town of Spadola, near Serra San Bruno, in a big white house on the road to the Taverna dei Borboni.

When that happened, it would be all over.

Luca had never felt so helpless. Or so tormented by his own thoughts.

At the end of every day, when the judge banged his gavel, Luca was led down the stairs and through the heavy door to the basement jail. A few words with Joe Sestito, the inevitable tasteless dinner delivered in a metal pail, useless prattle from O'Malley in the adjacent cell, and then the lights went out and the shadows of Luca's past came out to play.

On clear nights a shaft of moonlight slanted across

Joe Sestito's desk from the lone window perched high on the far wall. In the thin glow, as he lay on his cot between waking and sleeping, Luca heard his mother scream.

Saw her die as his father's body sagged against the tree selected by his executioners for their grisly task. Cringed as Luca told Humberto Orsini to beg forgiveness for murdering Matteo and Viola Lombardo on the edge of the olive grove.

Remembered all the words Luca should have said to Vito instead of helping to push Jimmy Zambrano's body into the river after finding him strangled behind the club.

Sometimes he heard Jimmy's voice, too, asking Luca to take care of his family.

When he could cast the voices into the void beyond the iron bars of his cell, Luca analyzed every glimpse of Tess in the courtroom. Was she sad, upset, despairing, disgusted, hopeful? Each fleeting moment when their eyes met was an opportunity to convince himself that she would soon abandon him and a desperate prayer from the depths of his soul that she wouldn't.

They'd exchanged coded notes via Freshman. He kept the one she'd sent after Howland testified in his pocket.

48 72 32

The solution was eight, the same solution as the code he'd sent her. The counting game was a frail reed on which to base his hopes of a future with her when this was all over, but right now it was the only thing he had.

Yet at the same time, Luca knew that remaining loyal to him was destroying her. Tess, his *Tessa* was being dragged through the mud. The best thing for her to do would be to renounce Luca and reclaim her life.

If she wouldn't do it, he'd have to do it for her.

78 43 61

The solution was two. Not one heart, but two. Tess would understand.

When the trial resumed, if it continued to go badly, Luca would give the note to Freshman to pass to her.

The lack of sleep and physical activity was killing him. Two weeks of being confined to the cell or sitting in the courtroom made Luca so restless that his muscles twitched at night as he tossed and turned on the unforgiving cot.

His fellow prisoner apparently suffered no such

discomforts. Every night, after nattering on about the news of the day, O'Malley snored like a freight train. The night watchman shone his lantern inside the jail every two hours, invariably waking Luca if he'd been so lucky as to fall asleep, but O'Malley always droned on.

That night, O'Malley held a one-sided conversation with himself about the evening edition of the *Lido Daily Clipper*. When the lights went out, Luca lay on his cot, staring at nothing but seeing Tess.

Sometimes Hanna Gorski was with her; tall, blonde, and coolly elegant. The friends who buzzed around Tess when Luca first met her never came to the trial. Tess was an outcast now, he supposed, the way he'd been in Serra San Bruno as the traitor's son.

The glow of the night watchman's lantern swung across the jail floor for the second time, meaning that it was just after midnight.

Luca wanted to leap off the cot, grab the light with both hands and clasp it to his chest like a shield. He'd never been afraid of the dark as a child, but tonight when the watchman left, it was unbearable. O'Malley continued to snore. Dust motes swirled in the draft created by the closing door; white specks illuminated by borrowed moonlight. Luca began to count them.

He must have fallen asleep because he jolted awake

as a bulky shadow entered the jail. The visitor crossed in front of Joe Sestito's desk without bothering to glance toward Luca's cell. Silhouetted briefly as he passed through the shaft of moonlight, Luca saw a burly man with a policeman's nightstick although he wore no uniform.

The visitor went directly to O'Malley's cell. A key scraped in a lock. Luca heard hinges squeal, more footsteps, and then the clang of the bars snapping shut. Had the visitor locked himself in the cell with O'Malley?

"Wake up, you." The rumbly bass voice had a pronounced Irish lilt.

O'Malley's snores were replaced by a hacking cough. "Hey, what in the name of—? Chief Doyle?"

"In the flesh, laddie."

"What are you doing here?"

"We're going to talk, like Jesus and Judas. Sit up. You need to hear me proper."

Luca heard O'Malley grunt. "What's going on?"

"The Bison Club kicked you out."

"This is Henry Blick's doing." O'Malley was fully awake now.

"This is homemade trouble, Sean." Doyle's voice carried. "You never should have written that letter. It's time to face up to it and take your medicine."

"Henry Blick took up with a whore!"

"Aye, he married the lass. Mrs. Henry Blick is a fine lady now. But it doesn't matter if she was the bearded lady at a Belfast carnival. You're on the wrong side of things."

"I know what I know," O'Malley said in a voice laced with obstinacy. "He's going to be humiliated at my trial. I'm going to spew it all."

"There's not going to be any trial."

"No trial? Did you fix it? Am I getting out?"

"No, you're going to apologize and plead guilty."

"I'll do nothing of the sort!" O'Malley laughed. "I'm going to drag Blick and the whore through the gutter. She won't be so high and mighty after I'm done."

"The Post Office has you dead to rights for blackmail."

"I tell you she's a whore. Henry Blick married a whore!"

So much finally made sense to Luca. Ruth Cross had been Luca's English tutor and friend while living in the apartment above the Galliano Club. Whatever O'Malley knew, he'd used it to blackmail Ruth into having his way with her the night that Nick Procopio tried to break into the Galliano Club and kill Luca.

Apparently, when Ruth took up with Henry Blick,

O'Malley tried to use the information to get money out of the man. Luca suspected that O'Malley was also responsible for the damage to Ruth's apartment and the dancing school.

What a bastard. Ruth was a good person who deserved to be happy.

"Henry Blick can marry who he pleases." Doyle's booming voice went flat. "Doesn't mean he wants to pay you for the privilege of not talking about it. So tomorrow when the deputy comes in, you tell him you want to see your lawyer and apologize. You'll get two years in Sing Sing. We'll find something for you when you get out."

"I done your dirty work for years and this is all I get?" O'Malley exclaimed. "Who collected the so-called tax from every club and restaurant getting rich from bootleg liquor? Who kept out the scum that wanted to join the department? Made sure the Irish stayed in charge, eh?"

"You were a good soldier, Sean, and I protected you, didn't I? But you got cocky, tried to line your own pocket and that's where you went wrong." Luca strained to hear as Doyle's voice dropped to an angry whisper. "You hurt the department, Sean. Made me look bad. Got yourself kicked out of the Bison Club. Next they want to kick out all the police who are members. That includes me, Sean. Do you hear that? *Me*. Gerald Francis Doyle. Member of the Bison Club for over five years."

"This is between me and Blick."

"Not anymore." Something heavy tapped the bars of O'Malley's cell, making the iron resonate. "Now I've said my piece. You plead guilty tomorrow and take your medicine and we'll see you when you come back."

"You can't--."

Whatever O'Malley intended to say was cut off by a heavy thud and an exclamation of pain. Another blow prompted a gurgling crack, an agonized gasp, and the abrupt thump of a heavy body hitting the wall between the two cells. A swift tattoo of thuds and thumps was accompanied by labored breathing, cries of pain, and clumsy stumbles in the cramped cell.

The beating went on and on. The swish and thwack of the nightstick hitting its target took on a monotonous rhythm. Eventually there was silence.

"Get up, you gobshite," Chief Doyle said hoarsely.

O'Malley did not reply.

Luca silently turned over on his cot so that his back was to the bars. O'Malley's cell door clanged shut. Shuffling footsteps paused at Luca's cell. He felt eyes on his spine and breathed in the stink of sweat and blood. After an eternity, Doyle left the jail, leaving behind the stink of sweat and vomit.

The night watchman never came back.

In the morning, Luca heard O'Malley rasp that he'd fallen during the night and his arm was broken. Also, he wanted to see his lawyer and change his plea.

Joe Sestito's face was thoughtful as he handed Luca a steaming cup of coffee through the bars of the cell. Luca accepted it without comment. When another deputy came in to escort the prisoner, O'Malley limped out, hunched in pain and smelling badly. One arm was bent awkwardly at his waist. His face was a blood-smeared pulp. One eye was closed.

"I hope they fry you, Lombardo." O'Malley paused in front of Luca's cell. He smirked, showing bloody gums and a missing tooth. "Got no business with that girl, none at all."

"Go take your medicine," Luca said quietly.

CHAPTER 28

Midnight search

Hanna whirled around. She'd been so intent on listening for the lock tumblers that she didn't hear Tess creep up on her.

"Well?" Fists on hips, Tess radiated disapproval as moonlight glinted on her spectacles.

"I'm breaking into the Galliano Club," Hanna confessed.

"I can see that." Tess marched up the back porch steps and peered at the hairpins in Hanna's hand. "Why?"

"The club is closed." Hanna turned back to the lock and delicately inserted the hairpin again. It wasn't a cheap bobby pin, but a heavier brass one, the kind women with unruly hair used to create pincurls. Sam had taught her the many uses of that kind of hairpin years ago.

"It's two o'clock in the morning. Are you planning on robbing the place?"

"Of course not. I just want to look around."

"Why? What do you expect to find?"

Hanna levered the pin inside the keyhole until it encountered pressure. "Just give me a minute," she breathed.

The dead of night in back of the Galliano Club was a cold and lonely time. No light except whatever shone down from a hazy half-moon. Cold leached out of the gravel lot and bounced off the side of Tess's coupe parked nose toward the brick. It seeped through Hanna's coat and up the legs of her pajamas.

Tess similarly wore a coat over her nightgown. She shivered as the wind tossed her red curls. Hanna had been more prepared and wore a hat.

The lock gave a soft snick and released. Hanna pocketed the hairpin and turned the knob. "Five minutes," she said to Tess. "Just a quick look around."

"Fine." Tess marched in after her.

A long hallway stretched in front of them, pitch black except for a glow from the window in the saloon. "Find a switch," Tess murmured.

Hanna blundered forward, feeling along the walls. She encountered an opening, slid her hand around a doorframe and hit a switch. An office sprang to life. Desk, sofa, table-height safe, big bookcases and more sports memorabilia.

"This is Mr. Spinelli's office," Tess said, right behind her.

Hanna figured it was as good a place to start as anywhere. She went to the desk and opened drawers, rifling through items of no consequence.

"What are you looking for?" Tess planted herself in the doorway.

Hanna finished with the desk and tried the handle of the safe. Of course, it was locked and no mere bobby pin was going to open it. "I'm not sure. Something to do with Marta."

"Like what?"

"Don't you think the whole story about the letter to the editor of *The Red Book* sounds a little far-fetched?" Hanna demanded. All the suspicions she'd bottled up now came tumbling out. "About these women writing to your boyfriend? How everyone in the club told the same story, almost as if they'd rehearsed it?"

"You think they're all lying?"

"Don't you?"

"Why would they make up such a crazy story?" Tess spread her hands. "Look, I know you're upset about Marta's funeral and the police blaming Mr. Procopio, but--."

"Somebody is hiding something," Hanna cut her off. "Somebody they all want to protect but he damn well knows how to use his hands."

"You think Luca did it!" Tess exclaimed.

Hanna had to be honest. "Tell me it hasn't crossed your mind."

"It hasn't," Tess blazed. "What connection would Luca have to your sister? He's never been to Chicago."

"Maybe he has and you don't know." Although Hanna had only seen him in the courtroom, Luca was too damn handsome, too quietly charismatic. Sonny Zambrano talked about Luca like he was a god.

Marta would have followed him like a new puppy.

"You're looking in the wrong place," Tess said indignantly. "He's already on trial for fighting with James. Why not charge him with homicide, too?"

"What if I'm right?"

"Well, Miss Sneaky, go ahead and search the club. Find yourself some evidence." Tess swept her hand toward the saloon. "In fact, let me help you. What shall we find? Train ticket to Chicago? A lock of blonde hair with a note signed 'love you always, Marta'? Or maybe Luca doodled her name in the account books when he was entering invoices."

"Tess." The more sarcastic Tess got, the calmer Hanna became. "I've got to look. There will always be a question if I don't."

"Go right ahead." Tess flounced down the hall. A moment later the lights over the bar in the big saloon snapped on.

Hanna searched the office for another few minutes but found nothing of interest. Further down the hall she found a big pool room with two tables and racks of cues. No hiding places there. A tiny library held a desk, a few comfortable chairs, and newspapers threaded onto wooden dowels to keep them flat and prevent anyone from walking off with them. Some in English, more in Italian. Some recent, some weeks old. The desk held a pile of Western Union telegram forms and a homemade directory of Italian businesses.

In the saloon, the green wainscotting gave the room a warm and welcoming embrace. Hanna's eye was drawn to the tall bottle of golden Liquore Galliano above the bar that stretched nearly to the ceiling. The rest of the bottles in the display were empty, which was too bad. Hanna could have used a stiff belt of something alcoholic.

Tess was making coffee in an electric percolator and sawing into a block of cheese. Hanna examined all the pictures on the walls, even taking them down and making sure nothing was stuck to the back of each one. Tess poured herself a cup of coffee and sat at one of the tables with a plate of cheese and the mug. Hanna went into the tiny kitchen and opened every cupboard door before coming back into the saloon.

The work counter and the space inside the bar was a

wealth of nooks and crannies. A keg was set into a clever well under the bar. Glasses, mugs and plates were stacked and ready for customers. Even without Luca, it appeared that the place was well-organized and spotlessly clean.

Hanna moved to the work counter below all the shelves of empty bottles and that huge spear of golden Liquore Galliano. Sam had never liked the stuff, said it was too expensive for a good binge.

The October edition of *The Red Book* was still on display.

Conscious of Tess in her coat and nightgown and spectacles calmly eating cheese and drinking coffee, Hanna started at the end closest to the kitchen. A folded stack of bar cloths and aprons. A glass cake stand with a domed top waiting to be filled with donuts or pastries. Thick china mugs and a motley collection of spoons in an old coffee can. In the space underneath she saw big glass jars, a stepladder, and baskets of flags and bunting.

She pressed keys on the big brass cash register. A bell dinged and the drawer shot open. All the cubicles for change and bills were empty except for one holding five first-class stamps.

A shoe box sat next to the cash register. She lifted the lid and saw that it was full of envelopes, too many to count. Most were open although a few on top were still sealed. They were addressed Luca, although his name was written variously as Gianluca Lombardo or Lucky Lombardo. One envelope was even addressed to Mr. Galliano Club.

"Find something?" Tess called.

"Maybe." For a long moment, Hanna wanted to put the lid back on, pretend she hadn't seen them. But she left the lid where it was and brought the box to the table where Tess sat sipping her coffee.

"Letters," Tess said.

"What if some of them are from Chicago?" Hanna asked.

"Only one way to know." Tess took out a handful.

Hanna took another bunch out of the box. They soon devised a system, dispatching letters they'd read into a bowl. Both drank coffee and read interesting bits out loud to each other. Outside the club, Hamilton Street was absolutely silent.

After an hour, Hanna found what she didn't want to see.

Dear Mr. Lombardo,
Having read all about you In our local newspaper, I am convinced that we are compatible in almost every way. Because of this, I suggest we

meet to formalize such compatibility.

Prior to your trip to Newton, please send me your clothing measurements. I would be most pleased if you are six feet, two inches tall, with a waist approximately 38 inches in circumference. If so, you will fit into my late brother's clothing and a new wedding suit will not have to be purchased. As you can see, I will make a most frugal and sensible wife.

You need not have any reservations about my physical attributes. I am 64 inches tall with a waist measurement of 23 inches. I closely resemble the girl on the cover of the October edition of The Red Book magazine.

Miss Elizabeth Landry
Newton, Massachusetts

She silently passed the letter to Tess.

"This poor woman," Tess said at length. "Writing a letter to a complete stranger."

"I guess Sonny was telling the truth."

"They all were. The only thing Luca had to do with Marta was making the connection between her photograph in the newspaper and your picture on the cover of the magazine."

Hanna's emotions churned. She wished to God she'd brought a box of cigarettes along on this little nighttime escapade. "How is it that you're so sure? Aren't you just a little worried that your precious Luca isn't who you think he is?"

"He's not perfect," Tess retorted. "I know that. But I can be who I want to be with him."

"That's what all women think at first." Envy crawled into Hanna's throat. Tess was so sure. All Hanna could do was put up a good front.

"I know you're desperate to find out who killed Marta, but it wasn't Luca." Tess squeezed her hand. "We're still friends, you know."

Surrounded by letters written by lonely women to a man they didn't know, with the woman who loved him enough to defend him all night in her bedclothes, Hanna thought about the time she kissed Karol Dombrowski.

CHAPTER 29

A volcano waiting to erupt

A short column on page three reported that O'Malley resigned from the police department and pleaded guilty to the charge of misuse of the mails. Luca threw down the newspaper and hoped that Ruth Cross and her new husband were relieved that the policeman was headed for prison. O'Malley wouldn't bother Ruth again.

But as irritating as O'Malley had been, the jail was unnervingly quiet without him.

Luca had a few books and Sestito talked once in a while, but the hours of absolute silence were an agony to be endured minute by endless minute.

He missed the rush of beer in a pitcher, the bang of the door as people came and went, laughter and complaints and the clack of balls coming from the pool room. Vito shuffling around and claiming that the drink in his hand was the first one of the day. Arguing with Sonny over the kid's Latin translations and algebra homework. Bantering with Tony Bilotti and the other old-timers. Even sitting on the bar and reading the lady letters to Gio Tulipano and the rest of the regulars.

The small, routine tasks of organizing the cellar and accepting deliveries and making the sandwich of the day now seemed like all he could ever want to do.

The question of how Vito was faring on his own was an ever-present worry. Sonny could run the saloon, but he was only there after school and still had homework to do. How was Vito going to manage the beer deliveries? No doubt Rotolo was circling like a shark with a sack full of cash, waiting for Vito to have a weak moment. Would Vito sign away the club while Luca was in jail?

It was no use thinking about it. There was nothing he could do.

Tess was harder to block from his thoughts. When she testified, would they ask her if Luca displayed signs of immigrant psychosis? Was he a violent man?

Would she be forced to confess that he'd killed a man in Italy? Or that Humberto Orsini deserved to die?

Over and over again, their conversation unspooled in the quiet hours as he lay on the cot in his cell.

"I told you about my parents," he told her. "My father was an army officer from the north. Sent to Eritrea. He deserted and came to Serra San Bruno, our village in Calabria. Married my mother. When

266

the army caught up with him again, they executed him. A firing squad. They killed my mother, too. I was five or so and I saw everything."

His voice cracked. Tess waited.

"The officer in charge of the firing squad was named Humberto Orsini. When I was older, he came to our village. He was in charge of the army garrison in the area."

"How did you know it was the same person?"

"He had a scar. It was more than twelve years later but some things are never forgotten." Luca's voice was very quiet. "I confronted him. I had my father's gun. I wanted him to beg for my forgiveness. He stabbed me and I shot him. For a long time I told myself that it was an accident, that I didn't mean to kill him. But I did. I wanted revenge for my parents."

Luca dozed off, the newspaper on the floor of his cell. The next thing he knew, Sestito was unlocking the bars.

"A visitor from your lawyer's office." The iron hinges pealed as Sestito swung the bars open. "Must be a good lawyer if he works on a Saturday."

Luca rubbed the sleep out of his eyes and followed Sestito to the little private room where he'd met Mr.

Freshman. It was just big enough for a table flanked by two chairs on either side; heavy oak chairs with saddle seats and slatted backs that were more comfortable than the chairs in the courtroom. An interior window let the deputy keep tabs on what went on inside.

Benny Rotolo lounged in the chair opposite the door, playing with a gold pocket watch on a finely wrought matching chain.

Sestito shut the door. Luca stayed standing. "What are you doing here?"

"Nice way to greet a fella who's come all the way down to the courthouse on a Saturday night." Benny leaned back in his seat and kicked the chair across from him, sending it rocketing toward Luca.

"What do you want?"

Rotolo looked around. "This place ain't much. Just two cells and a deputy sheriff with a hard eye trying to give everybody the jitters."

Luca glanced through the glass to see the deputy seated at his desk again. "Sestito's all right."

Rotolo slapped a copy of the *Lido Daily Clipper* on the table along with a fountain pen and some writing paper. "You seen the paper today?" He turned the newspaper to show Luca the headlines that he'd tried to ignore. The words were printed in two sizes, the better to capture readers' attention.

BARE-KNUCKLE FIGHTER IN OUR MIDST

"Lucky" Lombardo, so Recently Lauded for Helping Discover Mill Foreman's Murderer, Revealed to Be Potential Danger to Community

Fought Foes to Standstill for Money!

"Not looking too good for you, eh?" Rotolo picked at his teeth with the nail of his pinky finger. "On trial for attempted murder and this Conover fella lets everybody know what a great fighter you was."

Luca folded his arms, having already read the newspaper, thanks to Sestito. "What's that got to do with you?"

"Well, us being business partners and all, I come to offer my help."

"We're not partners. You sell beer to the Galliano Club. That's all. I don't need your help."

"They're going to fry you." Rotolo grinned. "You tried to kill the First National Bank of Lido."

"I didn't try to kill anybody," Luca said with heat. "It's got nothing to do with you."

"And poor Miss Blue Hat is right in the middle of it." The other man's grin grew wider. "Tess Kennedy. I remember meeting her with you at the Candyland Supper Club. Real pretty girl. Maybe I should go offer her some sympathy. Let her cry on my shoulder."

Luca went cold. "Leave Tess alone."

"Not much you can do for her from here, Sheik." Rotolo glanced at his fingernail, flicked away a bit of something. "Or when you're in Sing Sing waiting for the electric chair."

Luca slowly sat down. "What do you want?"

"Now we're getting somewhere." Benny shoved the newspaper to the side and slid the writing paper and pen forward. "I think we can make a deal, Sheik."

"What sort of deal?"

"I went over to the Galliano Club. Talked to old man Spinelli. He's not doing so good."

Luca waited.

"He's a drunk," Rotolo said with a wink as if they were sharing a secret. "He can't run the place without you and everybody knows it. He needs to sell while he still can."

"Vito's fine," Luca said, knowing that he was wrong and Rotolo was right.

"He'll sell the club if you tell him to."

"Why would I do that?"

"Because you're smart, Sheik, real smart. Smart enough to know how this thing with the First National

Bank of Lido is going. You're headed for Old Sparky and that fat Howland fella's gonna marry Miss Blue Hat."

Luca didn't answer.

"You had a fighting chance before this Conover fella appeared. Before him and that doctor fella, you was just some jumped-up Italian, thinking he could snatch a society dame and no one would notice. Now you're a volcano waiting to erupt." He thumped the newspaper. "Go on. Read it."

"I was there," Luca said.

"So here's the deal." Rotolo lowered his voice. "You get Spinelli to give me the club and I'll take care of the judge."

"Bribe the judge?"

"Everybody's for sale in this burg. That judge is as crooked as a three dollar bill." Rotolo nudged the writing paper closer to Luca. "Here. Write Spinelli a letter. Tell him to sign the deed to the Galliano Club over to me."

"You think Vito is just going to give you the deed to the club building?"

"Jesus, Sheik." Rotolo snapped fingers in front of Luca's nose. "Being in the slammer has slowed your brainpan. I want the club and you want outta here so you can swan back into Miss Blue Hat's arms. Write

Spinelli a fucking letter. As soon as I've got the deed I'll get the judge to spring you. All fair and square."

"Why should I trust you?"

"What you should be asking yourself is what happens if your hotshot lawyer can't pull it off? What's going to happen to Miss Blue Hat?" Rotolo licked his lips. "I'll tell you what. She's going to marry Howland, if he'll have her after all is said and done."

"Shut up," Luca said savagely. "We're done."

"She spread her legs for you, didn't she?" Rotolo went on. "Real tight, was she? Howland's gonna be real disappointed when he finds out that you were there first. No cherry, just a pre-owned hole. Not that I'd mind having a shot at Miss Blue Hat, soften her up for the wedding night--."

Luca launched himself over the table at Rotolo and his hands closed around the other man's throat. Both chairs crashed to the ground and suddenly they were snarling and grappling, two wild animals fighting over a slab of dead meat. The table between them rocked wildly. The newspaper flew into the air, the printed sheets shooting apart and floating down like oversized confetti.

The door banged open. "Hey! What's going on?" Sestito yanked them apart, hard enough to throw Rotolo out of the room.

"You stay away from Tess," Luca shouted at Rotolo. "I swear, I'll kill you--."

"Shut up, Lombardo," Sestito said harshly. "You're in enough trouble as it is."

Rotolo was ordered out. Sestito marched Luca back to his cell. The bars closed with a clang.

CHAPTER 30

Another goodbye

It was hard to say goodbye to Marta but not as hard as Hanna expected.

Perhaps that was because Hanna had really said goodbye weeks ago when her sister's trail went cold. Back in Chicago, before the unexpected business about the portrait and the cover of *The Red Book* magazine.

Hanna felt empty as Father Nowicki intoned the Latin words that would send Marta to heaven. The hunt was over, the uncertainty gone. Revenge was the only thing Hanna had left to live for.

Father Nowicki shook incense over Marta's closed casket on the altar. The church was full. Lido's mayor and his wife plus dozens of other leading citizens filled the pews trying to look sympathetic and virtuous. They were obviously unfamiliar with Catholic rites, missing the usual cues to stand and kneel and sit, but it was a show of solidarity that Hanna would not have seen in Chicago. A terrible thing had happened in the city which they were so proud of, and the least they could do is show up and mourn and hope that it never happened again.

Across the aisle, Karol Dombrowski was there, along with a score of fellow Poles in similarly somber suits. None of the men looked comfortable in their high collars and knotted ties and few of the suits fit well. Hanna supposed that the men all worked at that mill with him.

Karol had murmured something sympathetic to her when he arrived at the head of the train of men, but Hanna had been too focused on maintaining her self-control to do anything more than nod. The only thing she registered was that if Karol had a wife, she didn't come.

Behind Hanna, Mrs. Rutherford gave a soft little sob and her husband murmured something indistinct. The Rutherfords, the Blicks, and so many other families had sent invitations to supper and coffee and ladies' luncheons. They were nice people, not what Hanna was used to, but they had tried their best to make her feel welcome. If they were surprised that she was living above the Galliano Club with Tess Kennedy, they didn't show it.

Next to Hanna, Tess dabbed at her eyes with a balled-up handkerchief. The girl was made out of sterner stuff than her sweet appearance would suggest. A college girl who could count things in her head as quick as lightning, used to work in a bank of all places, and drove a Ford coupe. Who had mired herself in scandal but still held her head high. Hanna liked her more and more.

Father Nowicki finished with the eye-stinging incense. Karol Dombrowski and the other pallbearers filed out of their pews. Marta's casket was lifted effortlessly to their shoulders. As the cortege passed Hanna, Karol met her eyes but his stoic expression didn't change.

Hanna felt a jolt, as if he'd silently willed her the strength to go on.

Tess stayed with Hanna as they left the church. "Do you want me to come?"

"No." Hanna wanted to be alone when she saw the casket placed in the mausoleum. The ground was too frozen for the gravediggers; Marta would be buried in the spring.

The mayor had provided a fleet of vehicles that would proceed through the town behind the hearse to the cemetery. People seemed strangely impressed that Marta would be buried in the town where her body had been found, rather than in Chicago. Somehow Marta belonged to Lido now. She was everyone's sister.

Although no one at the funeral had ever met Marta, the church was full and took time to empty out. Hanna stayed in the shelter of the doorway and accepted condolences. Mayor Peabody and his wife were first in line, followed by Chief of Police Doyle, then Quinn and his wife. A few others like the Rutherfords and Blicks.

Scores of people Hanna hadn't met, like a busty platinum blonde in a mink jacket, were simply there to gawk. They didn't know that Marta wanted to see the Lipizzaner stallions of Vienna and the Eiffel Tower. The toys she dragged around as a little kid or the pride she took in being a Harvey House waitress.

Karol escorted Hanna to the line of cars waiting behind the hearse. She sat beside him in the backseat as they were driven to a very old cemetery, generations of headstones canted with age and dusted with snow. The Blick family mausoleum was being made available for Marta.

The pallbearers once again hefted the coffin to their shoulders. Father Nowicki led the small procession from the hearse to a chapel with Gothic arched windows.

His robes whipped and snapped in the wind like flags trying to launch into the sky.

The door to the mausoleum opened. Hanna got a glimpse of a dark interior with deep stone ledges, each with a brass label holder below a crucifix. Marta's casket was set on a wide ledge. Father Nowicki slid a card into the brass holder. Hanna stepped inside the mausoleum to light a candle.

There was a leather-padded step to kneel and say a prayer. Hanna knelt in front of the crucifix, acutely aware of Marta's casket in the confined and freezing space. She tried to say a prayer, to take solace in the words she'd learned as a child. *Hail Mary, full of grace.*

But she didn't know what she was praying for. For Marta's soul to rest in peace? Or to find her sister's killer?

Despair clutched at her with a cold, bony hand. Every route she'd taken led to a dead end. The police and private investigator in Chicago left her with an empty bank account and a deepening sense of desolation and failure. Lido had given her a flicker of hope, soon snuffed out. The few clues—the camisole and tie—led nowhere. She'd pinned her hopes on Luca Lombardo's letter and the connection to the Galliano Club but even that left her empty-handed.

Hanna had run out of threads to pull and questions to ask. The only solution was to accept the police's explanation that a serial strangler in Lido had somehow lured Marta from Chicago to Lido.

It was a convenient answer, but it couldn't be the truth.

Whoever had taken Marta's life had taken Hanna's,

too. What was she left with? A bitter need for revenge. And then what?

As her thoughts spiraled downward into the black hole of Marta's hopes and dreams, Hanna pressed her hands to her face. The next thing she knew Karol was there, his arm around her shoulders, keeping her from falling to the unyielding stone floor.

CHAPTER 31

Old sins

Tess sat in one of the chairs from Aunt Evelyn's library with the tin box that Karol had taken from Luca's room in the boarding house. She pried off the cover and sifted through the contents. His citizenship papers. A thick roll of bills fastened with a rubber band, his rumrunning earnings. His dead wife's Italian passport. A leather portfolio with a military crest on it.

And the little pocket ledger with leather corners she and Luca had discussed before. He'd actually asked if she understood what it contained because he didn't. It was hard to imagine another man asking her to solve a problem that defeated him. Certainly not James Howland.

She flicked through the ledger pages, recalling the conversation about divvy sheets. Whoever had kept the ledger was recording the division of profits. A third off the top, then the remainder divided into four shares. Owen Fisher's handwriting had come as a surprise to Luca, but she recognized it from the time she processed a loan application for him.

Someone banged on the street door below the apartment. Tess gave a start and slammed the lid on the box before checking the window.

Sonny was on the sidewalk looking up. He saw her and waved an envelope.

"I'm going out," Tess called to Hanna, who was in the bathtub.

She replaced the box in the side table drawer, ran down the stairs and opened the door. "Hello, Sonny. Is everything all right?"

He held out the envelope. "A messenger brought this for you."

"Thank you. We were at the funeral for Hanna's sister."

"I heard." The young man grimaced. "Is Miss Gorski all right?"

"I'll let her know you asked after her."

"Any more news about Luca?"

Tess shook her head. "No, we're all just waiting until the trial resumes."

"I'm ready," he assured her.

"Me, too." Tess mustered up an encouraging smile. "We'll turn the tide, I'm sure of it."

Sonny loped off to the club. Tess went back upstairs, turning the envelope over as he went.

The logo of the Adirondack and Western Railroad

decorated the upper corner. Her name was scrawled in the middle. *Miss Tess Kennedy, Galliano Club*.

On behalf of Mr. Homer Bradshaw, Tess was informed that items belonging to her remained in the house at 112 West Park Circle. It was required that she remove them immediately. She was also required to surrender her house keys within 24 hours.

"What's going on?" Hanna padded into the living room in a robe, a towel wrapped around her head turban-style.

"There are things for me at my aunt's house." Tess showed her the letter, then got her coat.

It was strange to be back on West Park Circle. Tess drove past all the big houses, knowing that she was no longer welcome in any of them. In two short weeks her life had changed completely. Maybe it was for the better, maybe not. It was too soon to tell.

Aunt Evelyn's house was dark. No one had shoveled the front walk after the last snowfall, giving the place the appearance of being asleep under a cotton blanket.

She parked in the drive and stamped her way through the snow to the front entrance. Her key turned easily, and the front door swung open, revealing a blank and empty foyer. Tess felt for the electric switch and the chandelier threw soft light over the staircase and bare walls. The foyer table was gone. The closet was empty.

Beyond the circle of light, the living room was a shadowy cavern.

"Hello? Anybody home?" Tess knew the house was empty but couldn't help announcing herself. "It's me, Tess."

The darkness absorbed her voice. The house was a shell; an empty, loveless shell.

She walked from room to room, switching on the few overhead lights. A hat box with her name on it waited in the kitchen. It was full of odds and ends that Aunt Evelyn had saved for her. Programs from school presentations. A certificate of achievement. A ribbon Tess won in a spelling bee.

A small photograph taken the summer that Tess first came to live in Lido. A stone-faced teen in a white linen dress was all but dwarfed by the great wing chair in the photographer's studio. Curly red hair tumbled to her waist.

Some of Annie's odds and ends were in the hat box as well. Letters from cousins in Ireland. Lists of sewing items she must have planned to buy. Some writing paper and envelopes. Plain, not monogrammed like Aunt Evelyn's stationery.

Tess idly opened a pale blue envelope to find a heavy parchment document folded inside. She took it out and found herself looking at a Wells Fargo bearer bond.

Even in the dim light by the kitchen sink, Tess knew it was genuine.

This was the bond that Max Lauder had sent Aunt Evelyn so she could escape her loveless marriage. Annie claimed Max never sent it, but Annie was the conduit for the letters between Max and Evelyn.

A wave of anger swept over Tess as she realized what Annie had stolen. Not just the bond, but Aunt Evelyn's chance at real happiness. The housekeeper had intercepted and hidden the bond to convince Evelyn that Max didn't love her, dooming Evelyn to her loveless marriage.

Annie got to stay in the big house on West Park Circle, preening with importance in her role as housekeeper to the co-owner of the Adirondack and Western Railroad.

The anger subsided as Tess thought of her own future. She tucked the blue envelope in her purse, determined to keep it close. The bond had to be worth thousands by now. Twenty, even thirty thousand dollars. With that much money, she and Luca could do anything, go anywhere.

Once he was free.

CHAPTER 32

Witness for the defense

After his parents died, Luca's grandfather gave him a basket and sent him into the house that his mother had called a nest; the house where his mother cooked and sewed and his father read aloud each night. *Take what you can carry*, his grandfather had told him. Luca was five or six.

He remembered counting the items he took from the house. Eight items of clothing. Six books. Two embroidered napkins. One leather portfolio with a military crest. One gun, the same pistol that his father, an officer in King Victor Emmanuel's army, took when he deserted his troops in North Africa.

The day after Luca filled his basket, his grandfather burned the house down.

His defense was about to start, but the same desperate pain and loneliness he'd felt as that heartbroken child hit Luca hard as the bailiff brought him to the courtroom. The numbers were in his jacket pocket. If things went badly, he'd pass the note to Freshman and break it off with Tess. Set her free.

She was there with Hanna Gorski. Luca took his seat, willing himself not to show weakness.

"All rise!"

Judge Pepper swept into the courtroom. He made everyone wait as he shuffled papers, poured himself a glass of water from a pitcher, and adjusted his spectacles. Finally he looked down his nose at the defendant's table. "Well, Randall, are you ready to call your first witness?"

Freshman stood. "We are ready to call Mr. Guido Serra to the stand."

There was a method as to the sequence of witnesses. First Guido and the other club members who'd been there that night, then Sonny and Tess, followed by character witnesses like Vito, Karol, and other club members who knew Luca well. Building momentum to a big finish, Freshman called it.

Luca figured that someone had lent Guido the ancient suit, as he'd never seen the doorman in anything but a motley collection of trousers, sweaters, and collar-less shirts. The suit was cut for an even larger man, making the doorman somewhat of a comical figure as he lumbered up the aisle. Luca wondered if Guido understood the oath even as he repeated it with his right hand on the Bible.

Given that Guido was a witness for the defense,

Freshman got to ask questions first.

Mr. Freshman stepped to the witness stand. "Good morning, Mr. Serra. You are the doorman at the Galliano Club, is that correct?"

"Yes." Guido looked uncomfortable, pudgy hands clasped in his lap.

"Were you working the evening that the plaintiff, Mr. James Howland, came to the club?"

"Yes, I saw him."

"You were the first person to see Miss Kennedy arrive at the Galliano Club. She asked you to tell Mr. Lombardo that she wished to speak with him. Can you describe those events for the court, please."

"Miss Kennedy, she come in a nice green Ford." Guido's heavy accent added a vowel to the end of each word. "She say, I wanna talk with Luca. I tell her, wait here. Inside, Luca says who is it? I don't remember her name. Luca go outside. They talk. I no know if Luca he is happy or sad."

"Did you go outside with Mr. Lombardo?"

"Yes. We go outside."

"Did Miss Kennedy have a suitcase?"

Guido's smile faded. "I no remember."

"That's all right, Mr. Serra." Freshman nodded encouragement. "Once you were outside again, you saw Miss Kennedy and Mr. Lombardo talk. Then what happened?"

"A big car comes with the boys. They look for Miss Kennedy."

"By 'boys' do you mean James and Richard Howland?"

"*Si, si.* I see them come to talk. Everyone is loud, angry. And then they fight."

"Did you see who struck Miss Kennedy?"

The smile faded. Guido looked at his hands. "I think maybe is Luca," he said softly.

"I'm sorry?" Freshman said sharply. "Please speak up. Did you see who struck Miss Kennedy?"

"Luca," Guido said tonelessly.

Luca gave a start of disbelief. Guido had been right there when Howland hit Tess. Not a foot away from Luca, watching the same events unfold.

Freshman was very close to the witness. "Please remember that you have sworn to tell the truth, Mr. Serra. There are severe consequences to lying in a court of law here in America."

The courtroom was silent, the air heavy with apprehension. Guido continued to stare at his hands.

"Perhaps you did not understand the question." Freshman's voice gentled. "In your written statement to the court you claimed that the plaintiff, Mr. James Howland, struck Miss Kennedy. You were standing no more than five feet away when it happened. Was that a correct statement?"

"I don't understand English so good," Guido mumbled.

Mr. Freshman took a few steps away from the witness stand. "At any time during the night in question, did you see Mr. Lombardo restrain Miss Kennedy or prevent her from departing the vicinity of the Galliano Club?"

"I think maybe she's afraid."

"Yes or no, Mr. Serra."

"No."

A dozen more questions as Freshman attempted to get the situation back on track but Guido had gone from being a friendly witness to an uncooperative one. The doorman replied to every question with a bare one or two-word answer.

Eventually, Cromwell had his turn asking questions.

"Mr. Serra," he began. "Has the defendant Mr. Lombardo ever had to deal with unruly customers? Or members, I should say."

Guido nodded. "*Si,* yes."

"And how does he do that?"

"Luca has a baseball bat. Behind the bar. For safety, he say."

"Has he used it?"

"*Si*. Nick Procopio. He cheat. Luca make him go."

"So the defendant used violence on a club member. Struck him with a baseball bat?"

"*Si*. Luca, he plays baseball."

"Fine. And uses his baseball bat to inflict violence."

Once again, Muriel Howland cried out. "Oh, the brute!"

"Objection." Freshman said over her. "Counsel is taking the witness's statement out of context."

"Overruled." The judge snorted. "Take your seat, Randall. Muriel, pipe down."

The woman gave a dramatic sob or two, shook out a flag-sized handkerchief to wipe her eyes and subsided into silence.

Cromwell paced in front of the witness stand. Luca found that he'd clenched his fist so hard that his fingers hurt. He forced himself to flatten his hands against the table top.

"Let us return to the night in question." Cromwell's voice took on a silky quality. "Mr. Lombardo is a good fighter, isn't he?"

"*Si,* yes. Luca is a good fighter." A proud smile washed over Guido's moon face and he raised his fists in an imitation of a boxer, the right protecting his chest, the left outstretched to meet an imaginary opponent. "Very good."

"How did the fight end?"

"Luca he bang the man's head against the brick." Guido smacked his hands together, creating a loud popping sound that made everyone in the courtroom jump in their seats. "Bang, bang."

"He slammed James Howland's head into a brick wall?" Cromwell boomed out the question in a voice like a cannon.

Guido mimed his head hitting a wall. "Like that. Bang, bang."

"More than once?"

"Many times," Guido said and smacked his hands together again. "Bang, bang. I think Luca breaks the head."

"You saw the defendant slam Mr. James Howland's head against a brick wall?"

"*Si,* yes."

"Did you believe that was an attempt by the defendant Mr. Lombardo to kill Mr. Howland?"

"Luca so mad, he want to break his head. Break him dead."

Oxygen left the room with a collective intake of air. The gasp swelled; breaths were held in shocked silence. Luca was momentarily suffocated as the whole courtroom tilted on its axis.

"Please clarify what you saw for the court, Mr.

Serra," Cromwell's booming authority softened into a deliberate tutorial; a spider teaching an acolyte how to be trapped in a web. "Knowing that Mr. Lombardo had used violence before, did you believe he intended to kill either or both James and Richard Howland?"

Guido hesitated.

"Mr. Serra." Cromwell was very close to the witness stand, looming over Guido, menacing him with height and prestige and social superiority. "Do you believe Mr. Lombardo intended to kill either James or Richard Howland to prevent them from removing Miss Kennedy from his control?"

"I think maybe yes."

"No further questions."

"Defense has a few more questions for the witness, Your Honor." Freshman approached the witness stand, his walk swift and forceful. "Mr. Serra, as we have noted before, your testimony differs from the statement you gave the police before the trial. In that statement you specifically said you saw Mr. James Howland strike Miss Kennedy. When Mr. Lombardo intervened, Mr. Howland then struck him, causing Mr. Lombardo to defend both himself and Miss Kennedy. What you have said today is significantly different."

"I say the truth now," Guido said.

"You admit that you lied to the police?" Mr.

Freshman spread his hands in a gesture of confusion. "You previously lied when you said you saw Mr. Howland strike Miss Kennedy?"

"So many questions! I don't remember so good."

"You don't recall what you said to the police or you don't recall the events of the evening in question?"

"Luca hit her," Guido said doggedly and raised his fists again in a parody of Jack Dempsey. "Is a good fighter. *Si, si,* a good fighter."

CHAPTER 33

Miss Blue Hat

"Hey, Miss Blue Hat!" Benny called.

The dame turned around. "Were you speaking to me?"

Twilight was settling over the courthouse steps. The pine trees in the park across the way were dusted with snow, reminding passersby that Christmas was just around the corner.

"Begging your pardon. It's Miss Kennedy, ain't it?"

"Yes."

Benny gave her a little tip of his fedora. "Benny Rotolo at your service. We met at Candyland."

"That's right," she said slowly. "What are you doing here?"

Not exactly showing him a friendly face. Never really liked a dame in spectacles. Made even the hottest tomato look like a schoolteacher.

Miss Blue Hat included, despite the green saucers behind the glass. Her lips were two thin lines of disapproval. One gloved hand kept her coat closed at the throat like he was gonna start tearing at her clothes right on the steps of the courthouse.

"I'm just here checking on my pal Lombardo," Benny said. "Even his own doorman says he's a real violent fella. Things don't look so good for him."

"That doesn't seem to trouble you, considering how friendly you were at Candyland."

"I aim to buy the Galliano Club. Lombardo keeps getting in the way. If he gets sent to the slammer, I figure the place is mine."

Streetlights came on, bathing cleared steps and sidewalks in a waxy glow. The knee-high snowbanks obscuring every street curb took on a fresh luster. The snow shovel business was probably almost as big a money maker in Lido as the beer racket.

"The Galliano Club isn't for sale," she said.

"How would a pretty little dame like you know what's for sale and what ain't?" Benny scoffed.

"Mr. Spinelli would have told me. I live in the upstairs apartment now."

"Well now." Benny tipped his hat over one eye and gave her a dose of the pearly whites. "That puts a different spin on things. I'll be your landlord. Makes me want the place that much more."

"Luca is going to be acquitted," she said but there was a quiver in her voice. "The trial is going to be over soon. You'll see."

A trolley went by, the conductor wearing a cap with earflaps. The clang of its bell lingered in the frosty air long after the whoosh of the vehicle.

"Sorry to burst your bubble, sister, but Lombardo's gonna be found guilty as homemade sin. In fact, I'm going to make sure of it."

"You?"

"I've got dirt on Lombardo, see?"

"What kind of dirt?"

Benny sure had her attention now. Specs glinting, lips parted, both hands pressed to her throat.

Show off the green eyes, put some peroxide in her hair and she'd tart up better than any of Trixie's girls. Feisty, too.

"He's a real bad man," Benny said, drawing out the words. Made Sheik sound worse than Capone on a murder spree. "He's going away for a long, long time and I'm going to get my hands on the Galliano Club."

Paying off the doorman counted for something, but with any luck, Lombardo's lunge in the jail's interview room was going to be the final nail in the fella's coffin. Sure, Benny could testify that Sheik had a temper like molten lava but the real damning voice would be the deputy sheriff who saw Lombardo go for Benny over the table.

In Chicago, a slick jury would know that a cop was

on the take. But in Lido, the jury would fall for the testimony of a fella in uniform like a ton of bricks.

Miss Blue Hat was breathing hard. "What do you know about Luca?"

Benny winked. "That's between me and that Cromwell fella."

"What if I told you that somebody in your organization is cheating you?" she said. "If you promise not to talk to Cromwell or the Howlands, I can give you proof."

If she'd turned into a chicken and squawked at him, Benny would not have been more surprised. "Dames shouldn't bluff," he laughed.

"I'm not bluffing," she said. "Somebody in your organization is stealing from you. Stealing your profits."

"What do you know about my organization?"

"Say you'll leave Luca alone and I'll give you proof."

"Lombardo popped your cherry, didn't he?" Benny concluded, shaking his head in regret. "I hear dames get desperate for the fella that pops them. They'll say anything."

The green saucers behind the specs nearly fell out of her head.

"Lombardo getting jugged leaves the Galliano Club

all for me," Benny went on. "I ain't letting that opportunity pass me by. But I like your moxie, sister. I'll like it even better when I'm your landlord. We'll work out a new arrangement about the rent."

He winked again, turned his back on her, and headed for the Cadillac.

CHAPTER 34

Pink roses

The more time Hanna spent with Karol Dombrowski, the more she learned that he took care of others, whether it was family, friends, or the men who worked for him. Which is why she was with him at McSweeney's on Sunday afternoon, eating the meatloaf special and wondering how he would react to her suggestion.

"So ask me," Karol prodded.

"I'd like to go back to the river where Marta was found," Hanna said. "With flowers."

He paused, fork in hand. "The river? Why?"

"To say goodbye."

It was the sort of hopelessly romantic thing Marta would have loved. A final farewell in the form of a bed of roses to float away like a Viking pyre.

Karol pronged another bite of meatloaf. "It'll be freezing out there."

"I didn't expect you to understand." Hanna's defenses were up, the words a salvo over the top.

"I didn't say I didn't," Karol said, seemingly

impervious.

Hanna eyed Karol over the rim of her coffee mug as he mopped up gravy with a bite of bread. Any sane person would say that throwing flowers into a river was a silly thing to do or tell her to leave flowers at the mausoleum. Or even worse, advise her to wait until the ground thawed and Marta was properly buried before spending money on flowers.

Karol cleaned his plate before speaking again. "Will it make you feel better?"

"Maybe." Hanna waited. Sam would have mocked her until she dropped such a crazy notion.

"Finish your food," Karol said.

Hanna set down her mug and ate her meatloaf.

He took her to a florist on Liberty Street where even on such a blustery winter day the window shoppers were out in full force. Fulton's was one of the few places open on a Sunday and was doing a brisk business.

"What kind of flowers do you want?" Karol asked as the Ford nosed against the curb.

"Pink," Hanna said. She opened her purse and took out some bills. Van Dyke's paid even better than Gossard's. "Pink roses were her favorite."

"What about you? Do you like roses, too?"

"No." The word was another swift bullet meant to

hurt.

Karol's eyebrows lifted. "I thought all women liked roses."

"My late husband always bought me red roses after he hit me," Hanna said. "I left when he broke my arm. When he got drunk or in trouble he'd come around with more red roses and want me back. I never went."

An awkward silence filled the Ford. "It's a good thing he's dead, then," Karol said finally.

"Some men are better that way." Hanna's hands shook as she took out her lighter and cigarette case. "Dead, I mean."

"Thanks for telling me."

"I didn't mean to," Hanna snapped. "Nobody likes a hard luck story." She held out the dollar bills with her free hand. "Here. For the flowers."

"You smoke too much," Karol said.

He ignored the money and got out of the Ford, leaving treaded prints in the slushy snow before gaining the newly shoveled sidewalk. His shoulders, clad in the heavy overcoat, barely fit through the doorway. Karol doffed his hat as he entered the store and neatly combed blonde hair caught the sun before the glass-fronted door swung shut and glare obscured the interior of the store.

It took three tries before Hanna managed to light up, angry at herself for telling Karol Dombrowski things that were none of his business, just like his friends were none of hers. She was angry, too, because telling Marta goodbye yet again was no substitute for catching her sister's killer.

All the same questions that the Lido police had swept under the rug kept circling her thoughts.

What brought Marta to Lido in the first place? Even if Procopio was a rampaging beast, as Chief Doyle insisted, there was no reasonable connection between Marta, a Polish waitress in Chicago, and Procopio, the Italian mill worker who wanted his boss's job.

The door to Fulton's opened. Hanna flicked the half-smoked gasper out the window as Karol appeared with a bouquet of pink roses wrapped in butcher paper and secured with a fluttering length of embroidered green ribbon. As Hanna's mouth went dry with desire, she knew that her theory that a man had lured Marta away from Chicago was the only one that made sense.

Not Procopio, but perhaps someone who knew him and introduced Marta. Someone who was handsome and glib. As dangerous as Sam, with the same bad boy charm that seduced Hanna into the worst decision of her life.

Someone who was the complete and utter opposite of Karol Dombrowski.

He laid the blooms on the back seat, got behind the

wheel and handed Hanna a small white box trimmed in another yard of extravagant green ribbon.

"Not a rose," he said.

She opened the box to see a stunning orchid in shades of pale violet.

Leaning across his seat, Karol pinned the orchid to the collar of her coat with those big hands. As he worked the pin through the tweed, his face came very close to hers.

He smelled like soap and wool and quiet strength.

"Are you courting me, Karol Dombrowski?" Hanna asked softly.

With a final tug on the satin-wrapped stem to make sure the orchid was firmly attached to her coat, Karol settled back behind the wheel. "No."

"Are you sure?"

"No."

"I'm not good for you," Hanna warned.

Karol started the Ford.

As before, the dock was nothing more than a lonely stretch of worn planks jutting over the Mohawk and interrupting the brown tangle of vines, thickets, and wet leaves that lined the riverbank in either direction. No one else was there, and had no reason to be until the river froze hard enough for skating or ice fishing.

The planks were slippery. As Hanna carried the

roses Karol put a hand under her arm to make sure she didn't fall. Hanna leaned against him. Neither of them mentioned the bruising kiss that had taken place there not so long ago. The orchid fluttered in the breeze but stayed firmly pinned to her coat collar.

At the rickety end of the dock, where the cracked timbers wore a rime of speckled ice and freezing water, Hanna knelt on the hem of her coat and unwrapped the bouquet. The ribbon was carefully wound up and placed in her pocket to serve as a souvenir of the day she finally let Marta go.

The river churned past, the color of mud and lower than before. Patches of ice on the leafless branches dipping toward the water glinted like diamonds in the cold sunlight. Overhead, the sky was a piercing blue vault that absorbed the musical rush of the river and released it into the heavens. A symphony for Marta.

Having delivered Hanna safely to the end of the dock, Karol took a few steps back to give her little ceremony some privacy.

Hanna took a deep breath, her exhale a plume of frosty air, and carefully separated the long-stemmed roses. She wondered what the Vikings said in times like this. Or if it mattered.

"I'm so sorry, Marta," Hanna whispered, her voice barely audible above the restless gurgle of the river.

"I'm so sorry I wasn't there to help. You'll always be in my heart. Always, always."

Still on her knees and swallowing around the lump in her throat, Hanna selected a rose and tossed it into the river. Instead of floating romantically away, the pink bloom ended up in a knot of icy vines sucking at the water's edge.

This time, Hanna gathered three roses to make a weightier offering to toss. Still on her knees, she scooted forward, leaned out as far as she dared and threw the stems with the force of a pitcher eying Babe Ruth in the batting box. The roses floated downstream just as she'd imagined. Pink petals bobbed on the surface.

A face appeared below the very end of the dock and looked up at her, mouth open in a silent plea for help.

For a strange and confused moment, Hanna thought she was seeing her own reflection in the moving water. Then a ghostly hand floated up from the depths and strands of inky hair swirled gently across a pale forehead.

All the air in Hanna's lungs erupted in a scream that seared her throat and brought Karol running.

CHAPTER 35

Sonny tells the truth

The coded message to Tess was still in Luca's pocket as various members of the Galliano Club took the stand as character witnesses. They lauded Luca's friendship, honesty, and the way he could count faster than an adding machine. Frank Conti and Gio Tulipano were particularly good on the stand. Their important positions at Lido Premium carried weight with the jury, too.

Cromwell found no chinks in their armor.

They were all from the large contingent of club members who'd been in the saloon the night Howland came, although none had come outside until after Howland hit Tess. The entire trial now seemed to swing on that detail.

Each member testified that they saw Guido come into the club to get Luca, that Sonny took over when Luca went outside, and that Guido rushed in shortly after to exclaim that a fight was happening on the sidewalk in front. The impression built that Luca had not gone looking for a fight, nor had he kidnapped or constrained Tess in any way.

Their testimony was a chance for Mr. Freshman to remind the court of Luca's past recognition. He'd helped identify Jimmy Zambrano's killer at nearly the cost of his own life. His sharp eyes connected the late Marta Gorski to the portrait of her sister on the cover of a magazine, enabling the poor girl to finally be identified after weeks of mystery.

Mr. Cromwell could do little to shake their testimony, except to establish that none of them had seen who struck Tess. To her, it seemed that the lawyer was groping for a way to swing the jury back to his side, but he could neither prove his client was telling the truth nor prove that Tess was lying.

Sonny was called to testify in the afternoon.

The young man was composed and confident as he took the stand and made the oath right after the lunch break. Mr. Freshman led him through the events of the night. Sonny's answers were well thought out and more detailed than those of other witnesses.

"You were behind the bar, you say," Mr. Freshman said. "Could you see out the front window of the Galliano Club?"

"Not well," Sonny said. "It was dark outside and the lights were on inside the club. There was too much glare, but I was aware of movement on the sidewalk."

"What prompted you to leave your post and go outside?"

"Guido, the doorman," Sonny said. "He opened the door so hard that it slammed against the wall of the vestibule and shouted that Luca was in trouble."

"Were those his exact words? Luca is in trouble?"

"But in Italian. Guido raised the alarm in Italian and then rushed outside again."

"This prompted you to go outside? What did you see?"

"I saw Luca squaring off against Richard Howland. James Howland was on the ground with his eyes closed. Miss Kennedy was also on the sidewalk, closer to the curb. I recognized her green Ford parked in front."

"You recognized Miss Kennedy? Had you met her before?"

"Yes. I knew that the defendant had a relationship with her. She was always very nice."

"So you went outside and saw the defendant engaged in a fistfight with Mr. Richard Howland. Can you describe the scene?"

"Miss Kennedy had her hands pressed to her face. Guido, our doorman, was right next to her. I came onto the sidewalk in time to hear Mr. Richard Howland say, 'I'm going to kill you, you wop. I was Golden Gloves at Yale.'"

"You are sure those were his exact words?"

"Absolutely. You see, I have ambitions to attend Yale myself."

The courtroom took on an unhealthy silence.

"What did the defendant say in response to Mr. Howland's threat to kill him?"

"Nothing. He was too busy."

A snort of laughter was met with a glare from Judge Pepper and a sniffle from Muriel Howland.

Mr. Freshman asked a few more questions, all of which Sonny answered firmly. Tess was so proud of him.

"Who did you believe actually struck Miss Kennedy?" Mr. Freshman asked.

"The man who was on the ground when I came out of the club. The plaintiff, Mr. James Howland."

"The plaintiff has testified that the defendant, Mr. Lombardo, struck her."

"From the way Miss Kennedy regarded Mr. Howland with fear and loathing, I firmly believe he was the one who struck her."

"Objection!" Mr. Cromwell popped out of his chair. "The witness is making an assumption based on personal bias."

"The witness based his belief on personal observation," Mr. Freshman retorted.

"Sustained," the judge said nastily and turned to the jury box. "The jury will ignore the witness's last remark."

A shiver of discomfort ran through the courtroom. Mr. Cromwell sat down and murmured something to James, who nodded.

Mr. Freshman clasped his hands behind his back as he addressed Sonny again. "You are currently at the top of your class at Lido Free Academy, aren't you?"

"Yes, sir."

"You are also one of the finalists for the upcoming Slingerland Speaking Contest, isn't that correct?"

"Yes, sir."

"How do you balance your schoolwork and working at the Galliano Club?"

"I go to the club directly after school. Luca makes me do my homework at the end of the bar before it gets busy. He helps me with algebra and Latin, too. When I'm done, I wash the dishes and clean up the icebox, things like that."

"When did you begin working at the Galliano Club?"

"Mr. Spinelli gave me a job after my father was killed, but Luca runs the club so I really work for him."

"What about after your father passed?"

"Luca gave my mother some money to tide us over

until the insurance was paid."

"Objection!" Cromwell was on his feet again, looking peevish. "The defendant's charitable good works in the Italian colony are not relevant."

"On the contrary." Mr. Freshman almost smiled. "The line of questioning establishes the defendant's character and if such a man, after years of supporting his neighbors, would suddenly become murderous."

"Sustained," the judge snapped. "If you have any more relevant questions for the witness, Mr. Freshman, do go on. If not, please say so."

"The defense has a few more questions for the witness."

"Please make them relevant."

Freshman nodded at Sonny. "Turning back to the events in question. You said you saw Miss Kennedy near her car which was parked in front of the Galliano Club. Did she make any attempt to leave the scene?"

"No, she stayed where she was until the Howland brothers left."

"At any time, did she appear coerced or restrained by Mr. Lombardo?"

"No, not at all."

"Miss Kennedy voluntarily remained with the defendant?"

"Afterward, she held onto him like she was never

going to let him go."

"How long did they stay in the club?"

"Not long. Luca got the key to the apartment upstairs, where Miss Cross used to live, and said they'd be up there. He carried her suitcase and they left. About an hour later, he came back into the club and took some food. Said she hadn't eaten any supper and that they were going to get married in the morning."

"Was Miss Kennedy alone in the apartment over the Galliano Club? Could she have left? Was her car still in front?"

"To my knowledge, she was alone in the apartment." Sonny stared at James. "She did not leave, although she could have. Nobody made her come into the club after the fight, either. She wanted to be with Luca. Nobody kidnapped her."

When it was his turn to question the witness, Cromwell approached Sonny like a bull charging through the ring to gore the matador. "You're in high school," he snapped. "A student who works part-time and owes his job to the defendant. Isn't that correct?"

"No, I owe my job to Mr. Vito Spinelli," Sonny replied.

Cromwell grimaced. "You were behind the bar that night and said you didn't see who struck Miss Kennedy. You did not actually witness the event, is that correct?"

"That is correct."

"So your claim that the plaintiff struck her is sheer conjecture, is it not?"

"It is a conclusion based on multiple impressions," Sonny replied coolly. "As well as my knowledge of the defendant and his affection for Miss Kennedy. I had no knowledge of the plaintiff and based my conclusion on Miss Kennedy's obvious antipathy for him. Had the defendant struck her, it is natural to assume she would have had more sympathy for the plaintiff, possibly even tried to help him. But she looked at the plaintiff like she hated him."

"No further questions," Mr. Cromwell said abruptly.

CHAPTER 36

Seem like a cheater to you?

"Owen, you're not eating," Cynthia said sharply. "Is something the matter?"

He hadn't been *darling* in weeks.

"Ah, no, not at all," he replied hastily. "Delicious. All of it."

"Well, I can't tell from the way you're picking at your plate."

"Work issues," Owen said vaguely. He pushed his fork into the mound of lumpy mashed potatoes.

"Don't you want some gravy?" Cynthia asked.

"Yes, of course."

"Look at the ladle," Cynthia beamed as he spooned beef gravy over the potatoes and slab of overdone beef. "It's the one for cream gravy. Gorham makes a different one for clear."

"Clear gravy?"

"Au jus." Cynthia gave the phrase her best French pronunciation. *Oh juice.*

Another bit of sterling silver they couldn't afford. "Lovely," he managed. The forkful of mashed potato tasted like paste.

He hadn't told her about the letter and never would. Thanks to Inspector Finch's arrogant, midwestern corn-fed cunning, Owen was invited to appear at the regional Post Office in Syracuse in three days to be interviewed about money orders sent to Gary, Indiana.

As soon as Owen read the summons, his mind went blank. Whatever he'd told Finch that day in the office vanished in a mental puff of smoke. He needed to say the same thing in Syracuse, of course. If the two versions weren't the same, Finch could arrest him for mail fraud.

Cynthia started going on about yet another charity event sponsored by that damn woman Osa Rutherford and her Women's Institute lot of rich do-gooders. Cynthia had pledged fifty dollars to the object of charity this week.

Somehow he managed to finish the meal and compliment Cynthia on her choice of canned peaches for dessert. When the meal was over, he tottered into the living room to suck on his pipe and pretend to read the newspaper. Cynthia went to clean the kitchen.

No sooner had Owen read the headline about another woman found strangled in the Mohawk River, than someone knocked on the front door.

Benny Rotolo was on the front porch, his black

behemoth of a Cadillac parked in the drive. "Hey, Fishy."

"I've told you before, my house is off limits," Owen said furiously.

"Not when I got a problem." Benny barreled into the house, tracking in snow and damp.

Owen closed the door. "Wipe your feet."

Benny ignored instructions. His wet footprints marred the carpet as he shrugged out of his overcoat and dumped it on the arm of the white sofa.

"Heard a rumor, Fishy." Benny dropped his hat on top of the coat. "Figured you'd know if it's true or not."

"A rumor?"

"Yeah. You think Broz is on the level?"

"Siwak?"

"Is he on the level?" Benny actually seemed disturbed, rocking on the balls of his feet, eyes flitting over the living room walls. "Seem like a cheater to you?"

"No. Siwak does what you tell him to do. Why?"

"Ever since . . ." Benny cut himself off. "But you didn't know nothing about that, did you?"

"I don't know what you're talking about." Owen didn't need this, not tonight. He wanted to show Benny the summons. Blame Benny for getting him mixed up in that stupid information racket with Al Genovese. But then Benny would just remind him who killed Genovese and that wasn't a road Owen wanted to go down ever again.

"Just tell me this. Is Siwak skimming profits from the beer racket?"

"No," Owen said. "Who told you that he was?"

"Somebody told me that we got a cheater in the outfit. Said they had proof, too."

Owen's mouth went dry. "Who told you?"

"A dame." Benny gave a harsh laugh. "Can you believe that?"

"Ridiculous." Owen forced a chuckle. "What woman would know anything about accounting?"

"Think she was bluffing?"

"Absolutely."

"What about you, Fishy? You been playing straight with me?"

"Of course." Owen spoke with the courage of desperation. "Don't I always show you the books? Income and outflow? Accurate percentages?"

"Yeah, you know all the fancy words."

"You'd take some woman's word over mine? I've been your partner from the start. Put my career and reputation on the line to get seed money from my employer so you could set up the brewery. You promised me shares in the Galliano Club." Owen was ready to go on but he'd lost his audience.

"Jesus." Benny was staring at the newspaper on the table next to Owen's favorite chair. "Another dame floating in the river."

Owen took it as a signal that the conversation was over. "You can keep the paper."

"Where's that pocket ledger, Fishy?" Benny left the newspaper where it was. "Still in your office safe?"

"Yes, of course," Owen lied.

"Let's go get it."

Owen gasped. "We can't. It's after hours. The building is locked."

"You got one excuse after another about that ledger, you know." Benny jabbed a bony knuckle into Owen's breastbone. "Makes me wonder if you lost it or something."

"I'll bring it to the pumphouse tomorrow," Owen heard himself say.

The answer mollified Benny who left shortly thereafter, taking the evening edition of the *Lido Daily Clipper* with him.

In the morning, Owen went to the office at the usual time. He said the usual good morning to Miss Camden. Nodded to Henry Blick before going into his office and feverishly hitting the keys on the adding machine. The clattering ratcheting noise always kept people away. He made a few telephone calls, too, making sure that a few called him back so Miss Camden would hear the instrument ring.

When Blick left to rub elbows with the unwashed workers in the mill, Owen closed his office door and put his plan into action.

The weekly payroll was in his safe. Owen extracted the cash and divided it into four bundles bound with rubber bands. He tucked two bundles inside his shirt where they'd be hidden by his vest and suit jacket. The other two went into his overcoat pockets. Folded carefully with the lining side out and draped over his arm, the bundles were invisible.

He closed the safe, turned off the lights and headed down the hallway to Miss Camden's desk. "I have to leave," he said calmly. "Mrs. Fisher fell on the ice."

"Oh, dear." Miss Camden was the picture of distress. "Is there anything I can do?"

"No, I just need to go home. Make sure she's attended to."

"You let us know if it's serious."

"I certainly will." Owen walked into the frigid air with the coat still over his arm.

The house was empty. Cynthia was at yet another charity breakfast arranged by Osa Rutherford. He packed a suitcase and added the bundles of payroll cash.

He thought about leaving a note for Cynthia but didn't. She had her Gorham sterling and her pearls and the new champagne bucket that would never be used.

All the things that were more important than him.

He drove to the train station and bought a ticket to New York City, the first stop on the way to a fresh start.

CHAPTER 37

Let's make a deal

Tess focused on not throwing up as she took the witness stand. A vice clamped her throat shut, and she could barely swallow. She raised her hand and put the other on the Bible and swore to tell the whole truth and nothing but the truth, just the way she and Hanna had rehearsed last night.

Her voice was calm and steady.

Not flighty.

Mr. Freshman stood up and approached her. "Good morning, Miss Kennedy. Thank you for coming this morning."

Tess nodded. Answering Mr. Freshman's questions would be the easy part. All she had to do was answer honestly and simply. Then, not let Mr. Cromwell trip her up.

She was ready. Hanna had coached her last night, trying to pitch all the curveballs that Cromwell was sure to throw at her.

Luca sat straight behind the defense table. Ten feet away. His future was in her hands.

"Miss Kennedy, for the court, please state your full name and address."

"Tess Elizabeth Kennedy. I currently reside at 601 Hamilton Street." Tess stopped herself before she explained why. Don't volunteer information, Mr. Freshman had cautioned her and in the first question she'd nearly done just that.

"Prior to her passing, did you previously reside at 112 West Park Circle, with Mrs. Evelyn Kennedy Thompson?"

"Yes."

"Was Miss Annie Harper the housekeeper there?"

"Yes."

"And were you previously employed as an account manager at the First National Bank of Lido?"

"Yes."

He gently led her through the details of her life with Aunt Evelyn, meeting Luca at the bank, and finding out that both her job and her engagement to James had been arranged by Aunt Evelyn and Preston Howland.

"Please recount to the court in your own words your discussion with Mr. James Howland on your last day of employment in the bank."

Tess took a deep breath. "I tidied up my account books the way we all did at the end of the day. Then I spoke to James in his office. I usually avoided going into his office as much as possible but what I had to say had to be said in private. I didn't want to embarrass him."

"You were engaged to be married to Mr. Howland but disliked being alone with him?"

"That is correct." Tess felt bolder and more in control. "The marriage had been arranged without my knowledge or consent. I eventually consented because it was my aunt's dying wish to see me married to him before . . . before she passed."

"How did you feel about Mr. Howland?"

"I disliked him. We had nothing in common."

"I see. Please tell the court what you told Mr. Howland that particular day."

"I went into his office but I didn't sit down. I returned his ring and told him that we weren't compatible and that I couldn't marry him."

"How did Mr. Howland respond?"

"He said I was being silly and to put the ring back on. When I didn't, he said he'd sue me and make sure I never worked in a bank again."

"Were you frightened by his threats?"

"I expected him to make threats."

"Why is that?"

"James felt that he owned me. If I broke off the engagement he'd be embarrassed."

"Objection!" Cromwell directed an icy smile toward her. "Hearsay. The witness cannot possibly--."

"Sustained," Judge Pepper interrupted. "Randall, keep your witness from fantasizing on the stand."

Tess felt her face flush.

Freshman cleared his throat. "Did you tell the plaintiff of your future plans?"

"No," Tess said, forcing herself to stay calm. She adjusted her spectacles. "I told him that I was resigning from the bank. Then I collected my things and left."

"Did anyone see you leave?"

"Everyone," Tess replied. "All the account managers. All the tellers. Everyone stared as I left."

"You subsequently decided to elope with the defendant. How did you come to that decision?"

"I knew that he wanted to marry me and I wanted to marry him."

Mr. Freshman led her through the familiar timeline. When she met Luca. Aunt Evelyn's permission for him to court her, and the events leading up to the night that Tess packed her suitcase and headed for the Galliano Club.

"On the night in question, you departed the house on West Park Circle and drove to the Galliano Club in your own vehicle to find the defendant. Is that correct?"

"Yes. I knew Luca would be working."

"What did you do when you arrived there?"

"Women aren't allowed in the club so I asked the doorman to go find him for me."

"The doorman being Mr. Guido Serra?"

"Yes, although I didn't know his full name at the time. I just knew his first name was Guido."

"So Mr. Serra went inside the club to get Mr. Lombardo."

"I waited on the sidewalk outside. When Luca came outside, I told him I'd broken it off with James and if he still wanted to marry me, well, I wanted to marry him, too." Tess felt her cheeks grow warm again, but for a good reason this time. "We decided to find a justice of the peace and get married right away."

"Where was Mr. Serra as you had this conversation with Mr. Lombardo?"

"By the door. We were a little ways away, closer to the curb where my Ford was parked."

"Were you able to proceed with the elopement?"

"No. James and his brother drove up." Tess lifted her chin. "James wanted me to leave with them. I told James that I still wasn't going to marry him and that he should leave. I know I shouted at him. That's when he struck me."

Mr. Freshman crossed to the defense table and picked up a cardboard folder. "With the court's permission, this photograph of Miss Kennedy was taken the following day to show the bruise resulting from being struck by the plaintiff."

He passed it to Judge Pepper who looked at it without commenting.

"Let's continue, Miss Kennedy." Freshman clasped his hands behind his back. "Tell us what happened next."

"Before James could try it again, Luca hit him. James fell, and his brother said how he was Golden Gloves at Yale and would kill Luca. They had a terrible fistfight right on the sidewalk in front of the Galliano Club. Everyone came out to watch. When Richard fell, James swung on Luca again. Luca banged his head against the wall and the fight was over."

"Miss Kennedy, let's review some of the details you've provided. First, are you sure that it was James Howland who struck you?"

"Yes, I'm quite sure." Tess squeezed her hands together.

"Did anyone else see him strike you?"

"Yes. Luca saw. Guido must have seen him, too. And his brother, of course."

"You're quite sure?"

"Yes."

Mr. Freshman slowly crossed back to his table and

leafed through some papers. Tess realized that he was again giving the jury time to make connections. In this case, to realize that James and his brother had lied.

At length, the lawyer came back to the witness stand. "Miss Kennedy, from your vantage point on the sidewalk, observing the fight, did it appear that Mr. Lombardo intended to murder either James or Richard Howland?"

"No."

"Miss Kennedy, at any time did the defendant prevent you from leaving the vicinity of the Galliano Club, either before, during, or after the conflict with the Howland brothers?"

"No."

"You testified that you went there of your own volition. Did you remain there of your own free will?"

"Yes."

"What is your current relationship to the defendant, Mr. Lombardo?"

"He is my fiancé." Tess straightened her spine. "My plans as regards Mr. Lombardo are unchanged and I believe he feels the same."

"And your current relationship to the plaintiff?"

"We have no relationship and I regret very much that we ever did." Hanna had suggested that extra bit of fizz.

He asked her a few more simple questions about witnessing the fight and then it was Mr. Cromwell's time to ask the questions.

"Miss Kennedy, were you aware of the defendant's past as a bare-knuckle prizefighter?"

"Yes," Tess said. "Much less skill and professionalism than collegiate-level Golden Gloves boxing."

Low laughter rippled across the courtroom. Tess waited.

A brittle smile crossed the lawyer's face. "Miss Kennedy, how long did you work for the First National Bank of Lido?"

"Almost two years. I joined right after graduation from Vassar."

"Mr. Howland testified that his father and your aunt arranged not only your engagement but also your employment. Is that correct?"

"Yes, but I was unaware of that fact until recently."

"You were employed at the bank for nearly two years, without being aware that you were expected to marry Mr. James Howland? Is that true?"

"Yes."

"That's quite hard to believe, that you could have worked there, interacting with Mr. Howland every day, and not be aware of your own pending marriage to him."

"Objection!" Mr. Freshman stood up. "Badgering the witness, Your Honor. Miss Kennedy has already admitted that she did not know of her aunt's arrangements with the Howland family on her behalf."

"Sustained." Judge Pepper shrugged.

Cromwell gave Tess another brittle smile. "Miss Kennedy, let us turn to the events of the evening you say you planned to elope with the defendant. You packed a suitcase. What did you put in it?"

"In my suitcase?"

"Yes. What was in it?"

"Clothes."

"You did not expect to return home that evening?"

Tess squared her shoulders. This was what Mr. Freshman meant when he said the trial would be about her. Mr. Cromwell was going to make her out to be a loose woman and she wasn't going to let him.

"I was on my way to marry Mr. Lombardo," she said. "A change of clothing seemed to be in order so I wouldn't have to wear the same thing over and over on my honeymoon."

Another titter of laughter rippled across the courtroom. Judge Pepper banged his gavel. "Silence!"

"All right, Miss Kennedy." Mr. Cromwell paced a bit. "There you were, with your honeymoon suitcase, asking Mr. Lombardo to marry you. According to you, you'd just severed your engagement to Mr. James Howland. What was the defendant's reaction?"

"He was happy."

"He didn't feel that he was getting used goods?"

Tess gasped, as did a number of other people in the courtroom. The judge banged his gavel and called for silence again.

"So perhaps the court should consider a different scenario." Cromwell waited until he was sure all eyes were on him. "Miss Kennedy, you have been described as flighty, even unstable, by many witnesses. Perhaps the defendant was not pleased with being second best in your lineup of potential husbands and struck you."

"I saw who hit me."

"Three men have testified that the defendant hit you."

"They are mistaken."

"Are you accusing three witnesses of perjury?" Cromwell looked around; hands spread in false bafflement. "Three different men. That's a very serious charge, Miss Kennedy. Please think carefully about your answer."

"I've never been struck by a man before in my life, much less be socked hard enough to get a black eye." Tess was unable to keep a tremble of anger out of her voice. "I'll never forget who did that to me. The plaintiff, James Howland, hit me."

For the third time, the judge gaveled the courtroom into silence.

Mr. Cromwell's smile was tight. "After the altercation with the Howland brothers, where did you spend the night?"

"In Miss Cross's apartment over the Galliano Club."

"Alone?"

"No."

"Who joined you?"

"Luca."

"The defendant."

"Yes."

"Did you have carnal relations?"

The courtroom was rocked by a universal gasp at such an audacious question.

"We considered it our wedding night," Tess said, chin held high.

"Yes or no, Miss Kennedy. Did you and the defendant have carnal relations following the altercation with the Howland brothers?"

"Yes."

Cromwell rocked on the balls of his feet. "Were you coerced by the defendant?"

Tess knew that he was driving her into a corner. If

she said she was coerced it would substantiate the charge of kidnapping. If she denied being coerced, she'd be branded an immoral harlot, which would nullify any favorable impression her testimony made on the all-male jury.

"Miss Kennedy?"

"No," Tess said, staring directly at Luca. "I was not coerced."

"Court is adjourned for lunch," Judge Pepper bellowed and banged his gavel. "Mr. Cromwell, you may resume your cross-examination when we return in an hour."

Tess drank a cup of coffee at McSweeney's, too nervous to eat anything. Had she ruined everything? Was Luca's defense now going to be that much more difficult? What else would Cromwell throw at her?

As she entered the courthouse for the afternoon session, stamping snow off her galoshes, Tess was shocked to see Benny Rotolo deep in conversation with Mr. Cromwell. They were making no attempt to be discreet but stood in the middle of the open area, where moody daylight cast odd parabolas on the floor from the windows in the cupola.

Tess leaned against a pillar to keep her legs from buckling under her. No doubt Rotolo was telling Cromwell about Orsini, the man Luca killed in Italy so long ago, the man who'd executed Luca's parents.

The two men shook hands as if sealing a deal. Tess couldn't breathe. Somehow, she'd known all along it would end like this. Her reputation in shreds and Luca sent to Italy to be tried for murder.

All because Aunt Evelyn wanted Tess to marry James Howland's money.

Barely knowing what she was doing or where she was going, Tess went into the courtroom. There was still thirty minutes left in the break and the place was mostly empty. Cromwell wasn't there. James sat alone behind the plaintiff's table, looking rather forgotten and forlorn.

Tess didn't even think about being brave or not as she crossed to him.

"James, we need to talk."

"Are you finally embarrassed by your shameful conduct?" James demanded.

"Don't make me apologize here, in front of policemen and everything."

James stood up. "Mr. Cromwell said I'm not to speak to you."

"Don't you want to hear me grovel, James? Tell you how wrong I was?"

"Well, it's about time."

"But in private."

James followed her out of the courtroom. She led him down the hall to the small interview room set aside for Mr. Freshman to use to speak to clients and witnesses.

Tess ushered him in, closed the door and leaned against it. "We both know you and Richard lied on the stand," she said. "And somebody convinced Guido Serra to lie, too."

"Mother said that you can't prove it," James said but at least had the grace to redden in embarrassment.

"Of course she did," Tess said. "Listen, I want you to withdraw the charges."

"Withdraw!" James exclaimed. "Why would I do that? We're winning."

"Because you lied."

"Three to one," James scoffed. "Your side isn't looking too good right now, is it?"

"Drop the charges and I'll give you this." Tess took out the pale blue envelope and showed him the Wells Fargo bearer bond.

James stared at it hungrily. "My God, it's got to be worth thirty thousand dollars!"

"Do you want it?"

"Of course I want it." James blinked at her. "You're serious?"

"Drop the charges and it's yours."

He took a step backward. "Father would kill me."

"Not if you make the bank loads of money," Tess said. "He'd really respect your financial good sense. Make him swell with pride, the way he does when Richard walks into the room. Mr. Golden Gloves won't be so golden anymore."

"He'll want to know why I'd drop the charges now."

Tess had a ready answer. "Because you know how much this is hurting your mother."

"She cries all the time about it," James admitted. He was almost transfixed by the bond. "God, a Wells Fargo bearer bond."

"Drop the charges and it's yours," Tess said again.

James tore his eyes away from the bond. "This is a trick, isn't it? Lombardo gets out, then comes after me for the money."

He actually sounded afraid of Luca. "He won't know," Tess assured him. "I'll tell him the same thing you did. That you couldn't put your mother through any more drama."

"I think you're trying to play a trick on me."

Tess stuffed the bond back in the envelope. "Look, James, say you win the trial and Luca goes to jail. You'll walk away with nothing. Meanwhile, I'm rich. If I invest now, in six months I can buy a controlling share in the bank. Your bank."

James stared at her. Tess could almost hear the gears grinding in his head.

She waited, heart pounding, the bond still clutched in her hand.

"It's a deal," James finally said. "We do it for my mother."

"Agreed."

James held out his hand.

"If you double-cross me," Tess said, giving him the envelope. "I'll give Wells Fargo the serial number and say you stole it. You won't be able to cash it in."

"You're getting off too easy," James said, tucking the envelope into the inside pocket of his suit jacket. "This was never about hitching yourself to some greasy dago, was it? You were never going to marry him and go live in some immigrant gutter. You just wanted to be out from under your aunt's thumb and free to be a silly flapper. Everything was going your way until Cromwell made you out to be a harlot and now you just want it to be over."

It didn't matter what he said as long as he kept his end of the bargain. "You're right, James," she murmured.

He stalked out. Tess closed her eyes and sucked in air. Her heart was beating so hard that she felt shaky. She forced herself back into the courtroom.

Cromwell was seated at the plaintiff's table. James bent and murmured in the attorney's ear. Cromwell gave a start. James nodded and spoke again.

A moment later, Cromwell cut his eyes to Mr. Freshman at the opposite table.

Mr. Freshman likewise gave a start as Cromwell and James spoke to him. Luca was brought back into the courtroom. Heads close together, Mr. Freshman passed word to him.

Tess saw Luca nod.

"All rise!" the bailiff declared.

Judge Pepper took his seat, banged his gavel, and declared the court back in session.

"Your Honor," Cromwell said. "A matter of some gravity has arisen. May counsel approach the bench?"

"All right, yes," Judge Pepper said testily. "What now?"

"Your Honor, my client has decided to drop all charges against Mr. Lombardo," Mr. Cromwell said, a certain tang of humor in his voice. "Should a single condition be met."

Muriel Howland gave a shriek. Tess pressed a hand to her mouth before she did the same. What a fool she'd been, to believe James would keep his word.

"Drop all charges?" Judge Pepper thundered, adjusting his spectacles as if better eyesight would help him understand such a surprising development.

"What?" Preston Howland leaped to his feet as his wife made hiccuping noises.

The judge pointed his gavel at them. "Sit down, Preston. Let me get to the bottom of this. Muriel, don't start the waterworks now."

"My client is willing to drop all charges on the condition that the defendant Mr. Lombardo agree to marry Miss Tess Kennedy." Smugness positively leached out of the attorney at the prospect of condemning a Vassar graduate and former society girl to the depths of hell through marriage to a common immigrant. "Your Honor could perform the ceremony now, if that is acceptable to all parties."

A hundred incredulous stares searched for Tess, pinning her to her seat. Even Luca turned to look. She was surprised to see confusion and something like fear in his eyes.

"Well?" Judge Pepper boomed. "Randall, is your client amenable?"

"Yes, Your Honor. However, I believe the decision is up to Miss Kennedy."

Tess stood up dizzily. Her legs were stiff as she moved up the aisle, counting steps to distract herself from the stares and murmurs of incredulity thrown at her like spears meant to wound.

Luca stood up as she approached. James snickered.

"I accept the terms," Tess said.

She and Luca waited silently side by side, as the Lido city clerk was sent for and told to draw up a marriage license. James remained at the plaintiff's table with Mr. Cromwell. Muriel cried noisily. Preston appeared ready to burst with indignation. No one left.

The clerk came back with a large scroll and inked their names in the appropriate places. Luca signed, then Tess, and the scroll was handed up to Judge Pepper. The rest was a blur. Tess said "I do" in a hollow warble and barely heard Luca when it was his turn. There was no ring.

Judge Pepper barked out "Man and wife." The case of Howland versus Lombardo was officially closed with another bang of the gavel. The defendant was free to go.

The bailiff intoned his mantra of "All rise" and the judge swept out.

The courtroom erupted in a mad scramble of rushing and shouting. The double doors were flung open and all the reporters who had been covering the trial vied to be first to file their story for the evening newspapers. Preston Howland shouted at James who merely smirked. Weeping, Muriel rushed up to her son. Richard scratched his head.

Mr. Freshman said something about having them come to his office tomorrow. His instructions were lost in the hubbub.

Tess couldn't breathe as the crush pressed in from all sides. Luca put his arm around her shoulders and the tumult carried them out of the courtroom like two corks bobbing on a stormy sea.

CHAPTER 38

Road rage

Cromwell had been real pleased when Benny told the sob story about being Lombardo's friend, right up to the moment he visited the guy in jail to take him a copy of the newspaper and Lombardo had swung at him. The lawyer was a smart fella who understood that Benny could pound the final nail in Lombardo's defense.

So how had the trial ended the way it did? Benny couldn't believe he was left empty-handed yet again. Old man Spinelli was still clinging to his club. What's more, Fishy hadn't showed up at the pumphouse for a coupla days in a row.

"Something smells bad, real bad." Benny unknotted his tie. Threw it on Trixie's bed. He needed to let off some steam badly enough to break the rules Trixie had laid down after his last session with Annunziata.

"Where does this Spinelli live?" Trixie asked.

"What?" Benny moved behind Trixie as she sat on her little vanity stool. Her face was reflected in the mirror. He slid a hand around her throat. Caressed the line of her jaw.

Trixie swiveled around, breaking his hold. "Go talk to him at home. Maybe he'll be alone."

"Alone." Benny savored the word. "Nobody around to rescue him."

"That's what you want, isn't it?" she asked. "He won't want to sell the club where everybody can hear how much he's getting for it."

Benny jingled the change in his pocket as Trixie turned back to the mirror and began to darken her eyelashes with the end of a burnt cork. She had a point about Spinelli not wanting to talk money at the club. Everybody in East Lido would know all the details within an hour. The office inside the club wasn't so private, not with the pool players eavesdropping and the bartender lurking nearby.

That was something to remember when the office belonged to Benny.

"I'll be back later," Benny said to Trixie's reflection as he headed for the bedroom door. "You look real pretty. Don't use it all up on the paying customers."

The headlights of Benny's Cadillac cut two cylinders of light through the night as he drove north. He found the intersection where Clark Street went over the Boone Street tunnel. It wasn't really a tunnel, just an underpass but Lido was sure proud of this little speck of engineering.

Hudson Street branched off Clark. The houses were newer than in Fishy's neighborhood and smaller. The street was freshly paved. Blue glass insulators on top of the electrical poles winked in the moonlight. An automobile awaited in front of every house. Even if he didn't know the address, Benny would have known Spinelli's house by the Packard. It was running with the lights on, warming up the engine the way everybody had to when the temperature dropped.

Lady Luck was with him. Benny glided to a stop in front of Spinelli's house as two people came out and headed for the Packard. Spinelli wore a Homburg hat pulled down to his ears. The scrawny dame in a raccoon coat had to be the wife. A regular ball and chain.

"Hey, Spinelli!" Benny swung out of the Cadillac and slammed the door. It was loud in the quiet neighborhood.

"What do you want?" Spinelli was belligerent, no doubt to impress the wife. But his words were slurred and he swayed on rubber legs.

"You know what I want." Benny waited by the rear bumper of the long Packard. "Let's go in the house. Talk a little business."

"I don't got no business with you." Spinelli wrenched open the passenger side door of the Packard and the wife got in.

Benny let the old man fuss with the raccoon coat and close the door. But when Spinelli came around to the driver's side, he got an eyeful of the Colt Pocket Hammerless in Benny's right hand. "Listen, old man," Benny said with heat. "Time is up. You shoulda took the cash offer when I made it because now you ain't getting nothing. Where's the deed to the Galliano Club?"

Maybe drink made the old man into a fighter, because he whipped off that Homburg hat and threw it in Benny's face. Spinelli followed up with a punch that knocked the gun away and made Benny stumble into the snow at the edge of the drive.

The next thing Benny knew, the Packard lurched backward, swung into Hudson Street and took off like a bat out of hell, nearly sideswiping the Cadillac. Benny snatched up the gun and vaulted into the Cadillac. The engine hadn't cooled yet and it turned over on the first try. He put it into gear, stamped on the accelerator and shot off in hot pursuit, the Colt on the passenger seat.

The Packard was a heavy beast and Spinelli was fishtailing all over the tarmac as Benny caught up. He nosed the Cadillac right into the Packard's bumper, matching Spinelli's frantic swerves to throw him off. Benny snatched up the Colt and steered with it in his right hand as he cranked his window with his left. The next time Spinelli swerved to the left, Benny reached across his own steering wheel and fired a couple of rounds. Spinelli jacked to the right as the little mirror near the top of the windscreen exploded into silver fireworks.

Benny cut his wheel hard to follow just as they gained the peak of the overpass. He stamped on the accelerator and smashed into the spare tire mounted on the rear of the Packard, catching it in mid-swerve. The Packard leaped off the overpass and hung for a moment silhouetted against the night sky. Then the heavy engine tipped the vehicle and it plunged out of sight.

The noise of the crash was louder than a train wreck.

Benny skidded to a stop and jumped out of the Cadillac in time to see a huge fireball billow up from the mouth of the Boone Street tunnel. The flames brightened the entire surrounding area, creating a flickering red daylight. People ran out of the few farmhouses that flanked the road, screaming and shouting, but the wreck was fully engulfed. The poor saps couldn't do nothing except mill around in a panic. Benny stared at the flames, transfixed by the terrible glory of the fire.

Nobody got out of the Packard.

CHAPTER 39

Homecoming

Luca didn't remember shedding his clothes or undressing Tess, only the moment that they were joined together, skin-to-skin in the apartment over the club. He didn't remember if he said a word or if she did, or if there was any need to speak.

They fell asleep afterward, his arms locked around Tess under the blankets and their legs tangled together. The bedroom was dark and chilly when he woke with his pulse jackhammering against his brain.

A dozen long inhales helped him realize that he wasn't back in the prison cell with O'Malley snoring on the other side of the cinderblock wall. Tess was on her side facing him, warm and soft, red curls tumbling over her cheek. Her spectacles were on the little table on the far side of the bed. Luca went to smooth the hair from her face but his hand was trembling so badly he couldn't touch her.

He eased out of the bed and found his shirt and trousers. Padded out of the bedroom and got himself a glass of water in the kitchen, hoping he wasn't having a seizure of some kind. The curtains in the living room were open, flooding the room with moonlight reflecting off the snowy scene below. Hamilton Street was blanketed in white.

Luca dropped into an upholstered armchair and pressed the heels of his hands against his eyes, drawing in cold air in an effort to calm himself. The transition from prison to free man had come with no warning, no real closure. And somehow he was married, too.

It slowly occurred to him that the apartment looked completely different from the way it had been before. It was fancy now, with layers of warmth, comfort, and color. Hanna Gorski must have helped, although she wasn't there now. He dimly recalled coming up the stairs and being introduced. Karol had been there, too. They'd left after a round of congratulations, saying something about Hanna accepting a standing invitation from some people named Rutherford to stay with them.

Luca had questions for Karol, not only about Hanna but about Rotolo and Fisher, too. But they could wait.

"Are you all right?" Tess squinted at him from the bedroom doorway, a blanket draped over her shoulders.

Luca shook his head. "But I will be."

Tess knelt in front of him. The blanket puddled on the floor around her. "What can I do?"

Luca touched her then, sliding a hand into the silky

curls, unable to believe she was really his now and forever. "We're really married?"

"Marriage certificate and all." Tess pressed his hand against her cheek. "Guess we don't have to fuss over getting married in church now."

"Tell me what happened," he said. "Why did Howland drop the charges? He was winning."

"His mother," Tess said. "It was too much. You saw. She kept crying and carrying on."

"I didn't want you to testify," Luca said softly.

"I had to," Tess said. "Not just for you. For me. They were trying to show that I was some flighty brainless idiot. Well, I'm not and I needed to show that."

Luca hoisted her, blanket and all, onto his lap and crushed her against his chest. As her body molded to his, Luca gave a silent prayer of thanks. Relief and wonder replaced the anguish and uncertainty of the past few weeks.

"You stayed," he said, lips pressed against her hair. "All my life, everyone I've loved has been taken away. Except you."

"I'm pretty tough," Tess sniffed. "But now you're stuck with me."

Luca tightened his arms around her, rested his cheek on the top of her head, and closed his eyes.

"One," Tess whispered.

"One," Luca replied. He'd make sure she never regretted her choice.

His trembling ebbed away. Tess's breathing grew soft and regular.

The crunching sound of a heavy vehicle moving through the snow on Hamilton Street floated up to them. Luca carried Tess back to bed.

The next morning, the apartment was a snug sanctuary. Luca made fried eggs and bread for their breakfast as Tess told him how she and Hanna had furnished the apartment with items from the house on West Park Circle after her aunt passed. She also provided all the details about Hanna Gorski that hadn't been in the *Lido Daily Clipper*. How Hanna didn't believe the official conclusion that Nick Procopio had killed her sister. How she'd even spoken to Maria Teresa Procopio. Tess hoped Hanna never went back to Chicago; they were close friends now. Luca decided that he owed Hanna a debt of gratitude for standing by Tess when the rest of Lido pulled away.

Pounding on the street door below made both Tess and Luca bolt up from the table, jarring plates and making their half-empty coffee cups rattle.

Luca went to the parlor window. "There's two policemen downstairs," he said. "Howland must have changed his mind."

"No," Tess exclaimed. "That's not how it works."

He took her hand and they went down the stairs together.

Two policemen were jammed together under the striped awning.

"Good morning." The taller policeman's face was red and chapped with cold. The ankles of his heavy wool uniform trousers were soaked from the snow. "Do you know anything about the owner of the Galliano Club?"

The policeman wasn't anyone Luca recognized from his stay in jail. "Vito Spinelli is the owner," he said.

"Do you know him?"

"Of course. I work at the club."

The policeman raised his eyebrows. "Are you Luca Lombardo?"

"Yes."

The policeman's eyes traveled past Luca to Tess. "Mrs. Lombardo?" he asked respectfully.

"Yes."

"I regret to inform you that Mr. Spinelli and his wife were in a car wreck last night near the Boone Street Tunnel. Killed. Both of them."

Luca felt Tess's hand grip his even more tightly.

"There's not much left to identify," the shorter policeman said. "Because of the fire. But we need you to come to the morgue and identify what you can."

He gestured to a police car waiting at the curb.

"We'll get our coats." Luca's voice was rough.

They left the two police officers waiting under the awning, climbed back to the apartment and found their coats. Before they descended again, Luca wrapped her in a long, wordless hug.

"Maybe they're wrong," Tess said when he released her.

They weren't.

Two days later, Luca learned that Vito had left him the building encompassing the addresses 601 and 601 ½ Hamilton Street, as well as the lot immediately in back of it. He also inherited the Galliano Club business, to include all of its financial assets and outstanding debt.

The lawyer made him sign a paper, then handed Luca a savings account passbook. Vito's name was carefully written in familiar script.

There was just enough in the account to pay for the funeral.

CHAPTER 40

Unexpected guest

Hanna had met Vito Spinelli a few times. He'd been nice enough, considering that Tess had presented him with a fait accompli in terms of being his new tenants, but always unbearably sad and a little tipsy. But the Italian community of East Lido had obviously adored him.

Saint Rocco's church was filled to bursting for the double funeral, with throngs in the vestibule, in the side aisles and even more outside in the snow. The pews were packed, almost everyone in black, even the children. Stained glass windows cast multi-colored light into the church that was immediately absorbed by the sea of dark wool. Dozens of statues of the saints looked down on the congregation with stern faces, reminding everyone of the heavy burden of sainthood.

Instead of the quiet reverence Hanna associated with Marta's funeral and that of Tess's aunt, the mourners at this funeral were loud. They wept loudly, consoled each other loudly, shuffled their feet loudly. Even the men.

From her vantage point in the middle of the church,

Hanna looked around. She and Karol were outsiders. Both too tall, too pale, too dry-eyed.

Tess was in the front pew with Luca. Sonny Zambrano and his mother sat with them.

The two coffins were on the altar, both closed the same as they'd been in the funeral home. Portraits of Vito and Louise faced the congregation, displayed on easels amid scores of floral arrangements. A third photograph of a young Army officer was propped between the portraits. Hanna had learned from Tess that it was of Ciro Spinelli, the couple's only child who'd died in France.

Karol caught her eye as the organ crashed into a chord that vibrated through the church and rose above the weeping. He put a hand under Hanna's elbow as they stood for the procession of priests and altar servers and saltings of incense that made her eyes sting.

The Mass went on forever, with constant sobs that punctuated every prayer. At long last, Luca led the pallbearers up to the altar and led the slow march of the two caskets out of the church. The distraught congregation shared their grief with the small receiving line made up of Luca, Tess, Sonny, and Sonny's mother.

Hanna wondered if Tess knew that the funeral was a coronation of sorts. Her friend was the new queen of

East Lido because Luca Lombardo was certainly the king.

Throughout his trial, Luca had been an enigma to Hanna. Silent, composed, unsmiling, barely reacting to the tension. But his eyes had always searched for Tess as he was led in and out of the courtroom. Hanna felt their connection like a physical thing; a steel cable strong enough to hold up bridges and anchor a love beset by hurricanes.

In the tumultuous days since his release, Hanna saw more steel in the way Luca took charge. He had the ability to quell ambiguity and leave order in its wake.

But Tess was with him now and without her, Hanna was at loose ends. Karol and the Rutherfords and the Blicks had become friends, too, yet the funeral made Hanna see that she was still a stranger in Lido, wasting her time looking for a killer who was smarter than she was. Yes, she had a job at Van Dyke's, but staying in Lido meant she would always be looking over her shoulder, wondering if Marta's killer was watching her and laughing up his sleeve. He could be the man across the store being measured for a new suit. Trying on shoes and buying socks.

Yet could she give up and go back to Chicago? What was waiting for her back there?

Aware of Karol's guiding hand on her waist, she

drifted out of the pew and into the aisle.

The press of bodies emitted the cloying odor of garlicy breath, damp wool, and unending grief. Hanna was grateful when someone pulled open the other half of the double doors. A gust of cold air swept in. Beyond the doors, the stone steps beckoned, as did the rumble of traffic on Hamilton Street.

A woman in a smart mink jacket was in the press of mourners, a black cloche partially concealing platinum curls. Hanna's fashion sense registered the quality of the outfit.

As they got to the doors, the woman veered away to avoid being funneled toward the receiving line. Hanna recognized the rhinestone clip on her hat.

It was the same woman in the same outfit she'd worn to Marta's funeral.

Hanna kept the mink jacket in sight as its owner made her way down the steps. Hanna got the impression of someone who was even more of an outsider than Karol and herself. Had the woman known Vito and Louise Spinelli? Many strangers had shown up to Marta's funeral and it never occurred to Hanna that they'd come for any other purpose than to gawk. Perhaps this woman was a professional mourner.

Somehow, Hanna didn't think so.

"I need to take a walk," she said to Karol.

"A walk?" Karol frowned. "It's freezing."

"I'll meet you at the club." The Galliano Club was opening its doors after the funeral for whoever wanted to come and pay their respects to Vito.

Karol caught her sleeve. "In five minutes, I'll drive you anywhere you want to go."

"Just stop," Hanna hissed. "Just stop being so goddamned decent all the time."

The mink jacket was nearly out of sight, walking rapidly. Hanna skimmed down the steps of the church and followed.

After two blocks, the mink turned left toward the river. The next right turn took them into an area of small businesses. A feed and grain warehouse, an automobile garage, a brick factory with the legend *Mens Silky-Fibre Underwear* painted between the first and second-story windows.

Hanna kept her distance, cursing under her breath and ruining her shoes in the snow. The mink went past an iron scrapyard, full of broken wheels and plows. A sign advertised *Fresh Coffee 24 Hours* in blue neon. A couple of Fords were parked nose-in against the side of the building.

The mink went inside.

Hanna didn't hesitate but marched in, too. The place wasn't big. A counter fronted by empty stools. A row of booths. Strong smells of grease and burned coffee.

A man wearing a paper carhop hat, a burning cigarette in his mouth, leaned over the counter. "Best coffee in Lido," he said leadingly.

He needed a shave, a bath, and an ashtray.

"That's what I've heard," Hanna said as she slipped into the booth where the mink jacket was studying herself in a silver pocket mirror.

The woman snapped the compact shut. "What the hell?"

"My name is Hanna Gorski." Hanna took off her gloves. "You came to my sister's funeral."

After a long pause, the woman shrugged. "Lots of people went."

"I thought you might like to introduce yourself to me." Hanna fished out her box of Lucky Strikes. "Smoke?"

The woman stared at Hanna but accepted a cigarette and a light. "Thanks." She drew hard, keeping her eyes on Hanna's face.

"Hey, Trixie." The slob with the cigarette ambled over, a pad of paper and the stub of a pencil in his hand. "Gonna introduce me to your friend?"

"Jesus, Bud." The woman named Trixie blew out smoke. "I'll take a cup of coffee and a slice of pie."

"Same for me," Hanna said.

He ambled away.

"Coffee in this place is thick enough to stand your spoon," Trixie said.

"I've had worse," Hanna replied.

"You're not a working girl." Trixie blew smoke through her nostrils.

"No."

"Then you won't have many friends in this dump."

"You two dames need anything else?" Plates laden with thick slices of pie clattered on the linoleum table top as he slung them down. He grinned at Hanna, the cigarette dripping ash.

"Get lost, Bud," Trixie snapped.

"Have it your way, Trix." Bud went back to his counter.

Trixie dumped sugar into her coffee from the glass dispenser. "Okay, I went to Vito Spinelli's funeral today thinking maybe I'd talk to Lombardo. But he looked busy so I left."

Despite the warmth of the place, Hanna felt a cold finger slide up her spine. "Did he get you pregnant? Sick with the clap?"

"Lucky Lombardo?"

"Yes."

"Him?" Trixie hooted with laughter and ground out her cigarette in the tin ashtray. "You're a surprise. All dolled up but thinking in the gutter."

"So why did you want to talk to him?"

Trixie's expression hardened. "I wanted to warn him. My man wants the Galliano Club. Says that now that Spinelli's dead, Lombardo is easy pickings."

"I don't think Luca plans to sell the place."

"You don't understand. My man isn't buying, he's taking."

"Your man have anything to do with my sister Marta? Is that why you went to her funeral?"

"You're a pushy bitch."

"Please." Hanna leaned forward. "I need to know. My sister is dead and I have gone through hell trying to find out what happened to her."

"I can't tell you anything."

"Do you need money? I can pay you."

"What good is money if a girl ends up in the river?"

Hanna knew what was behind the brittle facade because she'd perfected that same look of devil-may-care feminine toughness. "You're scared, aren't you? I can help."

"I don't need your help."

"Let me tell you about my dead husband Sam," Hanna said. "He thought red roses fixed everything. Even after he broke my arm."

Trixie lowered her eyes and slowly unwound the

scarf tucked into the collar of the mink. Her throat was mottled with dark bruises like fingerprints.

Hanna swallowed a gasp.

"He likes rough stuff." Trixie said softly. "He done in one of my girls playing rough like that."

It all made sense to Hanna. "The girl found at the old dock? She was wrapped and weighted just like Marta."

Trixie nodded. "I think maybe he did your sister, too. Before I met him."

"Is he from Chicago?"

"Says he was a torpedo for Hymie Weiss." Trixie adjusted the scarf to hide the marks on her neck again. "Now he runs the biggest beer racket in this part of New York. Got a bunch of Polish fellas to keep him company, all armed to the teeth. Says one day I'm going to watch him plug Al Capone."

"Tell me his name," Hanna asked.

Trixie shook her head. "I've already said too much."

"You just said he's killed two women," Hanna pointed out. "You could be the next."

Trixie gathered up her gloves and purse. "Look, I really gotta go."

"Please, wait." Hanna grabbed the other woman by the arm, stopping her flight. "I'll go with you to the police. Help you any way I can. Please. My sister deserves justice. That other girl does, too."

"Justice?" Trixie jerked her arm free as her voice dripped scorn at Hanna's ignorance. "Did you fall off the turnip truck yesterday? The cops are all in Benny's pocket. I'd end up in the river. You, too."

"That's his name? Benny?"

But Hanna was talking to the back of the mink jacket.

Through the window, she saw Trixie climb into a Ford and drive off.

Bud came over to the booth. "Two coffees, two slices of pie. Dollar fifty."

Hanna dug out the exact amount but paused before giving it to him. "Trixie's man. What's his name?"

"Mr. Big Tip," said Bud and pocketed the money.

The walk back to East Lido took forever. Snow began to fall again. Hanna lost her way twice before she saw a trolley that would take her back to the intersection of Hamilton and Union.

Saint Rocco's Church was completely dark as Hanna plodded past on numb feet. The conversation with Trixie played again and again in her head, a gramophone recording that told her everything except what to do next.

Her shoes were ruined and her teeth were chattering by the time she neared the Galliano Club. No doorman;

Luca had fired the oaf who testified against him in court.

Through the big front window, Hanna glimpsed familiar faces around a table, the last stragglers from the reception after the funeral. She pushed open the door and passed through the vestibule into the saloon, stumbling into blessed warmth on feet that had lost all feeling.

"Hanna!" Karol caught her before she fell. "We were just going to send out a search party! Where have you been?"

"She's freezing." Tess materialized at her side. "Take those shoes off and I'll get you a hot cup of coffee."

Karol half carried Hanna to a table littered with plates and cups. "Your feet are frozen," he said.

Luca collected up a stack of plates, making room on the table for the steaming cup Tess set in front of Hanna. Toby and Eileen Mary Gleason were there, too.

Hanna wrapped her hands around the cup as Karol draped his big overcoat over her lap. "I found out who killed Marta," she said.

"Oh, Hanna," Tess breathed, her eyes as wide as her spectacles.

"Do any of you know a fellow named Benny? He's a bootlegger from Chicago."

"Jesus wept," Toby exclaimed.

Luca dropped the plates with a thunderous crash, sending shards of china across the parquet floor.

CHAPTER 41

Spilling secrets

"What happened to Fisher?" Karol asked Broz.

"Disappeared."

"Rotolo have something to do with it?"

"Don't think so," Broz replied. "He's real steamed up about it. Doesn't know any more than me or you."

They were in the Warsaw Club again. The back room was deserted at this late hour. Karol heard tired conversations coming from the front. A couple of workers from Lido Premium were around. They'd eyed him with concern when he arrived. It wasn't as if he was going to tell them to go home or accuse them of slacking tomorrow, but now that he was the foreman, men he used to consider friends treated him differently.

"Fisher disappearing means that Lombardo is stuck with Vito Spinelli's debt." Karol leaned closer to Broz. "He's going to sell the Galliano Club to get out from under. Wants to sell quick, too. You think Rotolo is still interested?"

"Sure." Broz drained his beer. "Talks about the damn place all the time."

"Pass the word to him. Lombardo is opening bids on the place the night of the Slingerland Speaking Contest. Jimmy Zambrano's kid Sonny is one of the contestants and everybody in East Lido will be there. Means Lombardo can talk to buyers without any of the members finding out."

"They don't want him to sell?"

"Vito Spinelli was a big deal in East Lido. Everybody expects Lombardo to fill his shoes, not sell out."

"Gonna take the money and run?"

"He'll pay Spinelli's debts first."

Broz wiped his mouth with the back of his hand. "What's in it for you?"

"Lombardo's a friend."

"Saint Karol." Broz snorted. "Always trying to help a pal."

"Tell Rotolo. The night of the Slingerland Speaking Contest. Around eight o'clock."

"I'll tell him." Broz rolled his empty glass between calloused palms. "Real bad blood between Rotolo and Lombardo, you know."

"That's between the two of them," Karol said as if it didn't matter to him. "All I know is that Lombardo wants to sell fast. Things haven't gone so good for him lately and now he's got a mess on his hands."

"Hey, he's out of jail." Broz stood up and lifted his overcoat from the back of a nearby chair. "In my book that means he's still Lucky Lombardo."

Karol stayed another few minutes before heading to Holy Angels.

As agreed, Hanna was waiting for him in the last pew, almost lost in the darkness that enveloped the back of the church. Closer to the front, shadows played across the walls from the pillar candles on the altar and the tiny flames of the votive candle racks. Karol could just make out the little chapels flanking the altar; Mary and Joseph on one side and the archangels Michael and Gabriel on the other.

Michael was Karol's favorite, although he wasn't sure the devout were supposed to prefer one angel over another. But Michael was a warrior with a sword and a bronze breastplate as well as a pair of magnificent wings. A pillar of the church, the way Karol had wanted to be a pillar of justice.

Now, he was foreman of the biggest mill in New York and learning how to think like a businessman, but he was also championing safety and justice for his workers and in East Lido for his friends. Giving honest people a chance to live a good life.

Perhaps that had been God's plan for him all along.

Karol genuflected and slid into the pew next to

Hanna. In the semi-darkness, she was even more beautiful, candlelight revealing the smooth planes of her face and the curve of her mouth.

"Did you find him?" she asked.

"Broz showed," Karol said. "He's going to tell Rotolo."

"I want to hear him say he killed Marta."

"I'll hear it for you."

Hanna shook her head.

"Toby and Luca are right," Karol reminded her. "They know what he's like. We've got a better chance of getting him to boast to Luca than confess to you."

"The police won't arrest him."

"Toby knows a good cop named Dooley. With three witnesses, Rotolo's as good as in the electric chair."

"What if it doesn't work?"

"Then we'll think of something else."

Karol felt for her hand. Her fingers were cool and dry. "When this is all over," he said. "You and I should talk to Father Nowicki."

Hanna shook her head. "No. I told you before, Karol Dombrowski, I'm not good for you."

"I wasn't listening," Karol said.

She didn't pull away when he kissed her.

CHAPTER 42

Hanna finds a gun

Life as a guest in the Rutherford-Blick household was extremely pleasant. Hanna might have been living in a luxury hotel with gourmet food and solicitous hosts who wanted her stay to be as comfortable as possible. She was treated as a celebrity, the same as at her new job at Van Dyke's.

It was an unusual household. Two middle-aged couples, attended to by a cook and gardener who both lived in an apartment attached to the back of the house, plus two maids and a laundress who came in during the day. The Rutherford's children were all in boarding school and the Blicks were actually newlyweds. There was always someone in the big house, yet it was always peaceful and meals were always served precisely on time.

Jack Rutherford ran the Lido Chamber of Commerce, had something to do with a company called Lido Lumber and was the current president of the Bison Club, the politics of which were a frequent topic of dinner conversation. Hanna gathered that anyone who was anything in Lido either belonged to the club or devoutly wished to belong. Men only, of course.

Osa Rutherford was much more flamboyant and outgoing than her husband. One of the heirs to the Lido Premium fortune, she was the head of the Women's Institute. As far as Hanna could tell, this was a do-gooder heaven that funneled women into classes to learn domestic skills or lecture halls to hear speakers in pith helmets tell about crossing rivers with unpronounceable names.

Hanna liked both Jack and Osa Rutherford but she found Henry and Ruth Blick to be much more interesting. They occupied a suite on the west side of the house.

Henry was the Operations Manager at Lido Premium, making him Karol's boss. No one around the dinner table needed to tell Hanna that he was once a soldier. His shoulders were always braced and straight and his clothing was immaculate. Hanna knew a bit about Ruth, the former occupant of the apartment over the Galliano Club, and found her to be a kind woman who absolutely adored her one-eyed spartan of a husband.

Sometimes late at night, Hanna heard music coming from their suite. It was always something soft and slow, the kind of music for waltzing cheek-to-cheek. Hanna listened and thought about Karol. She didn't even know if he liked to dance.

The night before the Slingerland Speaking Contest, which they all planned to attend, the two couples went out for dinner at a restaurant called Babylon. Hanna ate by herself, then went exploring.

Ruth and Henry's suite was enormous. The sitting room was decorated in a more masculine and simple style than the Rutherford's public rooms, with a circle of oak and leather Stickley armchairs, a glass-fronted barrister bookcase, and a long oak dresser topped with a Victrola and records in a brass holder. White muslin curtains softened the space, as did a multi-colored Persian rug.

The bedroom was twice as large, anchored by a bed with a massive headboard that was taller than Hanna and carved by a master craftsman. A simple white counterpane covered it and the linen pillowcases were edged with a thick band of crocheted lace. An upholstered stool waited in front of the vanity, where Ruth's bottles of perfume and a small box of powder clustered on a silver tray. The carving on the vanity matched the headboard and framed a mirror that stretched to the ceiling. Exotically patterned rugs in shades of red and plum covered the floor.

Beyond the bedroom, a bathroom was a treasure

trove of white porcelain, with a modern toilet, a clawfoot tub, and a huge white sink with a gleaming brass gooseneck faucet.

The suite was at once both simpler and more luxurious than Hanna expected. She resisted the urge to fling herself upon the bed and test its softness. The impulse was replaced by the mental image of Karol against the pillows, watching her undress.

Hanna gave herself a shake. She didn't have time to daydream.

The suite had an infinite number of hiding places. Two closets, an armoire, dozens of drawers and cabinet doors. Everything inside was meticulously folded, hung, or stored inside a specialty compartment, from a walnut box for Henry's collar stays to bags of cedar shavings tucked into the toes of Ruth's shoes.

As quietly and quickly as she could, Hanna began searching the bedroom, betting that's where she'd have the greatest chance of success. She found what she was looking for in a wooden box stored on the top shelf of the armoire, alongside a stack of blankets.

Col. Henry Packham Blick was inscribed on a brass plaque set into the lid, along with a military insignia featuring an eagle swathed in ribbon. Hanna carefully opened the box. A hefty revolver with a polished wooden stock was snugged into a compartment lined with blue velvet.

She carefully lifted it out. The revolver was heavy and made her think fleetingly of the shooting lesson Sam had once given her. *US Army Model 1917* was engraved into the strip of iron running through the heel of the stock.

Two half-moon clips, each holding three brass-jacketed rounds, were nestled in a well under the velvet compartment.

CHAPTER 43

Target in the window

Luca walked Tess out the back door of the club to the green Ford coupe. It was still a jolt to see the sporty number parked on the gravel instead of Vito's big black Packard.

"I'm going to worry all night," Tess said. She looked like a winter doll in her royal blue cloche and brown velvet coat. "You be careful, all right? I'd like to be married to you for a long time."

"Marriage suits you." Luca tipped her chin up for a kiss.

"What about you?" she asked, her lips lingering close to his.

"I'm the luckiest man in Lido," Luca said.

"You're going to be the coldest man in Lido if you stay outside much longer." Tess kissed him hard, then tugged away.

"Go get Hanna." Luca opened the car door for her. "Tell Sonny good luck."

"I will." Tess got behind the wheel.

When the coupe turned out of the alley, Luca went

inside and locked the door. The club was empty and dim. Quiet, too, except for muffled thumps coming from the tiny library on the other side of the office. It was still Vito's office. Luca wasn't sure it ever would be his.

Nothing inside the library looked out of place. Desk, chairs, newspapers threaded onto wooden dowels, a tidy stack of Western Union telegram forms. Luca climbed on the desk chair, stretched tall and rapped on the pressed tin ceiling.

A moment later, four tin tiles lifted up and disappeared into the darkness of the floor above. Toby Gleason peered through the square hole left by the tiles.

"Jesus wept," he said. "Add master carpenter to the list of my finer qualities."

Luca grinned up at his friend. "Rumrunner. Blackmailer. Carpenter."

"And gentleman farmer."

Karol appeared next to Toby. "Ready?"

"Ready," Luca confirmed.

Toby and Karol lowered three of Tess's rescued carpets through the hole. Still standing on the chair, Luca caught each one. He spread them on the floor, one on top of the other.

The plan for Rotolo was based on the assumption that he wouldn't talk freely if he thought anyone else was in the club. Once Rotolo was there and his guard was down, Luca would signal his friends hidden in the dance studio. They'd drop through the hole in the ceiling to eavesdrop. The carpets would muffle their landings.

"Test the signal one more time," Karol said when the carpets were in place.

Luca trotted down the hall to the saloon, went behind the bar and stepped on the pedal near the work counter. A moment later, he was rewarded with three sharp raps from the library. Karol had rigged a wire all the way from the bar to the dance studio, cleverly hidden in the wall paneling, that switched on a bulb. The light would be the signal for Toby and Karol to sneak into the club through the trapdoor.

Luca went back into the library.

"It worked fine," Karol said, peering down.

"Here." Luca handed up the Commodore baseball bat he kept behind the bar in case of trouble. It had last been used when the late Nick Procopio started a fight and lost his membership in the club. That seemed like a lifetime ago now.

"You'll need this more than me," Karol said. "I'm with Toby and he's armed."

"The only thing I need is a way to get Rotolo talking," Luca replied.

"You know, when this is over," Karol said leadingly. "Me and Hanna--."

"We know." Toby's voice filtered out of the darkness. "Here. Close the tile."

The pressed tin ceiling was whole again a moment later. Toby had done a good job.

Luca put the chair back where it belonged and turned out the light in the little library. Back in the saloon, he picked up the sign that Tess made and put it in the front window.

CLOSED TONIGHT
ON ACCOUNT OF
SPEAKING CONTEST
GOOD LUCK, SONNY ZAMBRANO

The front door was left unlocked.

The only thing left to do was to pretend that he was going to sell the club.

He stayed behind the bar, wiping nonexistent water spots off a tray of beer glasses. The clock on the wall ticked away the minutes, slower than molasses. The mirrored wall above the bar reflected Vito's collection of bottles, all imported from Italy and emptied long before Luca ever came to work there. The eternal bottle of Liquore Galliano rose through the display like a golden arrow.

If that bottle could talk, what would it say about ownership of the club passing to Luca? Did he deserve what Vito had built over the course of so many years?

As he polished and repolished the same glass, the slow passage of time reminded Luca of the day they'd all waited so breathlessly for the double blast of the Lido Premium steam whistle. Two blasts meant that the mill had completed the legendary order for that Boston shipyard without a single accident and every worker would get that hoped-for giant bonus.

Just a few hours later, he'd found Jimmy Zambrano's body behind the club. The days since then had been a cascade of troubles that had to end tonight.

Eight o'clock came and went. Luca started on the glasses all over again. Maybe Broz Siwak hadn't passed the message after all. Or maybe Rotolo was planning something nobody anticipated.

Framed in the big front window, spotlighted by the hanging lights over the bar, Luca felt like a tin target in a carnival shooting gallery.

CHAPTER 44

Slingerland Speaking Contest

The lobby of the Strand Theatre was thronged with Lido notables, many of whom Tess recognized as they maneuvered to avoid her. The only exceptions were Henry and Ruth Blick and Jack and Osa Rutherford, but of course they were still hosting Hanna who was with Tess.

The East Lido contingent was there in force. Led by Carmella Zambrano, both Tess and Hanna were embraced and acclaimed. Tess was amazed to see so many from the neighborhood. Everyone had come to support Sonny, even Bruno, the ancient waiter at Bella Napoli. The ticket had probably cost more than he made in two weeks.

When the lights flickered, Tess and Hanna accepted programs from the ushers and found their seats inside the theater. It was a full house and every seat rapidly filled. Both women kept their coats on. The theater was unheated and the wooden seats were chilly. The vents under the seats which cooled theatergoers during the summer were closed, but a faint breeze tickled Tess's ankles nonetheless.

Tess leafed through the program booklet, which contained a short biography of each contestant and their goal for the future. Sonny was listed as "Giacomo Zambrano, Junior; son of Carmella and the late Giacomo Zambrano, Senior. His goal is to be an attorney and politician."

"Look," Tess whispered and showed Hanna the back of the program. Lido Premium was the main sponsor with an advertisement showing a drawing of the big mill building, topped with the legend **1/10th of All Copper Manufactured in the USA Comes From Lido NY!**

Hanna didn't respond. Apparently lost in thought, she stared at the curtained stage, hands locked on a new leather purse as if afraid someone might steal it. It looked costly. Tess expected that Hanna got a hefty discount from Van Dyke's, her new employer.

Only partially visible in the pit below the stage, the Lido Free Academy orchestra began tuning up. Carmella Zambrano, seated in front with the other contestants' parents, turned to gaze at the packed theater. Tess caught her eye and gave a little wave of encouragement. Carmella responded with a broad smile.

Tess wondered if Carmella would be willing to

teach her to cook.

The orchestra launched into an inspiring swing of brass and flutes. According to the program it was "On the Campus" by John Philip Sousa.

The curtain rose to thunderous applause. A giant banner strung across the stage proclaimed **1926 Annual Slingerland Speaking Contest.** Tess joined in the applause. Hanna kept her hands on her purse.

A stout wooden podium was centered on the stage and decorated with patriotic tri-color bunting. Eight young men, all wearing dark suits, were seated in a nervous row to the left. Sonny was in the middle, his posture worthy of General Pershing. A bevy of self-important academics sat on the other side of the stage.

As the music swelled, a color guard marched in, garnering more applause. The flagpole dipped and swayed to the tune, unfurling the Stars and Stripes and the dark blue New York state flag. The pennant of Morton College, sponsor of the scholarship that would go to one lucky orator, proudly displayed crossed white keys against a green background and the Latin inscription *Veritas Vincit.*

The music ended with a flourish. The flags were positioned under the Slingerland banner. Mayor John Peabody mounted the steps and crossed to the podium to yet more applause. He gave a short welcome and invited all to stand for the national anthem. The orchestra crashed into "The Star Spangled Banner" and the theater filled with singing.

Preliminaries over, Mayor Peabody congratulated the contestants, expressed his enthusiasm for hearing each and every one of their performances, and finally extolled the city of Lido for its high educational standards and the quality of its teachers. Next came the dean of Morton College who would be awarding a full scholarship to one of the fine contestants seated behind him tonight, in honor of the late Willis Slingerland, a distinguished Morton alumnus.

"I wonder if anybody knows what made him so distinguished," Tess couldn't resist whispering to Hanna.

She got a quick side glance before Hanna focused forward again, hands still clutching the fancy purse. Tess couldn't blame Hanna for being distracted. No doubt the same questions plaguing Tess were also running through her friend's head.

Was Rotolo at the Galliano Club yet?

Did Luca, Karol, and Toby hear him admit to Marta's murder yet?

What if Rotolo didn't talk?

Tess took a deep breath and tried to pay attention to the speakers.

Harold Bellows, the principal of Lido Free Academy, lauded Morton College for its generosity and support before introducing Anson Egerton, who taught Elocution and Oratory at the high school. Out of all senior boys, the eight young men on the stage had achieved the highest grades in his class. Tess wondered if any girls had scored higher, not that it mattered for the purposes of the Slingerland Speaking Contest scholarship prize. Morton College did not admit girls.

Repeating the information in the program, Mr. Egerton introduced each contestant, along with the title of their presentation, in the order in which they would speak. Each young man stood and bowed to the audience as his name was called.

Sonny was the second speaker after the intermission. He gave a nervous smile that widened as applause thundered from the corner packed with his East Lido supporters.

Introductions over, the theater was silent as the first contestant took the podium. After clearing his throat several times, student Gregory Fulmer launched into the famous soliloquy from Shakespeare's Hamlet.

To be, or not to be--that is the question:
Whether 'tis nobler in the mind to suffer
The slings and arrows of outrageous fortune

**Or to take arms against a sea of troubles
And by opposing end them.**

Gregory turned in a credible performance, but Tess found it hard to reconcile the stirring words with the jug-eared, freckle-faced slip of a boy delivering them.

Hanna fanned herself with her program, stroking the air with short, jerky movements.

The next contestant, Elmer Stonebrook, rolled his shoulders as he approached the podium like a swimmer preparing to dive off the Lido Dam. He was a good speaker, flashing his eyes across the audience as he gave a stirring account of the first flight over the North Pole, quoting Richard E. Byrd as published in the September edition of *National Geographic* magazine.

Elmer was a good speaker, making the most of a deep voice and subject matter that was exciting, patriotic, and familiar. Not only had the flight been in all the news for months, but Lido had been touched by Byrd's fame. Piloted by Floyd Bennett and carrying Norwegian mechanic Bernt Balchen, the explorer's famous Ford tri-motor airplane stopped in Lido during a multi-state tour that began with Wanamaker's department store in New York City.

Tess was captivated, sitting on the edge of her seat, as Elmer ended with both hands aloft to emphasize the power of flight. He would be hard to beat. When the young orator went back to his seat, Tess turned to Hanna, wondering if she'd been as impressed, but Hanna was still fanning herself with the program. Her face was oddly expressionless.

The next two speakers gave the audience the Gettysburg Address and the monologue of Ajax by Sophocles. Neither were serious contenders for the scholarship, in Tess's view.

The principal announced a 15-minute intermission.

Tess reached for her purse, only to realize that it was on the floor near her foot instead of wedged in between her coat and the armrest. She scooped it up. Together with Hanna and everyone else, she left her seat for the lobby where the girls of Lido Free Academy's Home Economics class, wearing white dresses and blue sashes, dispensed punch and cookies.

"My stocking is falling down," Hanna whispered as they neared the refreshments. "I'll be back in a minute."

Tess accepted a cup of punch. When she turned to leave the table, she found herself face-to-face with Mallory Pigeon, a friend who had been in the same graduating class at Lido Free Academy. Mallory had been a spectator at Luca's trial but never once spoke to Tess.

There was no avoiding her in the crush of people in

the lobby. "Hello, Mallory," Tess said coolly. "How nice to see you."

"Tess." Mallory forced a smile. "I didn't expect to see you here tonight."

"Why not?"

"Well, being a married woman now and all." Mallory trailed off. "I'm so sorry for you, Tess. So tragic."

"Tragic? What are you talking about?"

"Surely you realize," Mallory said awkwardly. "Married under duress in a courtroom. By a judge. To an Italian from East Lido who hardly speaks English."

"I chose to get married," Tess retorted. "There was no duress. And Luca speaks English as well as you do."

"That's not what people are saying." Mallory's expression suggested that she was one of those people.

"I can't help it if people are uninformed." Tess spoke loftily but knew her face was red.

Mallory made a show of looking around. "Is he here?"

"No, he isn't."

"I completely understand," Mallory said, radiating fake sympathy. "He wouldn't fit in."

"Enjoy the rest of the program," Tess said and walked away before she exploded. She gave her empty cup to the Home Economics students and stalked back to her seat to fume.

The lights flickered and the orchestra played a chord to let the audience know intermission was ending. Tess looked around for Hanna amid the dozens of audience members taking their seats for the second half but couldn't see her.

The lights dimmed. The principal welcomed them back to the program. Mr. Egerton of the Elocution and Oratory curriculum introduced Wendell Huff, a painfully thin young man with wire-rimmed spectacles who draped himself over the podium like a wet sock to declaim Macbeth's dagger scene.

Is this a dagger which I see before me,
The handle toward my hand? Come, let me
clutch thee.

Somewhat belatedly Wendell's hand shot out in search of an imaginary blade.

Hanna's seat remained empty throughout the performance.

Wendell ran out of soliloquy but remained one with the podium, gaping at the audience. Mr. Egerton peeled him off and sent him back to his seat.

It was finally Sonny's turn. Tess nearly burst with pride as he came forward. In a matter of weeks, she'd come to regard him as a younger brother.

Instead of positioning himself behind the podium, he stood next to it, one hand casually resting on the wood. His selection was **The Cask of Amontillado** by Edgar Allan Poe.

Squaring his shoulders in a manner that reminded her of a smaller, darker-haired version of Luca, Sonny swept his gaze over the audience and began in a strong, convincing voice.

The thousand injuries of Fortunato I had borne as I best could, but when he ventured upon insult I vowed revenge. You, who so well know the nature of my soul, will not suppose, however, that I gave utterance to a threat. At length I would be avenged; this was a point definitively settled . . .

It must be understood that neither by word nor deed had I given Fortunato cause to doubt my good will. I continued, as was my wont, to smile in his face, and he did not perceive that my smile now was at the thought of his immolation.

As Montresor led Fortunato into the crypt and Hanna's seat stayed empty, Tess opened her purse. Just as she feared, the keys to her Ford coupe were gone.

CHAPTER 45

Opening negotiations

"You sure he knows not to start shooting until I give the word?" Benny asked, with a flick of his eyes to the backseat of the Cadillac where Stan sat cradling his Tommy gun.

"He knows," Broz reassured him.

"Good." Benny settled himself behind the wheel again. Stan only spoke Polish, which meant that he took orders from Broz. Real rough around the edges, Stan was a cold-blooded shooter.

That's the kind of moxie Benny needed tonight. He had a couple of angles to propose to Lombardo. With or without the kind of encouragement that came from the Colt Pocket Hammerless, the sheik was going to accept.

They were parked half a block away from the Galliano Club. Hamilton Street was deserted. East Lido was a ghost town, like Edison had started rationing light bulbs. The only sign of life was the yellow glow of the Galliano Club's front window.

The part of him that had grown the Lido Outfit into

the biggest beer racket in upstate New York saw tonight as the perfect business opportunity. Yet the part of Benny that was still a torpedo for the North Side gang in Chicago smelled a trap. He wasn't going to be taken unawares if it was, not like Dean O'Banion who got shot up in his own flower shop while shaking hands with Frankie Yale.

"Come on." Benny decided there was no point in waiting around any longer. The Colt Pocket Hammerless was in his secret chest pocket. Broz had a sawed-off shotgun and the sack of cash. Stan had the Tommy gun and who knew what else stashed in his clothing. Stan clanked as he hauled open the door.

Lombardo was behind the bar. He looked up as Benny swaggered in, flanked by Broz and Stan.

"Hey, Sheik." Benny made a show of looking around the mostly dark saloon and pretended to be surprised. "The sign said you're closed."

"That's right." Lombardo put down his bar towel. "Everyone is at the Strand tonight. Sonny is competing in the speaking contest."

"You by yourself?"

"You see anybody else around?"

Benny jerked his chin at Broz and Stan. They fanned out.

"You got a reason for coming into my establishment

like this?" Lombardo asked. "Like the sign says, we're closed."

"I hear you're interested in selling," Benny said. "Old man Spinelli left you with a mountain of debt. Selling beer at two bits a glass ain't gonna get you out from under."

"If you weren't charging so much for beer, I'd be fine."

"That's the problem?" Benny hooted with laughter. "Problem is you're selling to mugs who don't got any money. That mill pays good for Lido but they don't got the kind of money to keep a place this big going for long. In another month you won't be able to pay the electric."

Broz and Stan came back. "Nobody's around," Broz said. "Back door is locked."

"You check the cellar door, too?" Benny asked. "Don't want nobody interrupting our little chat."

"Cellar door, too," Broz affirmed.

"Great." Benny sauntered over to the bar, both his overcoat and suit jacket unbuttoned so Lombardo could see the Colt Pocket Hammerless. "How about me and you have a cup of joe? Talk a little business."

"Sure," Lombardo said.

CHAPTER 46

A toast

The couple behind Tess whispered to each other. It was clear they disapproved of Edgar Allan Poe, premeditated murder, and the story's sometimes arcane language.

She turned around in her seat and glared them into silence.

Even as Sonny held the rest of his audience spellbound, Tess began to have a bad feeling about his performance. **The Cask of Amontillado** was not what the judges wanted. It wasn't patriotic or Shakespeare or historic, but a plot about a plot to trick a man and then kill him, involving Italians and drinking.

Or maybe she was ascribing to the contest judges her own panic about a plot to trick a man involving Italians and drinking which was unfolding right now at the Galliano Club.

"Drink," I said, presenting him the wine.

He raised it to his lips with a leer. He paused and nodded to me familiarly, while his bells jingled.

"I drink," he said, "to the buried that repose around us."

CHAPTER 47

To the future

Luca didn't have to be a genius to realize the problem. The percolator was on the other end of the bar from the signal pedal, which was wired to the light closest to the window, the only way Karol could get it to work.

There was no reason to be at that end. Sonny usually did his homework there and had left the space scrupulously tidy. Luca should have thought to put something there. Dirty plates or the evening edition of the *Lido Daily Clipper* that congratulated the Slingerland contestants.

Above the bar, the man-sized bottle of Liquore Galliano glinted in the half-light, as if to tell Luca how stupid he was. The shelves of empty bottles on either side echoed the sentiment.

There was nothing to do but fill two mugs and bring them to the table Rotolo indicated with a sweep of his hand. His thugs settled at the next table over. Luca guessed that the lean one was Broz, Karol's inside man and one-time co-worker at Lido Premium. The other one looked dangerous and made no effort to hide his Tommy gun.

"A nice cup of joe," Rotolo said after taking an appreciative slurp of the hot coffee. "Even better than when old man Spinelli made it."

"What about your boys?" Luca asked, lifting his chin at the other table. "Am I supposed to provide free coffee to everybody who drops in with a Tommy gun?"

"Nah." Rotolo took another sip. "The boys gotta keep their hands free. Know what I mean?"

"You must think this is a dangerous place."

Rotolo laughed and raised his mug in a toast. "You're the one who got himself arrested for what? Attempted murder?"

"They dropped the charges." Luca took a swallow of coffee but didn't taste it. He had to get Karol and Toby within earshot before maneuvering the conversation around to Marta's murder.

Exuding confidence, Rotolo leaned back in his chair. "Let's talk turkey, Sheik. We ain't been friends, but I blame Spinelli for that. Now that the old man's gone and you're in charge, let's forget the past."

"Drink to the future instead?"

"Exactly."

"What kind of a future?"

"We should partner up."

"Last time you were here, you wanted to buy the place."

"Sure, who wouldn't?" Rotolo grinned. "I'm willing to give you twenty-five percent."

"Twenty-five percent of what?"

"Of the new Galliano Club speakeasy. Girls upstairs. A jazz band over there. Instead of Spinelli mopping up all the good stuff, we sell it to the swells at three dollars a slug."

"Who owns the other seventy-five percent?"

Rotolo raised his mug. "Consider yourself my junior partner."

"I don't want to be anybody's partner. I got Vito's debts to pay."

"Think about it, Sheik. We make this place into a speakeasy with girls upstairs and you'll be a millionaire in three months. Buy Miss Blue Hat whatever she wants."

Luca drank some coffee and decided to play for time. "Okay," he said, slowly lowering the cup. "How much are you willing to pay me for a seventy-five percent share of the Galliano Club?"

"The building, too."

"That'll cost more."

"Name your price."

"Forty thousand," Luca said, pulling the number out of thin air. "But no girls upstairs. I'm not going to desecrate Vito Spinelli's memory by turning the place into a brothel."

"He's dead," Rotolo scoffed. "You're wasting my time, Sheik."

"Thirty-eight thousand and partnership."

"Twenty-five."

"Twenty-five thousand?" Luca exclaimed. "That's nothing."

"Place as big as this, the take should be five, six thousand a night. You'd be in for a twenty-five percent share."

"That's more than a thousand a night," Luca heard himself say. For an evil minute, he was sorely tempted.

"More money than you see in a month, eh, Sheik?"

"Thirty-five percent," Luca countered. He could talk numbers all night but that wasn't getting him any closer to either the signal pedal or a conversation about the women in Rotolo's life.

"Thirty-five." Rotolo stroked his chin. "That's sixty-five percent for me. Throw in ownership of the building and you got a deal."

Inspiration struck. "We'll make a contract. If Tess agrees, we're in."

"Can't make a move without the ball and chain already?"

"Tess is half-owner now." Luca figured that by mentioning his new wife, he could maneuver the conversation in the general direction of Marta Gorski. "The deed is in both our names."

"Well, don't that beat all," Rotolo was suddenly angry. "Should have told me that at the beginning, Sheik."

"What difference does it make?"

"I don't do business with dames," Rotolo snarled.

What do you do with dames? Luca swallowed back the retort. "Do you want the place or don't you?"

Rotolo glowered. "Forget the percentages. I want the whole place. You and Miss Blue Hat clear out."

"Sixty thousand for everything," Luca parried. "I'll throw in the percolator."

"Spinelli was ready to take twenty-two." Rotolo shoved his empty coffee across the table.

Luca scooped it up. "I'll get you a refill. Give you a chance to think it over."

To his chagrin, Rotolo followed him to the bar and hitched a foot on the rail as he took in the big brass cash register and the glittering array of empty bottles on the wall above. "How much did Spinelli owe on the place?"

"Can't write a contract without a pencil." Luca went

to the window end of the bar and made a show of rifling through Sonny's school notebooks and clutch of pencils. His foot found the signal pedal and pressed hard.

An electric shock coursed through his body, lifting his eyebrows and rattling his teeth. Luca dropped both paper and pencils as his heart stuttered and his fingertips tingled.

"Feeling jumpy, Lombardo?" Rotolo scoffed.

The pedal was sizzling. Luca bent down to retrieve the writing materials and managed to dump out a bottle of lemon-lime rickey from the supply under the bar. The pedal hissed and subsided into silence.

He straightened up to see Rotolo standing in the space between the bar and the work cabinet, pointing a gun at him. Luca put the empty bottle on the work counter and slowly raised his hands. The bootlegger must have seen the pedal and knew what it was.

"Jesus, what a damn clodhopper," Rotolo said, in obvious disgust at Luca's clumsiness. He holstered the gun. "Get your paper and pencil."

CHAPTER 48

Meeting Trixie's man

Hanna left Tess's coupe on Second Street and doubled back to the alley running behind the Galliano Club. Nearly every house along the way was dark. She held the big leather purse under one arm as she half-ran, half-walked on the slippery sidewalks.

The gravel lot in the back of the club was bordered by low snowbanks that reflected the milky moonlight. Across from the opaque blockiness of the building, bare branches of the maple trees were outlined in white. The night was very quiet and the crunch of her boots on the mix of gravel and frost was frighteningly loud.

The back steps were almost impossible to see in the dark. Hanna groped her way up, praying not to trip, and felt for the door.

She set down the purse and slipped off her gloves, the better to find the keyhole. Once she did, it was an easy task to maneuver the brass bobby pin into the small opening. A few cautious probes and she recognized the tension as the pin levered the tumblers.

A soft snick told her the pin did its job. The

doorknob turned silently. Hanna grabbed the heavy purse and slipped inside the club.

The hall was so dark she could only move forward with one hand on the wall but the layout was easy to recall. The office was on her right, the pool room on the left and the saloon was straight ahead where a light was on. Male voices made a low murmur.

An arm snaked around her neck from behind, cutting off her wind. Hanna was propelled forward even as she fought hard, twisting and choking yet clinging valiantly to the purse. A stream of crude Polish assaulted her, the man's breath hot on her neck. Something hard and unyielding jabbed her between the shoulder blades.

Hanna stopped struggling, knowing that her captor was a Polish version of her late husband and probably just as flinty and ruthless. The man jabbed her with the gun even harder. Stumbling like Sam on a bender, she reluctantly preceded her captor into the saloon. In a stream of guttural Polish, she heard him announce his prize to the room.

"Says he found her picking the back door lock," somebody translated.

"Friend of yours, Lombardo?" The speaker lounged against the big mahogany bar with a mug in one hand. Not a big man, he nonetheless exuded brash confidence.

Wavy dark hair, hard blue eyes, and a dangerous self-assured grin.

Hanna instantly knew he was Trixie's man. Marta would have been drawn to him like loose iron filings to a magnet.

Benny Rotolo wore an expensive suit, but not so expensive that the wool fabric could hide the outline of a gun tucked into a breast pocket. Sam had carried his guns the same way.

Luca was behind the bar. "Friend of my wife's," he said, his voice as expressionless as his face. His eyes flickered across the room, drawing Hanna's attention to the lean man who'd translated her captor's words. He was armed, too.

Two torpedoes. Rotolo liked to show off. Either that, or he was afraid of Luca.

"Cheating on Miss Blue Hat already, Sheik? Well, I got to hand it to you. You got good taste." Rotolo's back was to Luca as he sipped from his mug.

Hanna's vision tunneled until all she saw was the handsome man in his slick suit.

Everything else receded. The translator on the other side of the saloon. The thug who'd dragged her into the club. Even Luca, seemingly frozen in place by the big brass cash register, watching her over Rotolo's shoulder.

"Well, Sheik," Rotolo drawled. "Ain't you gonna introduce us?"

"Hanna, meet Benny Rotolo." Luca's jaw barely moved as he spoke.

"Tell me about the day you met Marta Gorski," Hanna said.

CHAPTER 49

In the crypt

The judge from Morton College looked nervous and fretful. Paying little attention to Sonny's masterful performance, he kept crossing and uncrossing his knees. With every shift in position, he pinched the crease in his trousers all the way down his thighs and over his kneecaps, then felt for the cuffs at his ankles.

Tess wanted to shout at him to stop.

At the most remote end of the crypt there appeared another less spacious. Its walls had been lined with human remains, piled to the vault overhead, in the fashion of the great catacombs of Paris. Three sides of this interior crypt were still ornamented in this manner. From the fourth side the bones had been thrown down, and lay promiscuously upon the earth, forming at one point a mound of some size. Within the wall thus exposed by the displacing of the bones, we perceived a still interior crypt or recess, in depth about four feet, in width three, in height six or seven. It seemed to have

been constructed for no especial use within itself, but formed merely the interval between two of the colossal supports of the roof of the catacombs, and was backed by one of their circumscribing walls of solid granite.

It was in vain that Fortunato, uplifting his dull torch, endeavoured to pry into the depth of the recess. Its termination the feeble light did not enable us to see.

CHAPTER 50

A woman's voice

Karol had almost given up hope of seeing the signal when the Edison bulb burst into life. The sliver of brightness sent a charge of urgency through the darkness of the abandoned dance studio where Karol and Toby lay flat on the floor.

As planned, Karol lifted out the section of flooring, carefully setting aside the pressed tin tiles of the ceiling underneath. Toby hoisted himself to the edge of the opening. Karol lowered him through and the Irishman landed noiselessly on the carpets.

Karol handed down Luca's baseball bat before easing himself through the hole and dropping onto the thickly padded floor.

He recognized a woman's voice and nearly had a stroke.

Hanna was supposed to be safe at the Strand Theatre with Tess tonight.

Toby blocked him from charging out of the little library. "Jesus wept," the Irishman swore in a whisper. "Where did she come from?"

Karol shook off Toby's restraining hand.

CHAPTER 51

Jog your memory

"I never heard of no Marta Gorski," Benny blustered.

"You met her at the Harvey House restaurant in Chicago," the dame charged.

"Never been there."

"The Harvey House in Union Station."

Benny snorted. "You're dreaming, sister."

"Maybe this will jog your memory. She looked just like me."

The dame whipped off her hat, shook her head to loosen blonde waves, and Benny recoiled like he seen a ghost. Of course, the last time he saw this dame's twin, her eyes were buggy and her mouth gaped like a fish out of water.

He forced a laugh. "You want attention, sister? This ain't the way to get it."

The dame's voice shook, but she tossed the hat to the ground with one hand and opened her purse with the other. "Marta would have fallen for you like a ton of bricks. What did you promise her? Marriage? Nice clothes? A chance to see the world?"

Benny had no intention of letting this go any further. He snapped his fingers at Broz. "Take her outside and stick her in the car."

The dame barked something in Polish at him. The effect was to nail Broz's feet to the floor.

"I'm not going anywhere," the dame said to Benny. "Not until you admit that you killed Marta."

"Broz," Benny said, reaching inside his jacket for the Colt Pocket Hammerless again. "If you know what's good for you, you'll get her out of here."

Luca planted both hands on the bar. "Rotolo, tell her what happened to her sister."

"You killed Marta!" the dame shouted. Her purse fell to the floor, leaving her with a big revolver in both hands like a shooter who knew the button business. "Admit it! You lured her out of Chicago all the way to Lido. When you got tired of her, you killed her and dumped her in the river."

"Shut up," Benny bawled and whipped out the Colt. "Shut up or you'll be just as dead."

CHAPTER 52

Fettered

Sonny's electrifying delivery made Tess think about Lon Chaney in *The Hunchback of Notre Dame*. The young orator wasn't in costume or hunched or limping but his performance gave her the same chills.

He almost made her stop worrying, but not quite. Hanna had gone to the Galliano Club, of course. Tess fought the temptation to go, too. She could rush outside and find a taxi.

But she'd promised Luca that she would stay at the theater until the end of the contest. She had to trust that he and Karol and Toby could wangle the truth out of Benny Rotolo.

Sonny moved away from the podium, bending toward the audience, inviting them into the crypt, making them experience the damp and darkness.

Even as her pulse thrummed with nerves, Tess knew that Morton College wasn't good enough for Sonny Zambrano. He was Ivy League material.

In an instant he had reached the extremity of the

niche, and finding his progress arrested by the rock, stood stupidly bewildered. A moment more and I had fettered him to the granite. In its surface were two iron staples, distant from each other about two feet, horizontally. From one of these depended a short chain, from the other a padlock. Throwing the links about his waist, it was but the work of a few seconds to secure it. He was too much astounded to resist. Withdrawing the key I stepped back from the recess.

"Pass your hand," I said, "over the wall; you cannot help feeling the nitre. Indeed, it is very damp. Once more let me implore you to return. No? Then I must positively leave you. But I must first render you all the little attentions in my power."

CHAPTER 53

Saint Karol

"Hanna!" Karol had imagined a dozen ways the plan could go awry, but never this, never Hanna pointing a gun at Rotolo as the bootlegger pointed one at her.

"Get out, Karol," Hanna said, not taking her eyes off Rotolo. "Let me do what I have to do."

From across the saloon, Broz and one of his boys from Gdansk had an arsenal trained on Hanna, including a Tommy gun, a weapon Karol had only seen in newsreels.

"You lied to me, Karol." Broz was across the room by the front window, a sawed-off shotgun in his hands with barrels like beady black eyes of death. His chin jerked toward Rotolo but the weapon stayed aimed at Karol. "You set me up to set him up. But I knew what you were doing the whole time."

"Jesus wept," Toby said cheerfully, joining Karol in the saloon. "We can draw lots to see who gets to start the shooting."

"Nobody needs to shoot," Luca said in a steady voice from behind the bar.

"All he has to do is confess," Hanna said.

"Shut up, Sheik." Rotolo focused on Toby. "You're mixed up with the wrong bunch, Gleason."

"Heard you're paying three thousand a month to Chief Doyle now, so I have," Toby said, his gun covering both Broz and the Tommy gun. "How much more to clean up this mess?"

"Shut your fat mick mouth."

Karol gently propped the baseball bat against the wall and held his hands up. "Nobody needs to be shooting tonight. Broz, you and your friend with the Tommy gun can just walk out the door."

"He works for me, buddy," Rotolo snarled. "Not you."

"Saint Karol," Broz taunted. "Always thinking you can fix the problem. Did you really think I was going to rat out Rotolo and come back to the mill?"

On the other side of the big saloon, the Tommy gun said something in Polish. Broz spit an answer out of the side of his mouth. Karol didn't catch the exchange.

"Looks like your little party's gonna backfire, Sheik," Rotolo said over his shoulder to Luca. "Once we shoot the place up, you ain't getting a dime for this dump. Get rid of your friends and this crazy dame and we can get back to business."

"No shooting," Luca said.

Tension was crushing them all. No one in the saloon was breathing.

"Tell me about Marta," Hanna said to Rotolo. She was abjectly beautiful in the dim light, a Valkyrie with feet apart and hands locked onto the revolver, blonde hair tumbling against the curve of her jaw. "Tell me what happened and maybe I'll let you live."

"She was nothing but a kid," Rotolo said contemptuously and licked his lips. "Followed me like a starving dog."

"You strangled her and put her body in the river."

"You can't prove it."

"I don't have to."

"Hanna," Karol breathed. Only he and Luca were unarmed; two marble statues watching a smoldering spark fan itself into a bonfire. "Please."

"I told you to get out, Karol," Hanna said. The big revolver was steady. "You don't need to be part of this. You still have a life to live. But when Marta died, part of me did, too."

The thug with the Tommy gun directed a stream of rapid-fire Polish at Broz. This time, Karol understood what was said. Should he shoot Karol first or the girl?

Everything happened at once. Hanna swung away from Rotolo and dropped to one knee. The big revolver barked; once, twice, three times. Her arms quivered with each recoil even as the Tommy gun delivered a rattling hail of lead that peppered the ceiling. The man from Gdansk fell backward, crashing into a line of chairs. Broz's gun boomed. Toby's gun answered.

Something bit into Karol's shoulder. Plaster dust billowed out of the wall.

Rotolo's face twisted in rage and confusion.

Karol dove in front of Hanna as the gangster squeezed the trigger.

CHAPTER 54

My task was drawing to a close

26 13 97. They were one heart.

As Sonny's masterful rendering of **The Cask of Amontillado** neared its climax, Tess knew without a doubt that something had gone terribly wrong at the Galliano Club.

Luca was in trouble. Her heart simply knew.

Tess felt like Fortunato as he was walled in by the evil Montresor, but she didn't have the option of screaming.

When at last the clanking subsided, I resumed the trowel, and finished without interruption the fifth, the sixth, and the seventh tier. The wall was now nearly upon a level with my breast. I again paused, and holding the flambeaux over the mason-work, threw a few feeble rays upon the figure within.

A succession of loud and shrill screams, bursting suddenly from the throat of the chained form,

seemed to thrust me violently back . . .

It was now midnight, and my task was drawing to a close . . . there remained but a single stone to be fitted and plastered in . . . In pace resquiat!

CHAPTER 55

Like Lou Gehrig

With a strength born of desperation, Luca lifted the huge glass bottle of Liquore Galliano off its perch above the bar. It weighed as much as an icebox, most of the heft in the flared bottom half.

He swung it across the bar top like Lou Gehrig straining for center field. The bottle scythed across the bar top, whooshing through the air into Rotolo's back. Luca barely managed to hang onto the unwieldy baton as it reverberated from the impact.

Rotolo's shot smashed into the mirrored wall where the Liquore Galliano had been on display not two seconds before. The mirror cracked and spit. The bootlegger shouted, staggered, and pulled the trigger again.

Luca launched another blow, the muscles up and down his arms screaming with the effort to swing the enormous glass bat. This time the thick end of the bottle banged against the side of the bootlegger's head. The impact of glass against skull was spectacular, causing a hollow ringing drumbeat followed by the ear-splitting crack of the bottle breaking in two.

The bottom half of the bottle, more than a yard in length, fell away from Luca's grip. It clanged against the brass footrail and shattered. A thousand needles of glass mixed with pungent golden liquor and sprayed across the parquet floor.

Rotolo's eyes rolled back in his head. He swayed and collapsed, sprawling spreadeagled in the puddle. His gun skittered away. Shards of broken bottle made a halo around his head.

A pause of stunned silence and then the shelves above the bar canted toward the now-empty central display space. **The Red Book** flew off its perch. Vito Spinelli's prized collection of empty bottles collided into each other, chiming and clattering and booming out a symphony of shattering glass.

Luca dropped the neck of the bottle of Liquore Galliano. His hands were covered in blood.

CHAPTER 56

Finale

Patriotism won.

Elmer Stonebrook took home the scholarship to Morton College with his speech drawn from the pages of **National Geographic.** Tess dutifully applauded, even as she made a swift mental note to calculate the distances Byrd had claimed to have flown to the North Pole and back.

Not that she thought that the man was a liar, it's just that the past few weeks had shown her how easy it was to trick people.

Carmella Zambrano gave her a ride back to East Lido, too consumed with consoling Sonny to pay much attention to the excuse Tess gave about a breakdown.

As Carmella's Buick puttered to a stop in front of the Galliano Club, Tess saw dim light in the big window. She vaulted out of the still-rolling vehicle and charged into the club.

Karol and Toby were there, along with two men lying face down by the pinochle table and another tied to a chair. The bar was drenched, glass encrusted the floor and the place smelled like cough medicine.

Blood was everywhere.

"Where's Luca?" she cried.

CHAPTER 57

The call

"There's no evidence to back up your claim that he killed your sister, Mrs. Vitello," Chief Doyle said. "Or that other girl. We got an identification on her, you know. Italian girl from a farm on Bell Road. Sister-in-law claims that the brother killed her before he disappeared."

"Yes, it was in the newspaper," Hanna said impatiently, knowing that Trixie Dawson was never going to set the record straight about the young woman from her brothel. "But Mr. Rotolo left Chicago the same time that my sister went missing. They must have met in Union Station. He took her on the train to Lido."

She was back in Chief Doyle's office with the heavy draperies, posed on the edge of a big leather chair in front of his giant desk. The chief's stomach was even more expansive and his nose was redder than before. Hanna knew he didn't want to have this conversation but she was damned if Rotolo was going to get away with Marta's murder.

Chief Doyle grimaced. "Rotolo says he never heard

of her."

"He's lying."

"Mrs. Vitello, your sister's case is settled. There's no reason to change the facts of what Nick Procopio did to his victims."

"So what happens now?" Hanna pressed. "Surely you won't let Rotolo go?"

"There's a warrant out for his arrest in Chicago. Killed a store clerk in cold blood last August. Two eyewitnesses and he left a hat with his name in the lining at the scene." Chief Doyle snorted. "Aye, thought he was cleverer than that."

"He's wanted for another murder?"

"We've agreed to extradite him."

"Back to Chicago?" It was an angle Hanna had never considered.

"As soon as the marshals get here, they'll escort him to Chicago to stand trial." Chief Doyle picked up his cigar as his secretary appeared in the doorway. "If there's anything else the Lido police department can do for you, Mrs. Vitello, you know where we are."

Hanna said something polite and left.

A version of Rotolo's arrest had made the front page of the *Lido Daily Clipper*. There was no mention of her. Hanna had read the account so many times, she'd memorized it.

Mr. Luca "Lucky" Lombardo, the new proprietor of the Galliano Club at 601 Hamilton Street, was in his establishment Saturday evening, with close friends Mr. Toby Gleason and Mr. Karol Dombrowski. The latter is the foreman of the Lido Premium Copper and Brass Rolling Mill.

Their evening was interrupted by Mr. Benito Rotolo, accompanied by Mr. Broz Siwak and Mr. Stanley Strobicki. The visit was intended to force Lombardo to sell his establishment to Rotolo. When Lombardo refused, weapons were drawn. Lombardo and Dombrowski suffered minor injuries. Siwak and Strobicki both perished at the scene. Rotolo suffered a concussion and contusions after being clubbed with a bottle. Gleason surrendered his weapon to authorities but will not be charged because he acted to defend others from mortal danger.

Onc of Rotolo's bullcts had grazcd his shouldcr and his hands were covered in cuts, but Luca had spirited Hanna out of the club and into Tess's coupe before the police arrived. With a bar towel tucked inside his coat to staunch the bleeding, he got her back to the Rutherford's house in time to replace Henry Blick's revolver in its commemorative box hidden in the armoire. The weight as she pulled the trigger and the cylinder turned would be forever printed on Hanna's memory.

Osa and Jack, accompanied by Ruth and Henry, arrived home from the Strand Theatre a few minutes after Luca drove away.

Still shaky from the shootout, knowing that she'd just killed a man to keep him from shooting Karol Dombrowski, Hanna had to pretend that she had enjoyed the entire Slingerland Speaking Contest. Of course, the young man who declaimed Byrd's North Pole flight was the winner.

A cup of tea was pressed into her hand as the conversation buzzed. It took all of Hanna's willpower to take a sip, nod and smile. After a decent interval, she announced that she was going to bed. Sleep was impossible as scenes from the Galliano Club jerked through her memory like a 2-reel melodrama in the hands of a drunken projectionist.

Rotolo, snarling and smug.

The man with the Tommy gun falling backward.

Karol protecting her from Rotolo.

The huge golden bottle winging across the bar and exploding into a thousand pieces.

The sight of Karol hurt and bleeding was the last frame of the reel. Thankfully, his injuries were only minor although she didn't know it at the time. A few shotgun pellets in his side and cuts from shattered glass. He was already back at the mill.

That night in the coupe hurtling toward the Rutherford house, Luca asked her why she didn't shoot Benny Rotolo. Hanna didn't reply, although she knew the answer.

In the end, saving Karol Dombrowski so that Hanna had a second chance at life was more important than revenge for Marta. It had been the right choice, although a hard one to accept.

But maybe she didn't have to.

Hanna walked into the post office and asked to place a long-distance call. She was directed to a numbered booth.

Seated on a small stool, she recited the number from a well-thumbed business card to the operator. The wait for the call to go through to Cicero, Illinois, felt like an eternity. Hanna had plenty of time to change her mind.

She didn't.

When the instrument jingled 15 minutes later, the man himself was on the other end. Yes, he remembered her.

Hanna delivered the details and was assured the little matter would be taken care of. Frank Nitti thanked her and the connection was broken. The call had taken less than two minutes.

CHAPTER 58

Left with nothing

A victory dinner to celebrate the club's reopening was an occasion for something special. Luca made chicken cutlets, teaching Tess how to dredge thinly sliced meat in beaten egg and breadcrumbs and then fry them in garlic-infused olive oil.

When the cutlets were crisp and golden brown, he heaped them on crusty bread with a layer of sun-dried tomatoes cured in olive oil. Added peppery arugula lettuce from Medina's fruit stand, a pinch of freshly chopped garlic, and a squeeze of lemon.

The towering sandwiches were greeted with proper reverence by Hanna and Karol, plus Toby and his wife Mary Eileen with little Patrick on her knee.

The six friends were in the saloon, gathered at the biggest table with glasses of beer and cider to accompany the sandwiches. A symbolic reminder of loss, the bare wall above the bar waited for new decoration Luca knew would never come.

With his shoulder stiff from Rotolo's bullet, it had taken five days to clear out the glass, sand out the nicks in the mahogany bar and repair the gouges in the plaster walls. The arc of holes in the ceiling would remain, the pressed tin tiles too expensive to replace.

The club would reopen tomorrow, but there would be no new shelves, no more repairs.

The sandwiches were acclaimed and devoured. Tess cleared plates and plugged in the percolator.

Luca took the letter out of his pocket and unfolded it.

"What's that?" Toby asked.

"The First National Bank of Lido is calling in their loan to Vito," Luca said. "We've got thirty days before we have to pay seventeen thousand dollars."

"James Howland is a bastard," Tess said as she set down the box of *pignolata* from Bella Napoli. Sprinkled with tiny candies, the fried cookie balls were drenched in honey and arranged into a wreath the size of a dinner plate.

Luca took her hand under the table when she sat down again. She'd been incandescent with anger when the letter first arrived, nearly running out the door to accost Howland before Luca stopped her.

"You have to pay it all at once?" Karol took the letter. Hanna leaned over his shoulder to read it, too.

"All of it," Luca affirmed. The thought of losing the club was sickening. "Seventeen thousand."

Karol passed the letter to Toby who gave a low whistle.

"Can they do that?" Mary Eileen asked. Little Patrick reached for the wreath of *pignolata* with both hands and she pulled him back. "Aren't there laws?"

Tess answered her. "It's legal. I've seen it before. The terms of the loan are such that if the borrower's status changes, making repayment doubtful, the bank has the option to ask for all the money back. Vito's death qualifies as a change in the borrower's status. Luca inherited all holdings connected to the Galliano Club so he's legally responsible for the loan repayment."

"But you don't have seventeen thousand," Karol said.

"Look around," Luca said. "In thirty days it will all belong to the First National Bank of Lido."

"We'll think of something," Tess insisted.

Toby selected a morsel of *pignolata* and fed it to Patrick. "You could sell more beer."

"Two barrels in the cellar and then the club goes dry."

"Jesus wept," Toby exclaimed impatiently. "Think, dago. Nobody goes dry if you make more."

"Make more beer?" Karol asked.

"*Oddio*," Luca swore. "You're talking about

Rotolo's operation by the river."

"His boys scattered like roaches. Left everything. Cases of malt. The equipment."

Next to Luca, Tess gave a little gasp. "You mean, become bootleggers?" she asked. "Could we make enough in a month to pay off the loan?"

"If we get Rotolo's list of customers we could do it in two or three weeks." Toby popped a honey ball into his mouth. "He was pulling in at least twenty thousand a month. Think about it. Twenty thousand in a month. Then there's the month after that. And all the other months until they get rid of Prohibition."

Luca gaped at the faces around the table. He'd been out of jail less than two weeks and had no intention of going back. He had to think of Tess.

At the same time he couldn't lose the club. But the risk . . .

"Twenty thousand dollars a month," Tess said wonderingly. "We could pay off the loan and build an empire. We could even send Sonny to Yale."

"Under one condition," Toby stipulated. "Pay the loan and never go near a bank again. Bloody thieves, all of them. We invest in land. God's not making more of that. Land and real things you can hold in your hand. No silly stock market where they play with money and dreams."

"A business empire that would be a sharp stick in the eye of a certain James Howland," Tess said with real vehemence.

Luca didn't want Tess involved in bootlegging, yet was the alternative any better? Ask her to sell all the beautiful things she'd saved from her aunt's house? Live in a rented room in some East Lido apartment while he got a job in one of the mills? Without a specialized skill, he'd be just another strong back to stoke a boiler or load a freight car, jobs at the bottom of the pay scale.

All while watching James Howland dismantle the Galliano Club. The beating heart of East Lido, the legacy that Vito Spinelli had entrusted to Luca.

"What about the police?" Karol asked.

Toby winked. "Leave the Lido police to me."

Before Luca could reach his own conclusion, Tess spoke up. "Well, which of us here knows how to make beer?"

"I do," said Hanna. She lit a cigarette with languid poise and blew a stream of smoke toward the pocked ceiling. "Everybody in Chicago does."

CHAPTER 59

Welcome to Chicago

Benny suppressed a flutter of anxiety as the train pulled into Chicago's Union Station. Chased out of town almost half a year ago by Al Capone's thugs, he'd always planned to come back. Trixie on his arm, pockets bulging with cash, his old North Side cronies falling at his feet.

Basically, parading into Chicago like he owned the place before rubbing Capone's nose in the dirt.

Instead, he was arriving in handcuffs, under arrest for the murder of some store clerk Benny couldn't even remember. Trixie never came to the station to say goodbye. Chief Doyle made up for her lack, glowering at Benny as the federal marshals chivvied him into the train compartment. No doubt the old buzzard was steamed about losing his three thousand a week.

The train chugged to a halt, the whistle blowing loud and long. Harris and Payne, the two marshals assigned to escort him, stood up and put on their jackets, jostling as the train gave a couple of final jolts. They'd kept him manacled the entire way from Lido to Chicago, removing the cuffs only for toilet breaks. Benny even had to eat a sandwich with the bracelets on.

"Think your friends are gonna be happy to see you, Rotolo?" Harris said with a leer.

"I bet he's got lots of good friends waiting to see him." Payne could have been the other marshal's twin. Two identical dead-eyed, humorless mugs with shiny badges and cheap suits from Sears, Roebuck. Played cards with each other for a day and a half, leaving Benny to stare at sliding scenery and think of ways to get out of this jam.

As the train slowed near Buffalo, Benny had offered Harris five thousand dollars to undo the cuffs and look the other way.

No soap.

Offered six grand to Payne in Ohio.

Same result. Nothing.

Benny had no choice but to pin his hopes on former associates in the North Side gang. Bugs Moran was in charge now. Probably had half the Chicago police department on his payroll.

Too bad the other half was in Capone's pocket, giving Benny a fifty-fifty chance of beating the rap and avoiding a trip to the slammer or an encounter with Old Sparky. He'd just keep denying the charges until Bugs paid off the cops to make evidence or a witness disappear.

He and Bugs hadn't been close but loyalty to the North Side and the memory of Hymie Weiss and Dean O'Banion had to mean something.

If it didn't, Benny would buy some loyalty of his own. Trixie was holding on to a big chunk of beer racket money for him. All he had to do is send the word and she'd wire him enough to buy a dozen cops and double that number of prison guards.

"You want to carry Rotolo's suitcase or should I?" Harris asked his partner as he hauled the two marshals' overnight cases down from the rack above their seats.

"I'm not walking into Chicago like his butler," Payne groused. "He can carry it himself."

In a surprise move, Harris unfastened the cuffs and made Benny pick up his own suitcase. The two marshals stayed with him as they left the train, each gripping one of Benny's arms.

Once on the platform, they both let go. The day was cold and bright, the sky a hard blue.

Benny grinned and tipped his fedora over his left eye because it always made the dames look twice. First glance was for the hat, the second for Benny's dark hair and blue eyes. A swell-looking tomato in a fur coat walked by, heels clicking out a warm welcome to Chicago.

Benny threw her a wink. She simpered but kept going.

The platform emptied out quick, porters running past with baggage piled on handcarts. Benny shifted the suitcase to his other hand and realized that Harris and Payne had disappeared. He could scarcely believe his luck.

Before Benny could scoot away, a rattling sound ripped through the air. Something socked him in the chest and kept punching. He staggered backward, slamming into the solid metal side of the train car.

He looked down. His suit from Marshall Field's was all torn up and leaking blood.

In his last few minutes of life, Benny saw two shooters spraying lead out of Tommy guns. Behind them, a short dapper type with a cigarette clenched between his teeth raised a hand in a mocking sort of salute.

The sunshine flickered and went out.

EPILOGUE

November 1956

"Ma," I said and held up the little linen-covered ledger with leather corners. "Did you lose this?"

Ma glanced up from the big accountant's book open on the desk. She was dressed for the big event in an emerald green taffeta shirtwaist dress and matching kitten heels, but squeezing in another five minutes of work before it was time to go.

"What is it?" she asked.

"Looks like an old account book." I gave her the little ledger and dusted off my hands. "I was looking for the bunting that Pa thought was in the storeroom and found this in a box. The tables are all set upstairs. The wine is breathing and the waiters have memorized the menu and the pairings for each course. All the desserts from Bella Napoli are in the kitchen but won't be plated until after the main course so nothing goes even the tiniest bit stale."

The fine dining room upstairs looked gorgeous. Everything sparkled, from the snowy tablecloths to the gold-rimmed china to every inch of polished silver. I loved managing the big events. Even more, I loved proving that I could pull them off flawlessly.

Ma gave me a *well done, Sophia* smile and adjusted her trendy cat-eye glasses. Her short nails were varnished a pale pink.

She was still athletic and energetic and quick to smile but people sometimes thought she was older because of the snow-white hair. When I was a girl, it was the color of a new penny. But during the war, when my older brother Matt kept threatening to lie about his age and join up instead of finishing school and the restaurant was a USO club, her hair lost all its color.

"I didn't find any bunting," I said. "We'll put up the crepe paper."

Ma wasn't listening. "Oh my God," she whispered.

"What is it?" I perched on the edge of her desk, smoothing my full black skirt over my knees. My party dress was taffeta, too, with a plunging surplice neckline and cap sleeves. I'd inherited Pa's tawny hair and black suited me.

The pocket ledger was open, revealing pages filled with faded numbers. I could see that the paper was thick and of a high quality.

"Go get your father," Ma said in a gasping sort of voice.

"What's the matter?" I slid off the corner of her

desk. "Do you want me to get you a glass of water?"

"Go get your father," she repeated.

"Tessa?" Daddy always seemed to have a sixth sense where Ma was concerned. Still the most handsome man in East Lido, he was wearing the new Brooks Brothers suit she made him buy when they were in New York City visiting my younger brother Ben in law school at Columbia University. "Are you ready?"

Ma shook her head. "Look, it's Mr. Fisher's ledger. The divvy sheet."

"What a find," Daddy said with a smile. "Where was it?"

"Oh, God." Ma took off her glasses and covered her eyes.

Daddy's smile faded. "Tessa, it's an old book from thirty years ago. Nothing to get upset about. Especially not today."

Ma shook her head.

"Sophia, tell everyone to go on to City Hall." Daddy steered me to the doorway. "Your mother and I will catch up."

"What's going on?" I asked, with a backward glance at Ma. Her shoulders shook as she sat behind the desk, her diamond ring glinting in the overhead light as she covered her face.

"Nothing to concern you, sweetheart," Daddy said.

After all these years, he still spoke with a soft Italian accent.

The office door shut behind me. I squared my shoulders. This was an unforeseen wrinkle in a very carefully planned day. Complex arrangements for the big event had been in the works for weeks. Who was driving in which car, protocol for the swearing-in ceremony, the seating for the big dinner party upstairs afterward.

Aunt Hanna and Uncle Karol were waiting in what Daddy called the saloon. My older brother Matt and his wife Celeste were there, too, all the way from their flagship store next door. They owned the entire chain of Panetta's Hardware.

My husband Patrick Gleason presided over the long bar, making everyone including his parents, a pre-event cocktail. I'd grown up calling my in-laws Uncle Toby and Aunt Mary Eileen. Five whole months of marriage and I still hadn't shaken the habit.

Greeting everyone with hugs and kisses took a minute or two.

"Sophia! You look like a dream." Aunt Hanna looked even more glamorous than usual in a white blouse and charcoal skirt made out of some elegantly slubbed stiff fabric. "Givenchy, darling," she murmured in response to the silent question posed by my raised eyebrows. "Fresh from Paris."

Aunt Hanna owned and managed Van Dyke's, the fanciest clothing store in Lido. Ma's dress came from her store, as did mine. We always got a discount and first dibs on new stock, too.

While lots of women worked outside the home during the war, Ma and Aunt Hanna were the only women I knew who had careers. If you needed advice on what to wear you went to Van Dyke's and asked for Mrs. Dombrowski. If you wanted to know how to build a financial empire, you talked to Mrs. Lombardo. But to know how to be an award-winning homemaker, you'd go to the Gleason farm. Mary Eileen was always baking something like soda bread or raisin scones, things Ma wouldn't dream of doing even if she had the time.

For as long as I could remember, our three families did everything together. I was nine or ten before I realized we weren't actually related. That the four Dombrowski kids and Patrick and his little sister weren't really cousins to me, Matt and Ben.

Our parents were best friends and investment partners. Every two weeks they held a business meeting, usually in Ma's office in the Galliano Club but sometimes in the Dombrowski's living room or at the Gleason farm. Daddy says that's how they weathered the stock market crash of 1929, the Depression, the lean years when the mills in Lido closed their doors.

The six of them just kept going forward, building and buying.

The Galliano Club was always their hub, transformed along the way from men's hangout to soup kitchen to USO club to Italian restaurant.

Now, we had the bar and casual eatery downstairs, which Patrick ran. The big spaces upstairs housed the fine dining room, banquet space, and the commercial kitchen. The floors were connected by a big curving staircase. Daddy said that a library was once situated where the staircase is now.

It was a tradition in Lido for a new bride to stand at the top and toss her bouquet down the stairs. Patrick's sister caught my bouquet. All eyes went to Luke Dombrowski, of course. They were engaged a month later.

"Daddy says for everyone to go ahead," I announced after a peep at the still-closed office door. "He and Ma will drive themselves."

Promising to save seats for them, everyone trooped out. Patrick and I were left alone in the saloon. We'd redecorated the place a year ago. The ancient wainscotting was black now and the walls above decorated with huge pen and ink sketches of iconic

Italian landmarks. My favorite was Venice where Patrick and I went for our honeymoon. We didn't make the trek to Calabria. Daddy insisted it was too miserable a place for newlyweds.

Patrick came around the end of the bar and put his arms around me. "What's going on?" he asked.

"I don't know," I admitted. "I was looking for that bunting and found an old ledger. I thought it was something Ma had lost. She said something about it belonging to a Mr. Fisher and got all upset."

Seven years older than me, Patrick was a black-haired Irishman like his father, with twinkling blue eyes and a way of telling stories that never failed to make his audience laugh.

I was only twelve when Patrick went off to war. Every letter his parents got was read and re-read by all three families. We followed him from Anzio to the Bulge and even to Berlin. After the war he spent time in Ireland and France, learning the whiskey and wine import business, which for some reason his father thought was hilarious.

When Patrick finally came home, he went to work for Daddy, building up the club's "cellar" and envisioning the fine dining program. I was at Vassar by that time, thrilled to be making a name for myself at Ma's alma mater but missing the Galliano Club like crazy.

Every time I came home, Patrick had brought in more business. He was a wonder. Funny, smart, making my heart flutter, until I thought if I didn't have him I would die. When we got married, both sets of parents helped us with a down payment on the sweetest little house in the world.

"Did I tell you that you look stunning?" Patrick gave me a long, lingering kiss.

I nestled closer. Seeing Ma upset like that had rattled me, but Daddy would set things right. He and Ma had the perfect marriage.

If Patrick and I were half as successful, we had a lifetime of happiness in front of us.

"You said what to Rotolo?" Luca asked incredulously.

"I told him that I knew someone in his bootlegging outfit was cheating him," Tess gulped. "I'd give him the proof if he stayed away from your trial."

"Oh, Tessa."

"I thought he knew about Orsini. If he testified, they'd send you to Italy to stand trial for murder there."

"He couldn't have known. You're the only person I ever told."

"I was so scared that something terrible was going

to happen to you." Tess found a handkerchief and wiped her eyes. "What would have happened if Rotolo had taken me up on the offer?"

"He wouldn't have honored a promise, no matter what you gave him." Luca gently tugged Tess out of her desk chair and into his arms. "All in the past. Not worth getting yourself upset now, Tessa."

"You're not mad?"

"Over what? The fact that you loved me enough to tangle with a bootlegger?"

"You make it sound like I was very brave." Tess smiled up at him.

"You were."

"I don't want you to think I had kept a secret. I just forgot until I saw the ledger."

"No secrets between us," Luca confirmed.

"No secrets," Tess echoed.

He kissed the tip of her nose and let her go. Tess made sure she hadn't gotten any lipstick on his lapel. Luca fetched his overcoat and his wife's mink stole and they set off to see Sonny Zambrano take the oath of office as the new mayor of Lido, New York.

In December 1926, the Lombardo-Gleason-Dombrowski consortium took over Benny Rotolo's beer racket. After paying off the bank loan that Vito

Spinelli took out against the Galliano Club, they supplied beer to upstate New York establishments. They adhered to Toby's rules against stocks and banking, and invested the profits in real estate, rental properties and commercial enterprises. Insulated against the stock market crash of 1929, by the time Prohibition ended in 1933, they were all millionaires several times over.

Sean O'Malley served two years in federal prison for misuse of the mail during which time his wife filed for divorce and Chief Doyle died of a heart attack. O'Malley never returned to Lido but became a barber, the trade he learned in jail, in Poughkeepsie, New York, where for many years he fruitlessly hunted for evidence of a woman named Ruthie June Crosswater.

Owen Forbes Fisher fled to California and got an accounting job in the motion picture industry. In 1942, he was found guilty of embezzlement and conspiracy to commit fraud. He died in jail.

Cynthia Fisher divorced Owen on charges of desertion and married Owen's university buddy Ted Lansbury. When he disappeared in 1933 after an altercation with gambling associates in Saratoga, she finally went home to her mother.

James Howland lost everything during the Depression when the First National Bank of Lido went bankrupt. His father Preston took the train to New York City and threw himself off the Empire State Building. His brother Richard became a traveling shoe salesman. James and his mother Muriel relocated to Albany and ran a boarding house together. He never married.

Trixie Dawson continued to run a house of ill repute in Lido until the freight yards and mills closed during the Depression. Having purchased a swath of coastal property along the Florida panhandle, she was one of the wealthiest residents of Destin, Florida when she died in 1972.

Ruth and Henry Blick were married for forty years. Following his retirement from Lido Premium, they divided their time between Lido and an estate in Panama overlooking the ocean. Osa and Jack Rutherford were frequent guests.

Enzo and Rosaria Russo bought the Genovese place on Bell Road and became the third-largest dairy farm in the Mohawk Valley. Their son Rocco made twenty-five runs over Germany as a navigator on a B-17 Flying Fortress, after which he enjoyed a long career with Boeing. Their daughter Matilda wrote the hugely successful Jake and June Tipton private eye series. Kidnappings and dramatic rescues were a signature feature of the books and movies.

Toby and Mary Eileen Gleason had two children

and pioneered upstate New York's farm-to-table movement. Their land holdings included vineyards in the Finger Lakes region and the abandoned Packham Foundry property on the banks of the Mohawk River. They converted the latter into an amusement park and picnic area.

Hanna and Karol Dombrowski had one daughter and three sons who all had successful careers in law enforcement. After serving as Lido Premium's operations manager for many years, Karol was voted president of the Lido Chamber of Commerce. He bought his suits from Van Dyke's, his wife's store known for elegance and quality.

Luca and Tess Lombardo always considered their wedding anniversary to be the first night they spent together, rather than the date on their marriage certificate. They had three children, all of whom went to college. Their youngest was a staffer for Senator Frank Church and played an important behind-the-scenes role in the 1975 Church Committee's investigation into intelligence abuses and the establishment of the permanent US Senate Select Committee on Intelligence.

The Galliano Club was the jewel in the crown of the Lombardo real estate empire, which eventually grew to seventeen commercial ventures and properties along

Hamilton Street.

Luca never told anyone about putting Jimmy Zambrano's body in the river.

Tess never told anyone about bribing James Howland with the bearer bond to drop the charges against Luca.

Hanna never told anyone about the phone call to Frank Nitti.

And they all lived happily ever after.

Acknowledgments

My grandfather used to buy red wine by the gallon. Once home, he'd decant the gallon into a variety of smaller vessels. The Sunday dinner table would be graced with wine in bottles that once held anisette, crème de menthe, Seagram's 7, or Canadian Club.

(Not to digress, but if my grandfather made you a mixed drink of any variety, he called it a "highball." Also, when I was little, he called me "Punkin.")

If you asked him what kind of wine was in the recycled bottle, the answer was always the same: "That good kind."

One Christmas my uncle gifted him a bunch of empty bottles with homemade labels reading *That Good Kind.* I'm not sure my grandfather found it as funny as the rest of us did.

I owe a debt of gratitude to my late grandparents, Joe and Ann Sestito, who inspired the Galliano Club series. Every Sunday after Mass, the extended family gathered in their kitchen where my grandfather could be persuaded to tell stories of being a deputy sheriff of Oneida County, New York, during Prohibition.

My uncle, Fr. Joseph N. Sestito (USN, Ret.) also is responsible for the big finale. In 1949, he wowed Rome Free Academy's actual Slingerland Speaking Contest with a masterful rendition of *The Cask of Amontillado*.

Sincere thanks go to Maria Rich of the Rome Arts Hall of Fame, who planted the seed for the series. Many others helped me with local research. I'm grateful for the assistance of Arthur L. Simmons III at the Rome Historical Society and Patrick Reynolds, Director of Public Programs at the Oneida County Historical Society. Thank you to Linda Iannone for a behind-the-scenes private tour of the incomparable Stanley Theatre in Utica and also to Thomas Wynne and Steve Hamilton of the F.X. Brewing Company for the fantastic tour of the West End Brewery, the first to ship beer after Prohibition.

With grateful appreciation I salute my editor, Kerry Watson. More thanks go to reviewer Shelby Robinson, as well as members of the Nashville Writers group who critiqued first drafts of many Galliano Club scenes, especially Kathleen Cosgrove, Lily Wilson and Nina Fortmeyer.

Thank you to my husband and children. Wouldn't trade you for the world.

Last, but not least, my thanks go to James R. Guy, president of the real Galliano Club in Rome, New York.

In September 2020, he kindly gave permission to use the Galliano Club name. The 1920 building still stands in the historical Italian section of Rome, smaller than the fictional club, but with the same twin doors and dance studio on the second floor.

To all who helped make the Galliano Club series a reality, you are "That good kind."

Carmen Amato
March 2023

452

About the author

Carmen Amato turns her 30 years with the Central Intelligence Agency into fiction loaded with danger and deception.

She is the award-winning author of the Detective Emilia Cruz police series set in Acapulco, the Galliano Club historical thriller series, two standalone thrillers and the Mystery Ahead book journal for mystery lovers.

Find out more at carmenamato.net.

454

www.ingramcontent.com/pod-product-compliance
Lightning Source LLC
Chambersburg PA
CBHW072018020726
47501CB00006B/1851

* 9 7 9 8 9 8 9 1 4 0 3 4 3 *